# Didn't I Say to Make My Abilities *Average* in the Next Life?!

## VOLUME 8

Mile—Goddess Phenomenon!

# Didn't I Say to Make My Abilities Average in the Next Life?!

## VOLUME 8

BY

*FUNA*

ILLUSTRATED BY

*Itsuki Akata*

*Seven Seas Entertainment*

DIDN'T I SAY TO MAKE MY ABILITIES AVERAGE
IN THE NEXT LIFE?! VOLUME 8

© FUNA / Itsuki Akata 2018

Originally published in Japan in 2018 by EARTH STAR
Entertainment, Tokyo. English translation rights arranged
with EARTH STAR Entertainment, Tokyo, through TOHAN
CORPORATION, Tokyo.

Seven Seas press and purchase enquiries can be sent to
Marketing Manager Lianne Sentar at press@gomanga.com.
Information requiring the distribution and purchase of
digital editions is available from Digital Manager CK Russell
at digital@gomanga.com.

Seven Seas and the Seven Seas logo are trademarks of
Seven Seas Entertainment. All rights reserved.

Follow Seven Seas Entertainment online at
sevenseasentertainment.com.

TRANSLATION: Diana Taylor
ADAPTATION: Maggie Cooper
COVER DESIGN: Nicky Lim
INTERIOR LAYOUT & DESIGN: Clay Gardner
PROOFREADER: Jade Gardner, Stephanie Cohen
LIGHT NOVEL EDITOR: Nibedita Sen
MANAGING EDITOR: Julie Davis
EDITOR-IN-CHIEF: Adam Arnold
PUBLISHER: Jason DeAngelis

ISBN: 978-1-64505-211-1
Printed in Canada
First Printing: March 2020
10 9 8 7 6 5 4 3 2 1

*God bless me?*
# CONTENTS

### Misato

A high school student. Died saving a little girl and was reborn into a fantasy world.

### Mile

A girl who was granted "average" abilities in this fantasy world.

### Mavis

A swordswoman. Leader of the up-and-coming party, the Crimson Vow.

### Reina

A rookie hunter. Specializes in combat magic.

# The Kingdom of Brandel

## *Eckland Academy*

### Marcela

Adele's friend. A magic-user
of noble birth.

### Aureana

Adele's friend.
A commoner.

### Pauline

A rookie hunter.
A timid girl, but...

### Monika

Adele's friend. The second
daughter of a merchant.

# The Kingdom of Vanolark

The Town of the Dueling Inns

The Turning Point:
The Return to Ascham

**Capital
Shaleiraz**

The Spice Incident

# The Kingdom of Brandel

Capital

**Fief of Ascham**

Invasion

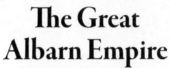

# The Great Albarn Empire

The Town Where Mile
Registered as a Hunter

**Capital**

## The Kingdom of Tils

Birthplace of the
Crimson Vow

## The Kingdom of Marlane

**Capital**

Mafan

THE DWARVEN VILLAGE
Glademarl

*God bless me?*

WORLD MAP

# Previously

When Adele von Ascham, the eldest daughter of Viscount Ascham, was ten years old, she was struck with a terrible headache and, just like that, remembered everything.

She remembered how, in her previous life, she was an eighteen-year-old Japanese girl named Kurihara Misato who died while trying to save a young girl, and that she met God...

Misato had exceptional abilities, and the expectations of those around her were high. As a result, she could never live her life the way she wanted. So when she met God, she made an impassioned plea:

"In my next life, please make my abilities average!"

Yet somehow, it all went awry.

In her new life, she can talk to nanomachines and, although her magical powers are technically average, it is the average between a human's and an elder dragon's...6,800 times that of a sorcerer!

At the first academy she attended, she made friends and rescued a little boy as well as a princess.

She registered at the Hunters' Prep School under the name of Mile and formed a party with her classmates. The Crimson Vow made a grand debut, but one problem after another came hurtling their way—from golems, invading foreign soldiers, and doting fathers to elder dragons, the strongest creatures in the world! Reina developed a crush, and even Mavis, their leader, received a wedding proposal!

The four have overcome many adversaries, but their greatest battle lies ahead of them. The empire to the south has suddenly launched an invasion of Mile's old home. The four now hurry on their way to the Ascham lands...

# CHAPTER 63

# The Fief of Ascham

**M**ILE'S SOUL was an amalgamation: the product of two souls that joined together one day three years ago— the souls of ten-year-old Adele and eighteen-year-old Misato Kurihara. However, in truth, Adele and Misato were the same person all along—the same consciousness and the same soul. During the time that she was Adele, Misato was still herself, merely rebooted from nothing, without her memories or faculties of reasoning.

To put it simply, Adele was the sort of person that Misato might have become had she been born into this world. That was Adele von Ascham.

Thus, when their spirits were finally brought together, there were zero incompatibilities. They were merely two instances of the same application running on the same operating system, simply with different output results based on varying input data regarding growth and education. In other words, on a software level, they were fundamentally the same.

And then, those two sets of results had been concatenated.

As such, neither of the sides had been subsumed. They were one soul, with two sets of memories. That was Mile.

Therefore, while Misato's personality was at the forefront—thanks to her portion of the experience having fundamentally more memories—Adele's personality was represented as well. Along with, of course, *her* memories.

*Most of the staff at the manor have been replaced with people who knew neither me nor my mother, but even those who were fired are probably still living on our lands. All of those former servants were so kind to me up until Mother and Grandfather died, and until they were forced out... And then, there's the fief of Ascham, which was looked after by Grandfather, Mother, and all of our ancestors before them, and all of the citizens who live there...*

Though Mile had made the decision to cast her old home aside—to have nothing more to do with it ever again—that was a rational decision that she had made as Misato. Adele's will, and Adele's memories, could not be so easily expunged.

"What do you look so puzzled for? It's not that complicated!" Reina called to Mile, who was deep in thought, her brow furrowed. "The Albarn Empire is to the south of Brandel, your homeland, but it also comes into contact with this kingdom, Vanolark, and also Tils, Mavis and Pauline's homeland and the place where we're all registered as hunters. By traveling west, we came to Vanolark via Brandel, which is to the northwest of Tils. There's also a route that passes through Albarn, but obviously, most people aren't interested in taking it, so we avoided it, too."

Reina had referred to Tils as "Mavis and Pauline's homeland" because, as the daughter of a traveling peddler, Reina had no idea where she had been born. Her father had never even given her any hints.

"Now, when it comes to our return, we obviously won't be taking the Albarn route, so we'll be traveling back on the Brandel side of the border. We'll have to avoid any places that have been touched by the invasion, of course. In order to do that, we need to pick whichever path will get us to Ascham the quickest."

As she spoke, Reina indicated a highway on the map that was a short distance from the border. It was a different route from the one by which they had come, which ran a bit farther to the north. Thus, this new route was slightly farther from the border.

The four agreed with Reina's suggestion and packed their things away into storage. Yes, it was time for that old standard, the Sonic Speed maneuver... Of course, all they had really packed away were the items that they had to carry by hand, so the move did not fully live up to its name, but their speed improved at least a little bit. This increase in speed was a manifestation of everyone's desire to move quickly.

Even if they didn't rush, they would probably still arrive before the Albarnian forces could reach Ascham.

In this world, wars took a very long time. One had to accumulate resources and then rally the interim forces (in other words, farmers) to battle, begin training them, and complete all last-minute preparations. *Then*, even after the actual military operations had begun, the marching and the battles themselves took time. It was common for both sides to end up at standoff for some weeks or to have blockades or sieges that dragged on for months.

In this case, it was clear that the Empire was probably gunning for a swift victory, but even so, their advance would be crippled by skirmishes, ambushes, traps, and surprise attacks, so the speed of their advance could never be comparable to that of an army on modern-day Earth.

Just a few days later, the Crimson Vow were already well within Brandel's borders. The Ascham fief was nearly on the horizon.

"That was a huge waste of money!" Pauline groused as they walked.

While thus far the Crimson Vow had spent every night camping out so as not to waste time, they did now and then swing by the larger towns they passed to gather information. They had made some paid inquiries at numerous Guild branches, but the information from each was more or less the same as what they had heard in the very first town. There was essentially no new information nor any further detail that the employees could offer... Indeed, from the second stop onward, paying for Guild information had been both a waste of money and time.

Pauline understood the value of information and would have gladly shelled out a half-gold at each guildhall if they had anything new to tell. However, no matter how many days passed and no matter how close they got to their destination, the information was all exactly the same as it had been on the very first day. So, Pauline's complaints of wasted money were more or less valid. Though one could argue that the "information" they had bought was that there *was* no new information, but still...

"We have to assume that either one Guild branch got their hands on the information and then transmitted it to all the other Guild branches, or that whoever initially sold them the report continued moving west, selling it to other branches as they went... In other words, there's only one source. Are we sure we should trust it...?" Mavis worried.

Pauline, however, felt more confident.

"I mean, this is information that the Guild was willing to sell to us, right? I can't imagine that they would buy any story unless it came from someone with the right credentials. Either they've been presented with sufficient evidence, or they have some other reason to deem the information reliable. Plus, they seem fairly informed as to the whole thing."

What Pauline said was not incorrect, but Mile could not help but retort mentally, *They said things like that on the evening news all the time, but just who are these "informed sources" they're always referencing? If you don't reveal who provided you with the information, you may as well be saying, "I heard it from a little old lady down at the tobacco shop..."*

Nevertheless, it was fair to say that the accuracy of the information was not a major concern here.

If the enemies were invaders from the Empire, pushing into the Kingdom of Brandel with unknown intentions and no formal declaration, then the kingdom could strike back without reservation. Other countries, if asked, would place all the blame on the attackers—the imperial forces. In fact, as they had not issued a formal declaration of war, they were technically an unknown group of armed attackers and could be treated as no better than bandits. Yes, they probably *were* bandits. That had to be it!

If the kingdom laid waste to a group like that, no one would care. The ones who would do the smashing could be the kingdom's own troops, or mercenaries—it didn't matter which, and it didn't matter who hired them...

"Now then, as previously discussed: today we are not hunters who took a request through the Guild but fighters who were hired independently. Therefore, we will not call ourselves 'hunters' but 'mercenaries.' It's not that we are misrepresenting ourselves by saying that we are *not* hunters, but rather that we are operating in the role of hunters who have taken on a job as mercenaries. As such, we aren't breaking any rules. On the off chance that someone says to us, 'Hey, aren't you all hunters?' we have to tell the truth: that we're registered as hunters, but right now we're working as mercenaries." As they walked, Mile ran through the plan once again.

The other three gave emphatic nods. They had already discussed this many times on their journey, but this was the final confirmation before they embarked on the real deal. It would have been surprising for anyone to pick this moment for questions or objections.

"Our party that we have formed as hunters is one thing, but as your leader, I would now like to put together a band of mercenaries. All who wish to be included, please raise your hand."

Three hands went up into the air.

"Thank you very much. Now then, I formally declare the mercenary band, the Order of the Crimson Blood, in operation!"

And so, they became the Order of the Crimson Vow through and through, cloaked in an ironclad deception.

Not even Reina, confident as she was, thought that the four of them were capable of getting involved in a war. All she had been thinking was that if they didn't do something right away, Mile would regret it for the rest of her life. Her intention was to let Mile act as recklessly as she liked but drag her back out before things got too hairy—using force if necessary.

*No one else needs to suffer a lifetime of regret from their own inaction. I know that feeling all too well...* Reina thought.

Mavis, meanwhile, fully intended to save the Ascham lands. *If it's for the sake of Mile, who always believed in my dreams, and who's saved me again and again, I'd forsake even the gods...*

No one could guess what Pauline was thinking, but a vague smile drifted across her face.

And as for Mile...

*I can't just abandon them. Even if it means I'll lose any chance I had of a happy, peaceful life...*

How could she be thinking such a thing when Misato's thoughts were at the forefront? Did that mean that her spirit was being poisoned by Adele von Ascham's childish sense of justice?

No. By her very nature, Misato Kurihara was the sort of person who would throw herself before a speeding truck to save the life of a little girl she had never even seen before. It was not peculiar in the slightest that she would feel the way she did now.

*If it comes down to the wire, I can announce myself as Adele... Better still, the Servant of the Goddess. I have to save all my people, even if that's what it takes. And I won't let a single one of my friends die in the process!*

She was fully and utterly committed to going into battle with just their band of four...

"Enemies from the Albarn Empire, huh?" spat Juno, the leader of the Ascham troops stationed nearest the fief's edge.

The imperial forces that had invaded so suddenly had already leveled the lands of Count Cesdol, which abutted with the national border. Their arrival on the Ascham lands was imminent. However, Juno did not regard these brigands, who had come barging in without even a formal declaration of war, to be real military troops. They were merely brigands. Such an appellation was more than sufficient for ruffians like them.

Though the Ascham territory belonged only to a viscount, it boasted far more troops than similar fiefs because it was so near

the border. Yet the strength of which they had boasted until just a few years ago had been greatly diminished of late.

"Damn that bastard son-in-law..."

Juno was, of course, referring to the man who had married into the Ascham family—the husband of the previous viscount's only daughter, Mabel.

After Mabel and her father were mysteriously attacked and killed, there was scarcely a person around who didn't have their suspicions. However, none were in a position to stop the usurper—a corrupt man whose only clout came from being the descendent of some count somewhere—who had waltzed in with his mistress and illegitimate daughter, slashed the budget for the fief's military upkeep, and redirected the funds toward his own luxurious lifestyle. As a result of all this, their combat resources had plummeted—manpower, equipment, and training alike.

Thankfully, all those who had schemed to push Adele out and take over the household—in spite of their utter lack of Ascham blood—had been discovered and brought to justice. In the end, they and their associates served only to wet the guillotine's blade. Adele, the rightful heir, had vanished for her own safety, but the king himself had personally dispatched a minister to manage the fief until her return. However, although the new minister was trying his darnedest, the fief's military strength was still nowhere near restored.

Besides, even at their most powerful, the fief's troops were still only the forces of a viscount. Even if it were only a fraction of the Empire's forces that they were up against, there was no way that they could be expected to have the power to repel troops belonging to the army of a large nation. At best, they could only hope to buy themselves a bit of time until reinforcements from the Crown, or from other territories, could arrive.

In truth, their chances of even getting that far were slim. Theirs was a backwater fief with little to offer, whose ruling family had been first embroiled in a scandal and then eliminated. There was not a lord or king in all the land who would be willing to march their troops out into the fray of a battle where they would certainly take great losses for the Ascham fief. No, they would be seeing neither hide nor hair of reinforcements until the others had rallied all of their defenses together and were prepared for a decisive strike...

In all likelihood, the place that would become the frontlines of Brandel's counteroffensive would be somewhere north of here at the forfeit of the Ascham lands.

Even if that counterstrike should be a success, their forces would have gone to battle not once, but twice, after being devastated by the imperial occupation. Their food and valuables would be plundered, their crops and fields trampled, and their population overflowing with orphans, widows, and casualties of war. At that point, any prospects of the future would be grim.

*Our beloved former lord and Lady Mabel would never forgive me... I made an oath. I swore to them that until my dying breath— no, even beyond that—I would pledge to be a god of vengeance, striking to protect the Ascham lands...*

Indeed, Juno—who had been taken in by the old lord, Adele's

grandfather, and grown from a poor orphan into the head of the fief's military forces—would lay down his life, his soul, his everything without a moment's hesitation for the sake of the house of Ascham.

It was twenty years ago.

Juno was ten years old, lying in the back alleys of the Ascham capital on the brink of death, when he was offered refuge from a life that was little better than that of a beast or insect. By the lord's mercy, he was granted the life of a human with honor and purpose.

Surely, there was no noble in the world who would go out of their way to take in a commoner—a filthy, half-dead orphan, no less—and yet, it had happened.

He was given a sword, an education, training, and a position as then-twelve-year-old Mabel's guard...or rather, as her playmate-slash-attendant, regardless of the fact that he was the younger of the pair.

"Juno, let's go into the forest and capture some kobolds! I was thinking of raising some as pets!"

"Ahaha! You fell for it! I tied the grass together right there! Now you have to sit through today's etiquette lesson for me. See you later!"

"Juno, I'm going to go take a bath in that stream, so I need you to watch me to make sure I don't drown or get snatched up by monsters or anything. Don't take your eyes off me!"

In all of Juno's days, there was no job that he completed as fervently—no job as rewarding—as that one.

For the sake of protecting the Ascham lands and the Ascham family, to whom he owed so very much, Juno toned his body and trained hard every day, until he finally attained his peak: the polished physical form of a warrior. Furthermore, he honed the knowledge necessary to defend Ascham from any enemy attack, whether by force or by more civil methods.

And yet, he had allowed Mabel and the Viscount to be killed, with no proof with which to cast blame on Mabel's husband, no matter how suspicious he might have been. Still, Juno was unable to step down from his post, thinking of what might happen should anyone ever try to lay a hand upon Adele, Mabel's daughter. If she were ever in danger, he would protect her at all costs—even if it meant being branded a traitor and a lord-killer.

He had allowed Adele to be taken away, once again unable to do a single thing.

*We can't be certain that Lady Adele has perished. There's a possibility that she lives on somewhere...*

He tried to reassure himself, but in truth, it was unfathomable. There was nowhere in this world where a defenseless twelve-year-old girl could live safely and happily all on her own.

The last time that Juno had seen Adele in the flesh was back when her mother and grandfather were still in good health and the girl herself was around eight years old. Just like her mother Mabel, about whom the words "head" and "cloud," were often

uttered in close proximity to one another, Adele was a rather—
no, *incredibly*—absentminded girl.

Though he was the commander, Juno was still but a soldier,
one who would never have much opportunity to speak with his
employers' young daughter. Indeed, even when he had the chance
to converse with her mother and grandfather, that did not mean
he exchanged words with Adele as well. At most, he was only ever
able to glimpse her from afar.

Juno recalled the day he had been taken into the viscount's
care—the day he had first met Mabel—like it was yesterday.

"Juno. You have to grow up strong to protect my father, me,
and all of the people of our lands, okay?"

With a great nod, he had given his assent to the young girl's
words, but in the end, he had already failed to uphold two-thirds
of that promise.

*Still, I will keep the other part of it, even if it costs me my life!*

There were 300 men in the Ascham forces. They were up
against roughly 5,000 from the Empire.

"Only 5,000? Let's make 'em regret thinking that a little rag-
tag band like that is enough to take us on!"

These final words were spoken not only in Juno's head but
uttered aloud. It was a commander's duty to assure his troops
that conditions were favorable and to instill a sense of confidence
in them.

*Of course, practically speaking, there's no way that we could
possibly win while fighting them head-on, and the difference in our
numbers is far too great to try and lay siege to them. Our only option*

*is to launch a surprise attack on the enemy headquarters and crush
them there...*

If they could take out the commander and other officers
in one fell swoop, they might be able to make it work. If they
killed the commander alone, one of his successors would just be
promoted in his place. However, if they could destroy their entire leadership in one go, that would be a different story. If the
enemies lost their ability to effectively mobilize their full forces,
as well as anyone who possessed authority, they would have no
choice but to withdraw at once. If that happened, then reinforcements were sure to arrive before a second wave of the invasion.

Just as these thoughts passed through Juno's mind...

"We're under attack!"

The front lines were suddenly struck.

"Damn!"

Now that he thought about it, the idea that smashing the
head of a snake would disable the rest of it applied to their side
as well. Furthermore, their own leadership was far smaller than
that of the enemy. If Juno, the commander, and Eden, his second,
were both taken out, then that was it for them.

There was no doubt that a head-to-head match would be
certain victory for the imperial forces, and even if their side
could somehow manage to hold up, it would be impossible for
them to snatch a win without taking casualties en masse. Why
did he assume that the idea of them leveraging their smaller
number to launch a surprise attack on the enemy headquarters
would never occur to the imperial officers? Why did he neglect

the possibility of the superior side launching a surprise attack of their own?

He had just been bitten in the behind by his own foolishness.

The enemy forces executing this surprise attack seemed to be a handpicked, elite group of around twenty or thirty in number, though it was impossible to discern a precise number in the midst of the fray.

"Calm down! There aren't that many of them. We'll just take them out one by—"

Before Juno could even finish speaking, a sword swung toward him.

"Guh!"

He managed to block the blade with his own sword in the nick of time, but out of the corner of his eye, he spied another enemy drawing a bow. If he tried to avoid the arrow, he would leave himself open to be hacked down by the sword. However, if he continued moving to repel the blade, he was sure to be pierced by the arrow.

"Damn it! This can't end here! I made a promise—a promise to Lady...!"

*Whoosh!*

As the arrow flew, Juno prepared himself for death.

*Ker-smack!*

"Huh...?"

Juno, the enemy swordsman, and the enemy archer all voiced their confusion in unison.

"By the hand of justice, we lend you our aid!"

Before them stood an elegant swordswoman with golden hair, who had just used her sword to strike down the swiftly flying arrow... A strange, peculiar figure, wearing a mask to hide her identity...

Without a word, the two imperial soldiers turned on the swordswoman.

"True Godspeed Blade!"

In the blink of an eye, both of the men had been struck with the flat of her blade. (In cases like these, striking with the part of the sword that would not cut someone straight through granted quite a bit more leeway.)

"Fireball!" A magical incantation rang out from the swordswoman's side.

No matter how skilled a fighter one was, an attack spell was no laughing matter. One could not fend off magic with a blade, after all.

If one were a combat magic wielder, one could get work any place, any time. Yet of course, those who would willingly enter into military service—let alone place themselves on the perilous front lines—were few and far between. Apparently, the imperial forces were willing to make that sort of investment. One of the enemy fighters rallied his own spell, but just when it was about to hit...

"Anti-Magic Blade!"

*Bwoosh!*

"Wha...?"

Inconceivably, the swordswoman's blade sliced the magical projectile clear in half. The attacking mage stood stock-still, unable to believe what he had just seen with his own two eyes. And then...

"Wind Edge!"

As the blade of wind went flying, the mage, with his inadequate armor, was struck down. Not only was the lady a top-notch swordswoman, but she was a combat magic wielder as well. How could such a person possibly exist?!

"K-kill her! Kill her now!!!" shouted the man who appeared to be the captain of the surprise attackers, judging the swordswoman to be their greatest threat.

Hearing this, the swordswoman coolly replied, "I shall never die! No matter how many times you fell me, I shall be restored and return to this battlefield, I will fight eternally to make my splendid dreams come true. For the sake of justice and the sake of my friends!"

She held her sword high above her head and declared, "I am invincible! No matter how many times I fall, I shall be reborn. I am the 'Reborn Knight'!"

Seemingly out of thin air, three girls then appeared at the swordswoman's side, giving their names in turn.

"Hunting down my enemies with ferocious tenacity, reaping their souls, I am the fearsome slayer, 'Magical Red'!"

"Guiding those souls to Hell, I am the holy 'Maiden of Darkness'!"

"Wh—? Pau—er, didn't we decide that your name was going to be, 'The Buxom Huntress'?!" the silver-haired child interjected.

"Y-you be quiet! Anyway, we aren't supposed to be 'hunters' right now, are we?!" the busty girl raged in reply.

Finally, the silver-haired child introduced herself.

"And I am she who quashes the superior side. They call me, 'Superior Mask'!"

The last time this particular character had made an appearance, her catchphrase was the complete opposite. Thankfully, the soldiers knew nothing of this. There was an entirely different question ringing through all of their minds:

***Why are they wearing those suspicious masks?!***

After the introductions were over, the four masked girls launched a high-speed assault. By spell and by blade, the imperial soldiers fell one after another. More importantly, the preceding hullabaloo had interrupted the flow of battle and granted the Ascham forces the chance to recover from the surprise attack, while the imperial troops were now, conversely, in splendid disarray. By numbers, the surprise attack force had no hope of winning—and almost immediately, the men lay prostrate on the ground.

The men who had been felled by the mysterious reinforcements were not gravely injured, but, as one might expect, those who had faced the Ascham soldiers were all seriously wounded, or even dead. Given that they did not have much leeway in the situation and no clear upper hand in terms of strength, taking their enemies hostage in the heat of battle was simply not possible. Even if it had been a possibility, it was probably not something that any of the Ascham soldiers were particularly inclined to do.

The enemies could plead all that they liked, but they would be shown no mercy. No soldier would ever be foolish enough to show kindness to an invader.

After all of the imperial soldiers had been dealt with, their own casualties tended to, and the remaining enemies taken hostage and sent back to headquarters, Commander Juno turned to the girls who had come to their aid.

"Wh-who are all of you...?"

The one who replied was the girl who looked to be the oldest of the group—the one who had come to Juno's defense.

"We are the mercenary band, the Order of the Crimson Blood. We've accepted a job request from someone indebted to an associate of the house of Ascham and come from another land to offer our assistance."

"O-our deepest thanks..."

Clearly, these were fighters who would not neglect to repay a favor that was done for them—and they were not afraid to leap into the fray of a battle that they had slim chance of winning. These were two things that deserved great gratitude...even if that name of theirs was a little bit peculiar.

Juno had not gotten a good look at the other members of the group, but now, he inspected them. They were all quite young, perhaps even underage, and...

"Wh...?"

Juno's body froze.

Radiant, flowing silver locks. A visage that, even obscured by her mask, gave the impression of someone who was kindhearted, if a little bit absentminded. Just like *she* had been, the very first time he met her...

The words spilled, unconsciously, from Juno's mouth.

"Lady...Mabel...?"

*Wasn't that my mother's name...? Hang on, this guy is probably the commander of the military, isn't he? If I recall, the commander of our forces was...*

Recalling faces was a weakness of Mile's. Other than that, her general powers of recollection were far superior to most. Thus, even though there was no way for her to recall Juno's face—a face that she had seen but a handful of times from afar, many years ago—she would never forget the words that she heard so often in conversation with her mother and grandfather: "Juno, the commander of our military," "Juno, whom my father rescued when I was twelve years old," "Juno, who protects us and our people."

Remembering these conversations, Mile smiled gently and absently uttered a phrase—a phrase that her mother herself had said to this man on the day when they first met:

"Juno, you must protect Ascham..."

The four members of the Crimson Vow disappeared back into the trees, leaving behind the man, whose face was now soaked with tears. There was a sound—perhaps a wail of anguish or a roar of delight. It resounded all throughout the woodlands where the Ascham troops had made camp.

Henceforth, there was one truth that the soldiers of Ascham came to know: a human can become a god of vengeance while he still lives and breathes. This was not a myth, but reality.

"Mile," asked Mavis sometime after, "was that man back there an acquaintance of yours?"

"Yes, though only by name. I think he was the commander of the Ascham military," Mile replied.

"So what the heck was that scream we heard right after we left him?" Reina asked suspiciously.

"Who knows? I think my mother was around the same age that I am now when she first met him. It sort of seemed like he'd mistaken me for her, and I guess I said something that she said to him back then. So he might have been remembering..."

"*You're a monster!!!*" the other three screamed.

"Huh?"

"Damn it! What are they *doing* out there?!" the colonel of the imperial forces shouted at his staff within the temporary walls of their grassland headquarters.

"Maybe they encountered some difficulties in locating the enemy?"

Even if their sneak attack had failed, it was most unlikely that *every single one* of the imperial soldiers sent out had been killed. If they made their retreat the moment that they realized failure was inevitable, then at least some of them should have been able to return to give a report. The fact that none of them had reappeared must have meant that they still had yet to actually encounter the enemy.

"I suppose we'll have to wait just a little while longer..." said the colonel with a shrug.

Just then, a single soldier came running towards him.

"I have a message! The supply convoy that was scheduled to arrive tonight came under attack! The units escorting the convoy only sustained minor injuries, but all of the goods have been destroyed!"

"*What?!*"

They were on the front lines and had just suffered a blow to their supply line. That was a huge problem...or would have been, for any lesser army. For superior forces like theirs, such a setback was a trifle. Even if they lost out on some of their supplies, their food and drink stores remained undiminished, and in a war that was being fought largely with swords and spears, there was no worry of dealing with insufficient shells or ammunition. At most, they might have to scrimp a bit on arrows, but with numbers like theirs, this was of little concern.

The convoy that had traveled out with them at the start had carried more than enough supplies to begin with, leaving them with adequate surplus so that they would have no trouble waiting until the next convoy could arrive. Even if they did begin to run low, they could simply raid the lands that they were occupying— or just have the soldiers tough out the shortages for a bit.

Why then had the colonel let out such a cry?

"How the hell did the enemy get *behind* us?! Or was this an attack from the people of the occupied lands?!"

Surely enough, the matter of the shifting battle lines was what had given the man pause.

"It could be either one... That said, it's not as though they actually attacked our main forces from the rear. They're probably just hurting for food and decided to brave the danger to try and pillage our supplies... If that's the case, and it *was* the Ascham forces, it should be easy enough to run them down. The fact that they would bother to get behind us, only to prioritize stealing our supplies over staging an actual attack means that they must be in pretty bad shape. Dwindling supplies mean that morale is low, and they won't have much longer in them! I bet we can just wait for the next supply convoy and then push right on through the fief."

"Hmm. I suppose that might be so..."

The officer's words cheered the colonel somewhat.

Neither the officer nor the colonel were idiots. They had had a plan for supplying their troops from the start—not even as a last-ditch effort. In truth, their recognition of the importance of logistics in warfare was relatively modern, even by Earth's standards.

As recently as World War II, there were many who would insist that procuring supplies locally was sufficient. Around the time of the Russo-Japanese War, military supply personnel were often belittled, with such popular sayings as, "If a wagon driver can be a soldier, then butterflies and dragonflies may as well be birds," and this attitude persisted even into World War II.

In this world, where most commanders were utterly unconcerned with whether their low-ranking subordinates even had enough to eat, there were very few who understood the necessity of maintaining weaponry or supplying ammunition. As a result, the commanders who focused on supply lines were relatively few. These men had kept some supplies in reserve, so a bit of a delay in resupply was not a problem.

A few days later, they still had not seen either hide nor hair of the surprise attack squadron, and the scouts who had gone to look for them had yet to return. The colonel was growing peevish when he received another report.

"The supply convoy was attacked! All the goods were destroyed!"

"Again?! You've gotta be kidding me!"

It was the straw that broke the camel's back.

They had carried quite a lot of food with them at the outset, and they had yet to exhaust their supplies of arrows or medicine in the course of battle. Technically, even if they experienced a bit of a delay in receiving their supplies, they had more than enough to mobilize. That said, if they were to attempt a proper invasion of the Ascham lands now, there was a possibility that they *would* begin hurting for supplies. What would hurt the most, however, was their comfort: the ale, high-quality foods, and other fresh items that the officers had reserved for themselves had already begun to bottom out.

"What are those convoy guards *doing?!* Send out some of our men and capture whoever is attacking—"

"A new report, sir! The supply stores of the 2nd and 3rd battalions have been destroyed! The 4th and 5th battalions have lost roughly half of their stockpiles as well!"

"Wh—?!"

The supply depots were manned not by the transport personnel but by members of the army proper. Now, those battalions most affected were entirely out of provisions—food, drinking water, and everything else. Even the colonel could see that this was a sticky situation.

"Take me there!"

The invading forces were a large-scale regiment, made up of five individual battalions formed of roughly 1,000 men each. The goods that had been brought in with the regiment had been divided up equally between the five battalions with each one maintaining their own individual depot. The fact that they had come under attack without their own forces even noticing meant that the enemy was capable of attacking the imperial forces from any side at any time. And that their attacks might even reach headquarters...

With this in mind, the colonel proceeded to each of the battalion's depots. What he saw was utterly unthinkable.

"H-how could this...?"

What the colonel had expected to see were ruined supply tents, and the smoldering, burnt-out husks of destroyed goods. However, what he found were clusters of supply tents still standing cleanly in a row, as though nothing had even happened...

However, each of these clusters had been utterly emptied without a single item left inside.

"What is going on here?!" the colonel shouted, laying into the commanders of each battalion as they arrived on the scene. "I would understand if the enemies had infiltrated and set fire to the depots. Well, no—I'd still have a lot of questions about whatever useless security measures allowed that to happen, but at least it would still make sense. How in the *hell* do you explain *this?!*"

Indeed, it should have been impossible for someone to simply waltz in and carry off such a large amount of supplies without anyone noticing. It would take innumerable perpetrators just to transport that much without the use of conspicuous supply wagons.

And yet, someone had accomplished this in almost no time at all, without being detected by anyone. Such a thing should not have been possible.

"Don't tell me that you lot..."

Realizing what the colonel must be thinking, the battalion commanders began to go pale.

"D-don't be ridiculous! There's no one who would be stupid enough to take advantage of the situation by siphoning off supplies from the front lines! Anyone who would try something like that wouldn't even make it home alive to be put before the military tribunal!"

Their death would be all but guaranteed—either by their inability to fight properly due to lack of supplies or the likelihood of their falling victim to their own enraged subordinates.

Even the colonel could not help but accept that logic.

"What in the world happened here?"

"We have so many of their supplies!"

Pauline looked very much like the cat who caught the canary.

"Seriously though, just how *much* can you fit in that storage of yours?" Reina stared in awe.

"Well, it *is* Mile..." Mavis seemed to have already realized that it was futile to think too hard about it.

Mile, of course, played it off with a laugh.

"This kind of seems like foul play, though..."

Just as Reina suggested, it was a bit underhanded. Mile had simply trekked into the enemy camp under the protection of an invisibility field, a sound barrier, smell barrier, and general detection barrier, scooped up the enemy's supplies into her inventory and trekked all the way back. It was incredibly easy work.

Transport units almost always had officers or some other kind of guards sticking closely to their wagons and carts, or even riding on them. As a result, sneaking in quietly to requisition an army's goods, even when they stopped to make camp, was quite impossible. Therefore, Mile had aimed for the middle of the day, when the convoys were on the move, to avoid any large-scale injuries.

By surrounding and entrapping the convoys with fire or earth magic and attacking them from the sides, they were rendered unable to proceed, their handlers forced to disembark the wagons and flee to the sides of the road. Once they had done so, it was safe to attack the vehicles with fire.

Indeed, both the attacks launched upon the imperial supply convoys and the mysterious disappearance of the goods from the depots had all been the work of the Crimson V—er, the Order of the Crimson Blood.

Naturally, the one who had proposed these attacks had been Mile, who knew all about the importance of cutting off enemy supply lines from the books, war films, and foreign dramas she had watched in her previous life, but Pauline had been all for it, too.

"What's the meaning of this?!"

"That's what *I* should be asking!"

An emergency strategy meeting had been called at the camp, and the atmosphere was tense, all parties present glaring at one another under the colonel's watchful eyes.

"Give us back our supplies at once! We might be part of the same army, but once the goods are distributed, if you let the enemy steal yours then that's *your* problem! You've got no right to come and try and take ours!"

"That's what *I* should be saying! The 2nd and 3rd battalions had everything taken from them, but the 1st battalion is unscathed. Seems pretty weird that the 4th and 5th both had half of theirs taken, doesn't it?! It's obvious that the enemy thieves got the

2nd through 4th, but then they ran out of time or reached their carrying limits and retreated. Then, as soon as the 4th realized, they rushed over and stole half the goods from us at the 5th and stashed 'em in their own depot!"

"I could say the exact same thing to you!"

"In that case, care to explain why the enemy would've skipped over the 4th and come over to the 5th? It seems natural that after the 2nd, 3rd, and 4th comes the 5th—and given that the 1st was untouched, it's pretty likely they tried to avoid the ones at the tail ends because it'd be too easy to spot them. You had better have a very good explanation!"

"Grrnh..."

The fact that the 5th battalion commander's words were growing steadily more polite was an indication of the fact that his anger was growing. Meanwhile, as for the commanders of the 1st, 2nd, and 3rd battalions...

"Just *what* is the meaning of this? How is it that we of the 2nd battalion, and the 3rd as well, now have utterly empty stores while the 1st is untouched—and in fact, has at least 30 percent more than we did to start?"

The 2nd and 3rd battalion commanders' faces were twitching, the veins bulging in their foreheads.

"How should I know?! I have no idea how this happened, I swear it!"

The commander of the 1st battalion would normally be enraged at such baseless accusations, but on this occasion, he appeared more mildly uneasy than anything else. The physical evidence of the imbalance aside, he had swiftly realized that to lob any strong words at the 2nd and 3rd, who had lost everything up to and including their food while they themselves had escaped injury, would be inexcusable.

Of course, the only thing that this restraint accomplished was to confirm the 2nd and 3rd battalion commanders' doubts about his behaviors.

Even if they were divided into battalions, such divisions were only temporary. They were still comrades, soldiers of the same regiment, in the same invading force. If anyone had lost their goods, the others should have been happy to redistribute their own.

However, to see those same comrades thieving from them and then pretending ignorance, and then trying to accuse *them* of stealing? Such things could be neither abided nor forgiven. They could give these so-called allies no quarter until they confessed to their crimes and returned the stolen goods at once.

Greatly vexed by this feud between his subordinate officers, the colonel gave up his investigation on the spot. He could already tell that, no matter what his findings were, restoring trust and morale among his men was already well nigh impossible.

"As things stand, the possibility of the Ascham troops infiltrating us and meddling with our supplies continues to grow, a fact that is made all the more dangerous by our current shortages. The next time that a convoy is scheduled to arrive, we will send a guard to meet it. Once we have received those goods and redistributed them, the invasion shall proceed. Do you understand me?!"

Thus was the colonel's decree. Whether or not the men were happy about it, no one could overrule him. The five commanders replied as one, "Yes, sir!"

"Very good. Now, when is the next convoy set to arrive?"

"Well, the next one is scheduled to have more guards, and it will be carrying a great deal more than usual to account for the previous two that were lost, so accounting for a slight delay, it should be arriving in four days."

"Very well. Five days from now, bright and early, our invasion begins. Spending all these days waiting on the damn surprise attack units was nothing more than a waste of our time..."

Later that evening, an officer appeared at the colonel's tent, looking queasy.

"S-sir! A-all the goods in our d-depot have—"

"What's this?! Speak clearly, man!"

"All of our supplies have vanished!"

*"How the hell?!"*

The colonel rushed to the depot in a panic, only to find it exactly as he had left it that afternoon. All of the barrels and crates that had contained food and other supplies were just as they had been. Seeing the confusion on his face, the officer explained.

"They're only the containers. Empty crates and empty barrels. When we checked them all this afternoon, the contents were still intact—there's no mistaking it!"

"………"

It was inexplicable, but it was just as the man said.

"We no longer have the leisure of awaiting the convoy. To wait for four days without any food would be far too dangerous. If this is all the enemy's doing, then there's a chance that they'll launch an attack on us at our weakest moment, and judging by how things have gone so far, it is possible that our next convoy, no matter how well guarded, will suffer an attack as well. I'm certain the enemy will come at us with their full force. If that should happen..."

The officer gulped.

"Our invasion begins tomorrow morning. First, we will head to the river to replenish our water, and then we set course for the capital. Spread the word!"

The officer rushed out.

Unfortunately for the soldiers, there was something they would not learn until they had already refilled their barrels at the river and were half a day away:

All of the metal bindings on those barrels had been ever so subtly loosened, and the wooden panels that formed them all cracked, just so. No matter what they did, they could not stop the barrels from leaking...

"What was that?"

"Well, sir, our barrels have been leaking, little by little. Currently, they are all nearly empty."

Hearing this latest report, the colonel was enraged.

"What is the meaning of this?!"

"The cask bindings have gone loose and the wooden panels are cracked, ever so slightly... It's not enough to be obvious when you first put the water in. They were leaking so slowly that we didn't notice it back at the river."

"And you're telling me that you just *now* noticed this, after we've already marched for half a day?!"

The colonel could scream all he wanted, but it wouldn't change the facts.

"Repair the barrels at once, and go get us some more water!" the colonel ordered.

However, his dithering subordinate replied, "B-but sir, we haven't the smiths to re-forge the bindings, and the other sections are all cracked, or have notches in them. These parts aren't something that just any layman can repair..."

"Well then, what do you propose we do?"

The subordinate, unable to respond, fell silent.

Even if they were to gather up all of the other vessels that they had on hand—in other words, their few buckets and wooden bowls and such—this would still achieve nothing. Even using all such items to draw water, the yield would be very small, and to carry them for half a day would only see their contents spilled. In any event, they had very few such containers to begin with. Naturally, even the colonel was aware that such an ordeal was not worth undertaking.

"Send for more barrels at once. I'm sure they can be requisitioned from the lands we're already occupying. While we're at it, gather up as much food as you can. I don't care if it's rice seed or seed potatoes—confiscate it all. It's the natural duty of the peasants to offer up anything that their leaders require. Now! Go!"

While they were at this, the colonel reasoned, they may as well stockpile as many barrels as possible. Some of their supplies had been stolen in their barrels, so their supply of containers was already insufficient. If they were empty, then a good number could easily be transported at a swift pace.

Yet, just as the colonel issued this order, one of the rations officers came flying into the command quarters.

"Damn it! If it isn't one thing, it's another!"

The officers in the vicinity looked quite uneasy. Without anyone noticing, the bindings of the barrels had been warped and the wood broken. All while their supplies had been under very careful watch...

Normally, they wouldn't go to the trouble of diligently attending to a lot of empty barrels and crates from which all the goods had already been stolen. However, as there was still a good chance that the enemy was slipping freely in and out of their temporary camp, the men had been instructed to keep a close watch on things. In spite of this, the barrels had been compromised.

If the enemies could just sneak in whenever they liked, then did that not also mean that they could slip in and slit their throats as they slept, without anyone noticing? It seemed only logical.

No matter how skilled and disciplined the soldiers in their employ, if all of the command staff were assassinated in the middle of the night... The colonel preferred not to imagine that scenario, instead preferring the theory that there might be traitors in their own midst who were colluding with the enemy. It was about a million times more appealing to imagine this work had been their doing.

However, the problems did not stop there.

Relations between the battalions were growing dangerously strained. Perhaps the worst they could possibly be.

What drove a soldier to brave inhospitable conditions and risk his life on the battlefield, surpassing his own limits to bring about victory, was the desire to protect his family and his motherland. More than that, his greatest strength came from the will to protect his comrades—the refusal to let a single one die.

Now, stricken with hunger and thirst, the commander's troops were calling the men of the other battalions thieves, traitors, and cowards. There would be no raising morale in circumstances like these.

To them, the others were not comrades, but enemies who had stolen their food, refused to share their own, and shirked their duties to their allies with the excuse that they, too, had been stolen from. No person who would steal another's life-sustaining food and water could ever be called anything but an enemy.

Worse still, among those who believed the other battalions to be their enemies, that line of thinking was sure to soon grow more entrenched. Next, they would grow distrustful of the other companies, then the other platoons, then the other squads. And then, each and every other man who would take from them the food and water that should have been theirs.

These men could agree to fight to the death for the sake of their homeland, alongside allies who they could trust. However, why would they ever agree to suffer and die for the sake of a bunch of thieving scumbags? It was a pointless death. A dog's death.

And once they were dead, those allies who lived on—who had stolen all their food and water—would go back home to take all the credit for their victory!

It was unfathomable. Who would die for something like that? No, they were going to make it back home alive...

Soldiers who thought like this could never give their all in a fight. They would prioritize their own safety over working together to defeat the enemy. And this was the true definition of *cowardice*...

"Looks like they're on the move," said Reina.

"Just as we predicted," Pauline agreed.

Just then, Mile interjected, "Guys, come on! Right there, you're supposed to sneer, like this, and say, 'All according to plan...' or, 'Just as the patterns divined...' or, like, 'Soldiers are nothing but trash!'"

The other three looked back at her in silence as Mile glared at them.

*I guess she's trying to put on a good face for us?* thought Mavis. Apparently, there was still much that she did not understand about the mysterious creature known as Mile.

"Let's get going!"

"Yeah!!!"

After having vanquished the imperial ambushers' units, the 300 Ascham troops broke up into 10 platoons of 30 men apiece and traveled around to the different hamlets of the fief, all while the imperial forces were still frittering around wasting time.

There was no way that an army of their numbers could ever hope for a straightforward victory against an army with scores more men. Therefore, they had no choice but to gather up all the civilians in their lands to fortify the capital's defenses, at least until reinforcements from the Crown, or other lords, could arrive.

The odds that those reinforcements would appear anytime soon were slim. However, even if the people were to abandon their lands and flee from Ascham, they would have no means by which to live, and the Ascham soldiers had not the slightest shred of intention of abandoning their homes in the first place. For them, there was no other viable option.

There were many villagers who refused to leave behind their homes and their farms and the lands where their ancestors were buried, so the soldiers had to convince those folks, as well as help move the sick who were too weak to move on their own, transporting the minimal amount of baggage possible. Bogged down by these details, the enactment of the evacuation plan did not go off quite as intended. But there was no meaning in a land without its denizens. To boast of Ascham was to boast of its people. Plus, there was the promise that Juno had made to Mabel.

"C'mon, sir, it's not like you have to leave this place behind forever! The royal troops and our neighbors' forces will come to help us, and also, the imperial army will be here soon!"

"I-Ish that sho, shonny...? Will I really be able t' come back to thish place? My wife's grave ish here... I can't help but think it would be better if I just shtayed here and died right beshide where my wife ish buried..."

As they rode along in the wagons, the old-timers had to be reassured of the same things again and again. It was a routine by now—just like gathering food or taking out the trash.

All of the watering holes were either concealed or rendered temporarily unusable. With some time and effort they could be re-dug as good as new, but no invading force was going to take the time to do such a thing.

"Hurry! The imperial army...no, the 'Albarnian bandits' will be here soon!"

Fiends who had not so much as issued a declaration of war could not be recognized as an army. 'Bandits' was a good enough term for them. Juno thought so, at any rate.

In just a few days, the imperial army would likely be on the move again. There was a chance that reconnaissance troops and other advance units might even start out before then, ahead of the main corps. Just like those units before... At any rate, whenever it was that they finally encountered the enemy again, Juno would not be surprised.

It was a little while after they had finished up evacuation preparations in one of the villages and were on the move again, helping to transport the villagers' things to the capital, that the first incident occurred.

"Sir Juno! We've lost sight of the children!"

It was a small fief, protected by a small army. There was hardly a citizen around who did not know the face of Juno, who often visited each settlement for the sake of training or assisting with other heavy labor. Several ashen-faced villagers had come to him to deliver this report.

"What?!" Juno shouted.

Upon inquiring further, he learned that a few of the naughtier children had suddenly vanished—and there was a very good chance that they had not gotten lost but run away on purpose.

"My daughter told me that she had forgotten something important back at home, so it's possible that they went back to the village..."

Hearing this, Juno summoned his deputy, Roland, at once.

"Roland, have half of the men continue on to escort the villagers. I will take the other half and search for the children."

"Yes, sir!"

By this point, Roland knew well enough that there was no point in wasting any time trying to stop Juno. There was not a member of the Ascham army who did not know that.

Juno and the fifteen men under his command headed back to the village, finally finding the five children. Just as they started to head back to catch up with the main troops, however—

"Soldiers of the kingdom! Don't let a single one escape! Make sure you bring a few in good enough shape to talk!"

With these words, several dozen imperial soldiers appeared.

Judging by what was said, the men intended to capture some of Juno's men and slaughter the rest. They would likely be tortured for information about Brandel without ever having a chance to send back word of their own circumstances.

If the enemy soldiers had been riding on horseback down the highway, they probably would have spotted them sooner, but they appeared to be recon troops or some other sort of forerunners, lying in wait and preparing a trap for the Brandel soldiers, so were moving quietly on foot. With their attention fully focused on finding the children, Juno and his men took notice of the enemy soldiers just a little too late.

With the children in tow, it would be impossible to simply make a run for it. They had no choice but to stand and fight it out. Surrender, of course, was never even an option.

"Keep the walls of the buildings at your backs and protect the children! If we can each take down—what, two or three of the enemy?—then it'll be over in a jiffy. Nothing to it!"

"You got that right, sir!" the soldiers roared.

There wasn't a soldier around who would be afraid of a skirmish like this one. Grinning at his subordinates' hardy reply, Juno plunged forth into the enemy ranks, a handful of his men following behind him. The remainder stayed behind as guard, keeping the walls and the children at their backs.

In the battle that would come to unfold, the Ascham forces

were vastly outmatched. In battle, Juno was a lion, but fighting against real, trained soldiers—ones who were skilled enough to have been selected as a vanguard, at that—was not the same as fighting against bandits, and no matter how fired up his men were, they were nowhere near the level to take on several men at once.

What left them at even more of a disadvantage, however, was that they were forced to split their resources in twain.

If they were to group up all as one, keeping the children in the middle, then the enemies would simply surround them and pick them off at their leisure. So there was no choice but to leave behind one portion of their forces to defend the children, while the other group went flying into the fray, whipping up a frenzy among their enemies. However, this meant that the men who were guarding the children could not move from where they were, and for now, the imperial soldiers were free to completely ignore them. Thus, the wrath of the imperial soldiers came down on the fragmented forces with full force, and it seemed clear that both would be quashed in their turn.

The Ascham soldiers' assumption—that the imperial forces would plan to target the children as hostages—had betrayed them.

It would have been one thing if the imperial troops were only a little over twice their numbers. However, here they were facing four or five times as many men, and they quickly found themselves at a complete loss. Juno managed to take down several of the imperial soldiers, and the other men gave everything they had as well, but they were outnumbered. Now they could only pray that the enemies would not lay a hand upon the children once they were through with the men.

After all, the men of Ascham reassured themselves, the enemies they faced were not truly bandits or cutthroats, but trained soldiers just like them. They were under the charge of a legitimately appointed commanding officer, and as such, it was unthinkable that they would act barbarically. And yet...

"We don't need those brats. Kill 'em all."

*"What?!"* the Ascham men shouted.

Anywhere in the world, there were good people. Likewise, anywhere in the world there were people who could best be described as human trash.

After felling the men who fought alongside Juno one by one, the imperial commander now ordered an attack on the soldiers who guarded the children. Naturally, the scope of that attack would include the children as well...

"You can't! I won't let you! Graaaaah!!!"

Juno raised a battle cry and swung his sword with all his might, but Lanchester's linear law was a cruel mistress. In a battle of blades and arrows, the results all depended on the difference in numbers between each of the sides—in a harsh, linear function. The only thing that could upset this was...

"Fireball!"

"Ice Needle!"

"Wind Edge!"

Indeed, the only way to combat such a reality was to introduce into the fray combatants who had the means to rain certain death indiscriminately upon a group of enemies, regardless of their numbers. This was certainly the case with a rifle or machine gun. In such a case, one side was operating on linear law versus another operating on square law. The two sides were so fundamentally different that there was no point in even trying to formulate an equation.

Magic suddenly began raining down on the imperial soldiers.

The men who had been heading toward the soldiers guarding the children flailed as they were bathed in a mass of fireballs, while the men who were keeping Juno's team in check were pelted with icy needles and scythe-like whirlwinds.

"Hell, are you all amateurs?! They're mages, just get there and knock 'em down before they can finish their next spells! Go!"

In close-range combat there was no hope for a mage who was attacked without time to cast their spells. However, that was only the case *if* they were attacked and *if* they were a mage.

"Wind Edge! Wind Edge! Wind Edge!!!"

"Wha?! She can cast without an incantation? More than *once?!*"

As far as Mavis herself was aware, her "Wind Edge" was not magical. It was merely a sword attack that utilized her spiritual energy, so as long as she could swing her sword, she could cast it as much as she liked...

Surely, this was breaking the rules. That said, the power of the Wind Edge was not enough to cleave through the trunk of an armor-clad enemy in a single stroke. Still, as the imperial soldiers' numbers diminished, and they tried to plunge toward the mages...

"EX True Godspeed Blade!" Mavis shouted.

Thinking that the power of her normal True Godspeed Blade would be insufficient against most trained soldiers, she had already popped a capsule of Micros… Just one, this time. She couldn't risk ruining her body at a time like this, when Mile was not present.

The imperial soldiers fell left and right. Luckily for them, she held her power back, striking them with the flat of the blade so as not to kill them.

"Impossible! How could a mere mage…?" the man who appeared to be the commander began to shout.

Mavis proudly replied, "I am a knight. A Magical Knight!!!"

While the imperial soldiers fell back, the Ascham troops took the opportunity to mobilize. Their enemy's numbers had been greatly diminished, and now, impeded by the magical attacks… they were sitting ducks.

Disregarding some more extraordinary exceptions, there was little difference in strength between most top-class soldiers. Thus, if one side had their strength lowered by even 20 percent, they were already in an untenable position. Imbued with new confidence, the soldiers defending the children repelled the enemy forces as one, swearing that they would not allow even one man to slip past them.

In the disarray, Reina and Pauline were able to wrap up their next spells, Reina launching another attack and Pauline providing healing to the injured Ascham soldiers. Anyone who approached either of the two were sent flying by the flat of Mavis's blade.

As the number of enemy soldiers continued to decrease, the number of battle-ready soldiers on the Ascham side was steadily increasing, thanks to Pauline's healing.

The match was quickly settled after that. After pinning down the enemy commander, who attempted to flee, Juno left his capture to his subordinates and headed over to where the three girls stood.

"This makes twice now that you've saved us," he said. "I can't thank you enough. Also..."

He trailed off in the midst of his thanks, looking around nervously.

"Wh-where's Lady Mabel...?"

*Ah.*

The three girls' faces fell.

"Unfortunately, she had a letter to deliver."

At Pauline's reply, Juno could not help but think, *Ah, she's sending a message to the gods up in Heaven.* It gave him the utmost regret that he was unable to meet her, but if she was on errand to the gods themselves, then there was little to be done. However, he could yet feel the depths of her love and grace in leaving her servants behind to protect them. So Juno mused, until...

"We just so happened to be able to help you this time, but please don't expect our assistance every time hereafter. That kind of dependent thinking offends the Goddess, and those who comport themselves in that manner will be denied her protection," the busty girl decreed, appearing to have guessed exactly what he was thinking.

Quickly, Juno bowed his head, amending his flawed, "dependent" train of thought.

"Now then, we shall depart."

With those words, the three girls left. Juno and his men watched, as they disappeared over the horizon.

"Mile told us to take it easy and get some food in a nearby village or something until she comes back from delivering that letter. And yet, here we are working for free!" Reina sulked.

Apparently, the fact that the trio had been present for the rescue mission was truly coincidental—in this instance, they had not planned on coming to the Ascham army's aid.

Of course, though Reina was vaguely sullen about it, they all knew that they had not intended to earn any money during this particular job in the first place.

"It may have been a coincidence, but I think it's still good that we could help. Let's recall that we saved an acquaintance of Mile's, the soldiers who technically work for Mile, and a bunch of children, who all live here," replied Mavis, ever the optimist.

"That's quite right. Besides, if the commander of the Ascham army died in a place like this, that would really put a kink in our plans. Still, this misunderstanding has really made things strange between Mile and that man... I get the feeling that the more they see each other, the worse Mile's going to feel, so perhaps this is all for the best."

And then there was Pauline, calm and collected to the last. "At any rate, it seemed like the Ascham forces were already well equipped in terms of food and water, and once they read that letter they'll have a surplus, which I think we can expect them to use their discretion in distributing. At this point, I think it's safe to say we can leave Ascham to them. After we reconvene with Mile, we can head toward the county south of here, which has already been invaded by the Empire."

Pauline spoke with a smile, but it was one in which there was not an ounce of mercy to be found.

Their task of escorting the villagers complete, all of Juno's men had returned to the capital. Now, with everyone back together, Juno once again took charge of the force. As they got into formation to repel the approaching imperial forces, a soldier approached Juno, carrying a message.

"A silver-haired girl asked me to deliver this letter," the man said.

"A message...?"

That well-developed brunette had said something about this, hadn't she? If Juno recalled...

*"Unfortunately, she had a letter to deliver..."*

Juno snatched the letter from the man's hands. The contents of the message read:

*The imperial forces have lost all of their supplies, including their food and water. In addition, all of their attempts at resupply have been interrupted. The following measures have been undertaken to prevent them from receiving any further supplies...*

Below this were spelled out various methods of surprise and rear attacks, and instructions for making incredibly wicked traps...

The name of the sender was not written, but Juno did not need a name to know who it was from. Anyone who read this letter, who had been vexed by Lady Mabel's mischief and the clever traps she had set in her youth, would immediately recognized the methods outlined in this letter as exactly the sort of thing Lady Mabel would do when fired up.

At the end of the letter was inscribed a single line.

"Oh, my..."

Juno gripped the silver-haired girl's letter tightly, tears flowing down his face.

"Oh, my word!"

Just as the people around him began to worry that there was something wrong, Juno shouted: "It's a divine decree! For now on, we of the Ascham army are the foot soldiers of the Goddess herself, under her command! We are a chosen army! Beginning at this moment, we are a divine force! The winds of justice, the will of the divine, and the Goddess's own protection flow through all of us!"

The men let out a roar, the likes of which only a howling storm could rival.

Juno was not the sort to stir his men up with empty lies, and by now, everyone had heard the tale of how the Goddess's servants had helped them stave off the imperial ambush just a few days prior—and furthermore, how those same servants had come to the aide of Juno's squad and the children after that.

Lady Mabel had ascended to heaven in order to protect her people. Now she was visiting her blessings upon them—and she had three divine soldiers accompanying her as well.

They could win. No, they *had* to win. The will of the universe could never permit a divine army under the Goddess's command to fall to the forces of evil.

And so, the spirits of vengeance began to multiply.

"Now then, we shall begin to enact our plan, as directed by our goddess. Thanks to her divine punishment, the imperial army has lost all of its supplies, down to food and water, and all further routes of resupply have been cut off. We shall obstruct the enemy from trying to produce any of their supplies locally and then retreat to wait until they are weak and exhausted.

"If we enter the battle at all, it will only be in small reconnaissance groups or as independent agents. The Goddess has made the lives and safety of the citizens of Ascham her priority, and we must never forget that you soldiers are her citizens as well. There will be no pointless deaths in this conflict. Do you hear me?!"

"*Yeaaaaaaaaaaaaaaaah!!!*"

Another valiant cry rose from the men.

"All right, then! While we retreat, we'll hunt all of the jackalopes and orcs that the imperial army might be able to use for food. Let's store up as many wild fruits and vegetables growing on the side of the road as seem edible, too. Now, let the preparations commence!"

The army hurriedly began the task of packing up camp.

"...And so, we'd like for you all to entrust your food and your barrels to the Goddess just for a short while. We'll be sure to return them afterwards, and if you don't comply, the Empire will certainly steal them away. Do you really think that those soldiers, who have lost everything—who are citizens of an enemy nation—are going to look kindly on you citizens of Brandel and leave you your seed crops for next year? They're going to take everything from you, force you to carry your own goods to the front lines, and demand women—perhaps even young children—to serve them. Hide everything, and then conceal yourselves in the mountains. It's for your own safety."

The so-called Order of the Crimson Blood was keeping busy, traveling to all of the larger villages along the main roads of the county of Cesdour, which abutted the national border, and which the Empire had already conquered. To the smaller villages, they sent on the villagers who had already been persuaded as messengers. The message they carried was, "Hide your food and everything else, and then hide yourselves."

Ascham was now in the hands of its army. If they were following the directions outlined in the letter, Mile calculated, then they should be making the same preparations there around now. They didn't have access to Mile's inventory, but with their forces concentrated together, they should be able to manage well enough.

And of course, the Crimson Vow had no reason to doubt a single particle of Juno's resolve. After all, at Pauline's suggestion, they had included a single line at the end of that letter:

**_Juno, you must protect Ascham!_**

It was quite the wicked gambit...

"Damn it! Where are all of those Ascham bastards?!" the colonel of the imperial regiment growled, not even attempting to hide his aggravation.

The troops had begun their fruitless march to requisition supplies from the locals and had now assaulted countless villages, only to come up empty-handed every time. All signs of the villagers had vanished, including their food and water. Not a single scrap had been left behind. They couldn't seem to find a trace of any wells, either. It seemed they had been buried, and all ropes and drawing apparatuses dismantled, leaving no indication that they had been there at all—to prevent the imperial troops from using them.

If all they had done was bury them, then re-digging them later would not be much of a task. With the combined efforts of all the villagers, the reconstruction would take no more than a few days. However, at present, the imperial forces did not have the time to spend days looking for the dig sites and then days more re-digging them themselves. Such time would be far better spent continuing to advance and tearing the capital down. Additionally, there was no telling how much longer it would take to build the simple housings required over the tops of wells—or if something more elaborate was needed, how long it would take to find the devices. For now, they had no choice but to press on.

"Where *are* all the Ascham troops? Don't tell me they all got together and circumvented us to stage a coordinated sneak attack..."

"No! If they did that, then there would be no one to defend against us invading the capital. It would be impossible for them to completely evacuate the city and hide all of its resources in the way that we've seen in these villages. If they lost their capital, then no matter how many hundreds of soldiers they had left, it would be the death of Ascham.

"Even if they managed to recruit all of the peasants, they would still have only a few hundred more soldiers at best. There would be nothing they could do against us if we'd already set up in their home base. They'd never go so far as laying waste to their own capital, after all."

The colonel nodded at his officer's words.

"In that case..."

"Well, sir, I believe we should ignore this clever ruse on the part of our enemy and proceed toward our destination."

"Indeed. Apparently, we were foolish to think that we could interrupt their chain of command with a surprise assault and move in to occupy the capital unscathed. Had we simply over-whelmed them with force from the get-go and moved straight in, we would have been relaxing and drinking fine wines by now," the colonel said, a bit disdainfully.

The officer shrank back. He had been the one to propose the surprise attack in the first place, but of course, it was the colonel himself who had judged this plan of action to be the correct one, and had directed his men to proceed with it, so the officer couldn't take all the blame.

"All right, men, roll out!"

After taking an extended break for lunch, the imperial troops began to move again. The only ones who had been provided meals—scraped together from the scanty food they had stored outside of the supply depots and the minuscule amount of wild grasses they had managed to harvest along the road—were the officers. For the rest of the soldiers, it was merely a long rest.

Initially, they had planned to hunt wild animals and monsters along the way, but for some reason, they could not catch anything. No doubt, moving with so many men kicked up too much of a ruckus, the officers assumed, thinking nothing odd of the situation.

"Gah!"

"Gwaaaah!!!"

The screams of soldiers rang out once more.

"Damn it, these bastards are persistent!" The officer in command of the vanguard troops let out a cry of rage.

Indeed, his men had just fallen into yet another trap.

First, they had come across what they had thought was the usual sort of crude pit that a child would trick someone into, but at the bottom of the pit were sharp bamboo spikes, slathered with poison. Then, they had stumbled upon what looked to be bothersome little rocks and tried to kick them out of the way, only to find iron rods embedded in the ground—iron rods, which had broken the men's toes. When they had tried to move a fallen tree that was blocking the road, and the men moved to put their hands under the trunk to lift it, they found the underside lined with innumerable thorns—naturally, covered in poison. When they tripped over an imperceptible wire, arrows came flying towards them, and they were assailed with great force by bamboo and shrubbery that had been bent for tension, with pointed stakes attached.

Most of these tricks were crudely made, hastily and clumsily fashioned, so there were of course misfires. However, there were others along this gauntlet that were elaborately and skillfully crafted, and these were no laughing matter—there were times they took fatal damage head-on. Thanks to those traps in this latter category, they had to treat every one of these traps with caution, and they had no choice but to proceed with great care.

Normally, in such a small fief as this, it would take them no more than a matter of hours to reach the capital from the border, but thanks to the traps, their movement was many times slower, and they still had a long way ahead of them. Having to make such a wild detour for the sake of getting water had not helped matters either. For the soldiers who were becoming overwhelmed with hunger and thirst, and would rather get to the capital as quickly as possible, all this was highly irritating. Of course, their irritation further clouded their attentiveness, causing them, yet again, to fall into a trap.

When looking at their numbers as a whole, it seemed of little consequence if they lost a battle-ready man here or there, but that still did not mean that they could afford to go around ignoring the traps' perils. And so, the average marching speed of the imperial forces fell to a halting crawl, less than even what a wobbling eighteen-month-old could muster...

The requisition troops that they had sent back to the occupied lands a few days prior had already returned. The men had found each of the villages along the highways completely deserted, devoid of food and water. Furthermore, it was not until they arrived—bringing with them the barrels that they had picked up from the villages and filled with water from the river where the regiment had previously stopped—that they found that almost none of the water they had put into the barrels remained.

Yet again, the bindings were warped, and the wooden panels were cracked with notches cut into them. Every single barrel had been compromised.

"The imperial troops should be arriving about now," said Reina.

"Yes," Pauline agreed. "We laid out plans for a lot of traps in that letter. Even if they couldn't put them all together... I think they should be arriving now."

The two of them stood at the top of an elevation from which they could see the Ascham capital. As mentioned, there had been a secondary sheet in the letter that Mile delivered, which contained blueprints for all of the plans that the Ascham troops had utilized to build their traps. It seemed that those men had followed their instructions exactly.

The imperial forces were exhausted, starving, and thirsty, and their usual cooperation was stunted by the discord sewn among them. Even so, the odds were still stacked against the Ascham forces.

5,000 vs. 300. That was seventeen imperial soldiers for every Ascham man. No matter how weak they were, winning against a force seventeen times your own in number was simply not possible. Furthermore, no matter how exceptional the fighting abilities of the Order of the Crimson Blood may have been, 4 vs. 5,000 was still just a little too much to ask.

Of course, if Mile were to get truly serious—if she were to fight without limits, without restraint—if she set out with the intent to slaughter every single one of those 5,000 men, then maybe, just maybe, it might not be so impossible. However, to do such a thing would leave Mile unable to retain a shred of happiness—with respect to neither her own mental health nor to international relations.

300 vs. 5,000.

4 vs. 5,000.

Both were utterly unbeatable odds.

So then, what of 300 + 4 vs. 5,000?

No matter how strong they were, it would be difficult for just four people to cause a ruckus among 5,000 men and defeat them all.

However, if those 5,000 men were weakened, and had already grown sloppy from the commotion caused by the four, and then 300 elite soldiers jumped into the fray...?

It was for the sake of just such a possibility that the Order of the Crimson Blood had put all their efforts into undermining the enemy on so many fronts. Now, they were on the cusp of the final, decisive battle. They would strike the imperial soldiers from behind even as they faced off against the men of Ascham, who would keep their own capital at their backs.

The imperial forces would not be setting a single foot in the capital!

"They're here. It's the imperial army!" announced Mile.

"So they are," Reina agreed as the two lingered in the shadows of the trees, observing the highway.

"I can see the imperial troops," said Mavis, "but where are the Ascham soldiers?"

There was silence. The four of them had all come to the same realization, but no one could drum up the nerve to put their concern into words. Finally, it was Mavis who voiced it.

Silence fell again. Indeed, in between the capital and the advancing imperial forces, there was no sign of the Ascham army... In fact, there was no sign of the Ascham army anywhere at all.

"Wh-wh-wh-wh-what do we do...?"

"Wh-wh-wh-wh-what should we do now...?"

"C-c-c-c-calm down, everyone..."

"That's awfully strange..."

Reina, Mile, and Mavis were babbling nervously; Pauline alone remained calm.

"I know for certain that we wrote in the letter that they should remove all of the people and supplies from the villages along the enemy's approach route, and that the final battle would take place at the capital. Even if this place is called a 'capital,' it's still really just a little country town, not a walled city. The lord's manor is just an estate, not a castle or a fortress, so it's not the sort of place where siege tactics would come into play. Judging from what happened before, I doubt they would ignore any part of a letter from Mile, and they've done pretty well in following all of our other instructions up until now..."

The other three were silent. Pauline was exactly right. They had all gone over the letter fastidiously before sending it, so there could be no mistake. They scratched their heads as they tried to imagine what the absence of the army might mean, but they came up with nothing.

They could not possibly have abandoned the capital and run.

"Oh! The imperial army is sending out a recon unit!" said Mavis.

Sure enough, the Albarnians, too, had found the lack of any military defense peculiar and had sent out a reconnaissance team of around thirty men to investigate. The men had just entered the capital and proceeded a short distance when...

There was a shout as arrows and spears and rocks suddenly came raining down from out of the windows up on the rooftops. The imperial soldiers fell one by one. And then, men armed with melee weapons came pouring from the doorways.

"What...?"

It was no surprise that the girls should be so bewildered. The men that appeared from the buildings were not armed with swords and spears, but with kitchen knives, hoes, what appeared to be mop handles, and the like—numerous objects that were clearly not weapons suitable for a soldier in any professional sense.

"Most of those men aren't soldiers, are they? They're just citizens of the capital and the villagers who took refuge there," said Pauline.

"Ah." Suddenly, something occurred to Mile.

"It's urban warfare. When Juno read that the final battle would be at the capital, instead of interpreting it as a battle taking place in front of the capital, defending it to the last, he must have thought that we meant that the battle itself would take place *in* the capital..."

"Wh-what are you talking about?!" Reina sputtered.

Mile explained:

"On an open battlefield, with no obstacles, the side that has the greatest number has the overwhelming advantage—even if it's an enemy that's been weakened a fair bit. So, Juno decided to move the battle to a place where it's difficult to leverage that advantage. You can't carry on a battle with any large numbers in a place full of obstacles, with obstructed views, and in narrow back alleys. On the contrary, the Ascham side knows the placement of all the buildings and the lay of the land—*and* they can get all of the peasants involved in the fighting..."

"Th-that's ridiculous! Fighting is a job for soldiers! What are they thinking making normal people engage with enemy forces?!" Mavis shouted. "If an army is defeated and a battle ends, then the country that claims a land and the people that govern it may change, but the citizens still live on. That is the nature of battle—of war! At this rate, all of these civilians—the wives and the elderly, the sick and invalid—all of them will all get caught up in the fight and die!"

Mavis could protest all she wanted, but the wheels were already in motion.

"That's what true, all-out war is," Mile said softly. "War doesn't care if you're a civilian or a soldier. It's not something that takes place just between governments and armies. Every citizen of a nation contributes to the war effort, whether it's economically, through labor, or in some other way. And sometimes, the contribution they make is their life," Mile finished. This world was not one where such notions had yet to become commonplace.

Pauline spoke. "The poison was too effective."

"What?"

"We leveraged the fact that they had mistaken you for your mother, risen to godliness. They must have thought that no matter what method they used, they were certain to win. They likely told the civilians something similar."

"So...this is all *my* fault..."

Mile began to pale.

"No, Mile, that's not true. I was the one who proposed that you write that in the letter in the first place! I hadn't expected them to go as far as this, so I failed to include any language prohibiting it. The fault is all mine. And so..."

"So?"

"So I will take responsibility. If I run straight into the enemy lines and spread my 'hot' magic all around, then I can probably cause enough confusion to—"

What she proposed was a suicide mission. No matter how much chaos she planted amongst the soldiers, it was a gambit from which there would be no return.

"Permission denied!" Mile swiftly shot down Pauline's harried words.

"The lands we stand on are the property of Viscount Ascham and one named Adele von Ascham. These are my lands, and those are my people. Therefore, they are *my* responsibility! And furthermore..."

A wicked grin flashed across Mile's face.

"Everyone's going to call Juno a liar if the Goddess herself doesn't appear at this final battle. Consider the poor man's reputation! I'll be right back!"

*Whoosh!*

The next moment, Mile had vanished.

"Mile...?"

"Mile...? Well, all right, let's follow..."

"Okay! Let's get ready to run!"

"What?"

Reina's enthusiastic reply shocked the other two. However, Reina gave no pause, continuing with a casual lilt, "Mile's getting serious. If we go now, we'll just get in her way. Plus, there's nothing else we can do, is there? Mile's gonna blow it somehow and come running back before we know it, all, 'Oh nooooo, I messed up again!' Am I right?!"

"...You're totally right," said Mavis.

"Th-that's probably true..." Pauline agreed.

Mavis gazed off into the distance and then spoke, "Anyway, it seems like she's getting along just fine down there..."

"Lattice Power Barrieeeeeeer!!!"

With a lattice barrier surrounding her body in a one-meter radius, Mile went charging through the middle of the imperial soldiers at high speed.

"Geh!"

"Gah!"

"Waaah!"

She continued plowing forward, knocking soldiers back one by one, all the way to the front—the space between the soldiers and the capital. Once she reached that point, she stopped, turning on a dime, and started *that*. Yes, *that*.

"*Goddess Formation Mile, transformation activate!* Refract and diffuse the light. Gather moisture into ice! Neutralize gravity and maintain formation...and complete! Final Fusion!!!"

Glimmering wings of ice appeared behind Mile's back, and a glowing ring of light formed above her head, both locking onto her.

"Cavorite, go!"

With the gravity around her negated, Mile kicked off, floating around ten meters up into the air. There she paused for a breather, staring upwards and huffing with exertion.

*Ugh, this is already getting out of hand! I'm wearing a mask, sure, but that doesn't mean that no one's gonna figure out who I am. And on the off chance that someone does guess my identity...*

*Why, if someone figures out who I am because of this, I'll have no chance of living a normal, happy life ever again!*

Realizing this, Mile was already at her wits' end.

She vibrated the air so that her voice would reach every last one of the imperial soldiers' ears.

"FOOLISH CREATURES!"

"Wh-what the heck is that?!"

"A bird?"

"A wyvern?"

"No, i-it's..."

"A g-goddess..."

The Albarnian troops were utterly shaken. Her voice booming, Mile began to speak again.

"Justice without power is meaningless, but power without justice is a grievous sin. And thus, as your goddess, I render upon you the punishment of death. Vile sinners, repent!"

Already, things were a huge mess. In her desperation, Mile began running through the relevant entries in her encyclopedia of phrases that she had always wanted to say.

"Sh-she's a fake! There's got to be some kind of trick here!" One man, who appeared to be an officer, shouted, trying to placate his disturbed subordinates. Yet, trick or not, there was no building or tall tree in the vicinity from which one could suspend a person in midair, and things such as cranes and piano wire had yet to be invented in this world. Moreover, most people in this world *did* believe in such things as gods and devils. Even this officer would never dare say that there was no such thing as a goddess.

All the same, he could not be expected to direct the army to pack up and leave just because a *supposed* goddess told them to. If he went back with a report like that, it would see him decapitated or hanged. Of course, such matters were no business of the rest of the soldiers. Punishing commanders and officers who could not handle the pressures of their job was one thing, but no official would dare to levy capital punishment on 5,000 soldiers.

Thus, the soldiers stood where they were, refusing to take another step.

"Men who would invade without issuing a declaration of war are no soldiers, no army. They are villains—brethren of evil! Such foul creatures would never be welcomed into the warrior's haven of Valhalla upon their deaths. The only invitation you lowlife brigands shall ever receive is a one-way ticket straight to perdition! Now, accept your divine judgement!"

Just then, a magical formation in the shape of the head of a wolf appeared in midair. From its open mouth, an enormous sound rang out over the imperial soldiers.

"Raucous Thunder!"

A divine, punishing thunderclap released from the wolf in the sky rained down upon all foes: Raucous Thunder.

### Flash! Ka-booom!

Silence fell.

The space around was filled with an almost terrifying silence, and the Albarnian troops stood, mute.

The people of the capital, who had heard everything thanks to Mile's sound vibration magic, were equally silent.

The only sound that rang out, both from outside of the capital and within, was the deafening quiet of fear. Some people sunk in terror and awe; others' eyes shone with hope and reverence. Yet everyone ceased moving and stared up into the sky.

*What do I do now?* Mile fretted.

No one moved a muscle. No one said a word.

*I can't just keep floating here forever...*

Currently, she was waiting for the imperial soldiers to turn tail and retreat. She certainly did not really intend to strike all of them dead with lightning. However, not a single one had made a move...

When Mile looked behind her, towards the Ascham troops,

she suddenly saw something particularly visible from her elevated vantage point.

To the north side of the capital, on the opposite side from the Albarnians' approach, was a mass of soldiers, already nearly upon the city. Their numbers were far more vast than those of the enemies to the south: a sea of soldiers four, maybe five times the numbers of the imperial regiment, perhaps even more. Considering that they were approaching from the north, it was quite impossible that they would be soldiers of the Empire. Which would mean that...

This group was the Royal Army of Brandel—a conglomeration of the king's own men and the forces of each noble's lands. In fact, Mavis had spotted them far more quickly than Mile, who had her back turned to the capital while she had been up in the air.

"Wh-what...? But Pauline and Mavis both told me that they probably wouldn't be sending out their troops just yet! Did those guys just speed up? They must have just noticed the Albarnian soldiers... Guh! *Oh crap, oh crap, oh crap, oh crap.* Never mind the Albarnians—I can't let them notice meeeeeeeeeeeeee!!!"

Mile muttered aloud to herself, but thankfully was no longer utilizing her sound vibrating magic, so no one else could hear her. Panicking, she descended straight down at once, plowing back through the imperial ranks and running straight back to meet up with Reina and the others.

"G-guys, we've gotta go, r-r-r-right now..."

"Time to retreat!" Reina directed, cutting in.

"Okay!!" shouted Mavis and Pauline.

Mile, a beat behind, mumbled, "Okay..."

Thus, the so-called Order of the Crimson Blood vacated the scene at high speed, running off to the south. Meanwhile, on the battlefield they left behind...

"Colonel! Enemy forces have been spotted to the north of the capital!" said an officer, relaying a semaphore message from the lookouts stationed up on an elevation, keeping an eye on the status of the battlefield and capital.

"What?! But all of the Ascham army is holed up in the capital." The colonel, still not quite recovered from the so-called goddess who had vanished as suddenly as she had appeared, expressed his disbelief.

"Th-that's not it, sir! It's not the Ascham army. They think it might be the royal army! We haven't been able to yet confirm the number of soldiers yet, but there are at least 20,000 and possibly far more!"

"Wh-what did you say?!"

If they were to rush in right now, at full speed and at full force, then they might be able to make it into the capital before the royal army arrived. However, if they were to then position themselves in the capital, where the three hundred men of the Ascham army were stationed, they would be surrounded by aggressive townspeople, trying to face off against an army many times their size. That would be a suicide mission.

Furthermore, the capital was not a fortified citadel. There were no walls surrounding it, no castles. With their supplies so diminished and even their archers short on arrows, there were few pros and many cons to entering a place like that. At the very least, the circumstances were not sufficient to satisfy the "Three Times" Rule of Offense—that one needed to possess an offense that was three times stronger than the enemy's defense in order to prevail.

Furthermore, fights had already been breaking out among the imperial soldiers, they'd barely had anything to eat in the past few days, and the water in their canteens had dried up ages ago. Their mages, having had to use their magic to come up with any drops of water they possibly could, were now in no state to do much more than move. Troop morale, physical condition, and loyalty were at an all-time low—there was no way that the Albarnians could take on an army of this size in their condition.

"Why?! Our analysts all predicted that the Crown would never respond immediately, that they would leave all their weak, remote territories to rot and set up their defenses just outside of them. They said that they would never act until they were completely ready to move! That was why we never mobilized any troops outside of this regiment and why we made it clear that this was not a full-blown play for the capital of Brandel—that intel was supposed to be reliable! Don't tell me that they figured out the second stage of our plan for when we would face off against the kingdom's counteroffensive?!"

Trying to forecast an enemy's movements boiled down to little more than personal opinion. Even when one was in possession of completely reliable information about the enemy and an accurate understanding of their psychology, one's predictions could still be way off. Needless to say, there were also many instances where the analysts possessed insufficient or incomplete information, and their enemies might try to outwit them—or they themselves might act on a sort of wishful thinking, assuming the circumstances to be in their favor.

"We have visual confirmation of the enemy vanguard! They're bearing flags of the armies of each noble household of Brandel, and—yes! Those are the king's colors, and the royal coat of arms itself!" the officer shouted.

The colonel was floored.

"*Why?* Why would they come at us with this much force, just for the sake of some insignificant little fief out on the borderlands?! The royal family, you say? I can't imagine the king spearheading those troops himself—could it be the first prince? The second prince is still too young, but would they really risk their crown prince, a sharp young man who carries all of the kingdom's hopes for the future, on a battle like this? Inconceivable! They would never do such a thing!"

Seeing the state into which the colonel had fallen, one officer, already resigned to incurring his superior's wrath, spoke up. "Colonel, your orders, sir! We haven't any time to delay!"

Whether he was going to tell them to attack or to retreat, he had to do it quickly. He could not simply let his men stand around and be run down by the enemy. Even if the order given was for a reckless assault that was certain to see them all annihilated, a soldier abided by his commander's word. This was the resolve that shone in the officer's eyes as he looked to the colonel.

"Soldiers, retreat! About face, on the double! Withdraw from the battlefield immediately!"

The officer looked at him peculiarly. It would not have been at all surprising for this particular colonel to instead give the order to attack. Realizing this, the colonel scrunched up his face in self-deprecation and muttered, "I don't care if historians of future generations label me an 'idiot,' but, 'the fool who sentenced 5,000 men to a pointless death' is a little bit much…"

Then, he raised his voice and bellowed, "Quickly, will you?! If we don't move out of here faster than the enemies arrive, they'll catch up with us from behind, and we'll be wiped out! Permission is granted to discard anything you don't need for the return trip. Now, *hurry!!!*"

The officers took off running in various directions. If they abandoned all of their weapons and supplies, there was at least a slim chance that they might be able to escape from the enemy army, which was still fully laden, with a supply unit in tow. As long as they could maintain enough of a distance for them not to be taken captive…

"Seems like we've bought ourselves a fair bit of distance. Let's change directions now and start heading east. If we went south from here, we would have to go straight through the Empire, which would mean keeping the the imperial army on our tails the whole time."

The Order of the Crimson Blood—or rather, the girls once again known as the Crimson Vow now that their mercenary duties were finished—had been moving south to avoid the armies of both Brandel and Albarn, but now it was about time for a change of plan.

Pauline, however, raised an objection to Reina's proposal.

"Just a minute now. There's something I'd like to take care of first. The imperial soldiers won't have any time to detour to the river, and at this rate it's possible they'll end up dying of thirst. There's no way that the water that a few low-ranking mages could produce would ever be enough to meet the needs of 5,000 men, along with their horses, who require even more... Most soldiers aren't necessarily villains or criminals, and I'd like to help them out a bit..."

It was rare to have mages fighting on the front lines at all, along with the other basic recruits. Anyone who had sufficient magical ability to use it in combat would not accept the position of common foot soldier, where the danger outweighed the pay. Even in times of emergency conscription, they could still file a petition for wages, and if they ever willingly took a position in the military, they were welcomed at the rank of officer, at least. In other words, there were very few mages on the scene in this instance.

Furthermore, the amount of water that could be produced via magic had a known limit. The amount of water that a human requires each day is around two liters. For 5,000 men, that was ten tons of water. Plus, every horse needs around thirty liters of water a day—the same amount as fifteen men. The elites of the army were much more likely to favor one horse over fifteen foot soldiers. Even if you were to bring together all those who could use enough utility magic to produce very small amounts of water, there was simply no way to compile enough magic to summon up ten-odd tons of water every single day. Never mind that drawing that much water all in one place would suck the air dry, creating an inhospitable desert.

Those who could use their magic for combat were also quite unlikely to want to use all their magical strength on something as trivial as gathering water. That was as good as ordering a soldier on the battlefield to abandon his sword, and there were few mages who would ever accept such a command. At best you might ask them to relinquish half of their magical stores to the task, or two-thirds at most.

In other words, to keep driving the soldiers on recklessly, without even enough water to function, meant that it was only a matter of time until corpses began to fall.

*"Whaaat?!"* the other three screeched, staring wide-eyed at Pauline.

"Who *are* you?!"

"Are you an enemy mage in disguise? Where's the real Pauline? What did you do with her?!"

"Reina, Mavis, keep away from her!"

*"Wh-wh-wh-wh-wh-wha..."*

The three then found themselves on the receiving end of a tirade from a massively enraged Pauline...

"Wh-what did you say?!"

The crown prince Adalbert, who was in charge of the Brandel royal army, was in shock.

"Well, your Highness, it was just as I said. A goddess manifested and granted us her protection. It was the spirit of the late daughter of the true line of Ascham, ascended after her death for the sake of her... Uhhoohoo..."

Juno, head of the Ascham military, began to weep.

Leaving the pursuit of the imperial army to the royal and noble forces, the Ascham troops had stayed behind to aid in the defense and restoration of their own lands, supporting the villagers in rebuilding their fields and homes. Currently, forces had been dispatched to each village, and Juno stayed behind to give his report to Adalbert, while the captains of each unit tended to their own men. Prince Adalbert, in turn, left the duties of pursuit to his subordinate generals and remained behind in the capital of Ascham as well.

There were a number of reasons why Adalbert had come to act as the leader of his father's army. First off, to have a counterassault led by the crown prince himself would serve to show the Empire just how serious they were. Secondly, his authority would help to maintain command over all of the lords' armies. If things went south, there was a chance that some grubby marquis or other might try to butt in and wrest control, but with Adalbert himself serving as commander, such presumptuous behavior was unlikely.

Plus, wiping out the imperial forces, who never showed any real signs of planning an invasion, with a number that was many times that of their own was a simple task. Upon doing so, they could boast that they were a country that protected even its most outlying citizens. It was a just cause, it would win them the support of these borderlands, *and* it earned a bit of clout for Adalbert, who had had no practical military experience until now.

Of course, given the dangers of this task, and the trouble that might result from Adalbert taking an injury in a place like this, the prince was not actually allowed to take charge of the pursuit. Instead, it was determined that he should "give direction from the capital of Ascham, which had held up so valiantly during the initial action."

It was an utterly absurd situation all around—but of course, that fact had also been taken into consideration.

Had this territory been the domain of any other noble family, then the imperial analysts' predictions would have been correct. The kingdom would not have rushed into battle at great pace, underprepared, yet overflowing with resolve. Instead, they would have undergone a far lengthier process of preparations and then made a heartfelt appeal to each of the noble houses on the grounds of creating a united front in the face of the Empire's act of aggression—all that before they would have even considered making a move.

Indeed, on first hearing about the invasion, the king had appeared mildly surprised but otherwise kept his composure. However, when he was told of the place that was being invaded, he instantly became distracted and enraged. He ordered an emergency dispatch at once, without so much as holding a conference, or even stopping to listen to anyone else's opinion on the matter.

Normally, the prime minister, cabinet members, and other high-ranking nobles would have been expected to raise a conscientious objection to the their king making such a unilateral decision, but for some reason they all immediately assented without a single protest, setting out at once to assemble the Royal Army—an emergency assemblage of the king's troops, under direct control of the king, along with a royal dispatch from each of the noble houses.

It would have been one thing if the kingdom itself was in danger, a neighboring country trying to nip off some little borderland would not have been a very pressing matter for anyone beyond those impacted directly—i.e., the people of the threatened fief themselves and their neighbors.

Of course, a counterassault would eventually be mounted so that the invaders did not try to worm their way in while the rest of the country sat on their hands, but the lords would take their sweet time about it, and the households farthest away would be inclined not to send any support at all until the very last moment, when it would absolutely unconscionable for them to do otherwise, at which point they would send as few men as they possibly could.

If they were far away, the best they could probably expect was a monetary reward afterward. It was not as though they had the chance to expand their territory, or even better, win promotion to a higher noble rank. Therefore, they would be slow to respond to the royal decree, finding all sorts of excuses not to comply—or rather, they *should* have been, but in this case, for some reason even the highest-ranking nobles had rushed at lightning speed to dispatch their standing armies in the name of the king's endeavor. Once this fact was known, even the smaller houses, who had dawdled as always, swiftly followed suit. They didn't know the reason behind it, but they did know that if they failed to comply it would look quite bad for them. Anyone who did not have the sense to intuit at least that much was not fit to serve as a noble.

Adalbert, of course, was fully aware of the circumstances. As much as the Goddess had cautioned them against spreading any word of her sighting, in an open place like that, with so many witnesses present, someone was bound to talk sooner or later. There were those who were out for the money, and those who were very faithful to those who they served, and those who thought that the wrath of a benevolent-seeming goddess was probably no big deal...

Of course, the fact that Adalbert knew exactly what was going on was just one more reason why he had been given the command of the king's army. Because he had been far away, he had neither gotten a clear view of Mile's 'Goddess' display, nor heard the message that she had broadcast with her magic. However, upon hearing the word 'Goddess,' the prince immediately lit up.

*A goddess...and a daughter of the house of Ascham! We've found her! The living avatar and holder of the Goddess's favor, the holy maiden Adele!!!*

Apparently, the commander of the Ascham troops was convinced that Adele was dead, but Adalbert, of course, knew better.
A girl with a goddess residing within her could never die so easily.

*And now, our country will have the protection of the goddess
who speaks through Lady Adele as well...*

"Lady Mabel surely possessed sufficient purity to have become
a deity, but to think that she would still be thinking of us..."

"What? But the daughter of Ascham is named Adele, isn't
she?"

"Hm? That's the name of the young heiress who went missing, Lady Mabel's daughter. The one who became a goddess and
granted us her protection was her late mother, Lady Mabel."

"Huh...? O-oh, I see, it was Lady Mabel, the goddess, speaking
through Adele's body then. That makes sense..."

That assumption was at least one that Adalbert understood.
However...

"No, the form she assumed was Lady Mabel herself."

"What? Then where is her daughter, Adele?"

"Well, a year and a half ago, Lady Adele vanished from her
academy in the royal capital, and we haven't heard from her since."

"Wh...?"

Later on, an investigation was held, and the former staff of
the Ascham manor, who had worked there for many years lead-
ing up to the events of four and half years before, gave testimony.
"That was our Lady Mabel, no doubt about it. She appeared to

us just as she looked when she was a girl, in her most precious days. Besides, the way she was conducting herself was outside of all common sense. That could not have been anyone but our dear lady!"

Indeed, until she was eight years old, Adele had little contact with anyone beyond her immediate family, her wet nurse, and her nanny. After her mother and grandfather passed away, even those two were taken away from her, replaced with new staff who were introduced to "the sole daughter of the house of Ascham"—the usurper's daughter, Prissy. Hardly any of them had any direct contact with Adele at all.

After that, as Prissy was introduced again and again as the Ascham heiress to outsiders, memories of Adele began to fade from everyone's consciousness. Even those who were fully aware that Prissy was not the rightful heir could not be expected to remember the face of a young girl who they had only glimpsed now and then from afar so many years ago. Plus, the wet nurse had already left the capital, and the nanny was now employed minding some other family's daughter. As a result, neither had been included in the investigation.

However, with Mabel, it was different.

Mabel, who had possessed such many and varied nicknames as "the garden that blooms all year round," and "the girl whose very eyes can make you happy." "Mabel the Tomboy," "the girl who thinks of crazy things," "Mabel the Dandelion," and so on and so forth, had made quite the strong impression on most citizens of the fief, particularly with the way she conducted herself

during what were known as "Lady Mabel's Wandering Years,"
when she was about twelve or thirteen.

It had not been readily apparent until she was around eight
years old, but in the years since, Mile had come to resemble her
mother to a striking degree. This of course included that splendid
silver hair of hers, which appeared amongst the women of the
Ascham bloodline, every now and then.

Furthermore, thanks to her father and stepmother, who had
them burned, not a single portrait of Adele remained. What
instead hung upon the walls of the manor were innumerable
portraits of her stepsister, Prissy, hastily drawn up by an amateur
painter.

In other words, when the people of Ascham looked upon
Mile—or rather, Adele, as she was now—the only personage that
came to mind was the late daughter of the house of Ascham, Lady
Mabel von Ascham.

The fact that she had grown up since then, that she had gotten
married? None of that mattered. No matter what age she was, in
the hearts of her people, Mabel was, "our dear young Lady Mabel."

And now, she was Lady Mabel, the goddess.

Even including those who had seen her right up close, there
was not a single person who doubted that the goddess who had
manifested in order to protect Ascham was Lady Mabel herself.

Meanwhile, Adalbert, who thought he would be able to
confirm the whereabouts of the avatar of the goddess, *Adele* von
Ascham, was in distress.

*Wait, so it* wasn't *Adele who appeared here? Or is it that her mother Mabel was the goddess residing in her? Or did her mother become a goddess and then ask a different goddess to protect her daughter? I don't get it! What should I do...?*

"By the way, Mavis, did you say that you saw the crest of the royal family among all the flags of the Brandel army stationed in the capital?" asked Mile.

"Yeah! For someone training to be a knight, it's crucial to be able to distinguish the flags of the different royal families, even if they're from other countries. It's pretty unlikely that his Majesty himself would be out here heading up his army, but it'd probably be one of his sons, or someone along those lines, in charge of his forces—and as such, serving as the commander of the whole of the national army," Mavis confidently replied.

"Wh-why would they do all that?"

"I don't know. As far as both Pauline and I are concerned, such a thing should be unthinkable... Still, there's no doubting it. That was most certainly the crest of the royal family. I, Mavis, would stake my own name upon it!"

"Wh...?"

Mile was nearly speechless.

It was not that she could not believe what Mavis had said, however—an entirely different matter was now swirling around in Mile's brain.

*C-crest of the Royal Family... M-Mavis-sama...*

The imperial troops were booking it with all they had. They set such a desperate pace that even calling it a forced march would be an understatement. That said, they were not expecting to have to fight when they reached their destination, and if any troops caught up with them, they would die. In circumstances like this, they had no choice but to muster up the last dregs of their energy.

As they already had no intention of fighting, all that mattered right now was getting back home. The imperial soldiers, who had been granted permission by their commanding officers to ditch anything that was unnecessary—and who had already had many of their consumable goods stolen to begin with—were now quite agile, so much so that outrunning an army that was fully laden with equipment and supplies might not be a total impossibility... if the soldiers had been in top form, that was.

Already they had been traveling for days, subsisting on the few morsels of food that they had been carrying when the supply depots were ransacked, along with the scant amount of water that the mages had been able to produce, and whatever animals and vegetables they had managed to gather along the road. However, most of the soldiers had not had much luck with hunting and gathering, and the water that they had all drawn into their own canteens back at the river had long since dried up. Furthermore, their hasty retreat left them no time to double back to a water source. If they did that, the pursuing Brandel forces were certain to catch up with them and their capture would be assured.

So the soldiers plodded forward, their feet moving almost automatically, as they suffered both thirst and starvation. At the very least, if they could leave Ascham and make it into Cesdol, which lay along the border with the Empire, there would be villages where they could find food and wells. All they had to do was meet back up with the troops they had sent ahead to maintain control of Cesdol, who could split their remaining supplies with them.

With these thoughts in their dazed, half-conscious minds, the vanguard troops plodded on, but when they lifted their downcast faces and set their gazes ahead, they saw before them...

...A *tent*. And in front of the tent, a long table. Behind the table were three girls seated on stools. Behind them, between the girls and the tent, were barrels and crates.

Upon the tent, the entry flap of which was closed, hung a wooden sign:

Traveling Restaurant – House of the Holy Maiden.

From all the men, there rang out a chorus of disbelief.


"Do you have any water?" asked one soldier, standing before the long table, his voice shaking.

One of the girls, who was quite developed but of questionable age, replied with a grin. "Yes, water will be five silver a cup. Ale is one half-gold, and wine is two."

"*That's expensive!!!*" the men shouted.

As you may recall, five silver pieces was equivalent to roughly 5,000 yen in modern Japanese money. One half-gold piece was an extravagant 10,000 yen.

"That's way too expensive!" a soldier screamed, but the girl simply replied, "Supply and demand. That's one of the most basic tenets of commerce. If you don't like the price, you don't have to buy it. It's as simple as that. The only patrons we're interested in serving are those who agree that the price is right. Plus, consider how difficult it must be for a group of young ladies to carry this water all the way to a battlefield to sell it, would you? Do you really think that we could sell this water, which took us days to transport, for the same price that you would find in a city market-place—all the while keeping in mind the risk of being embroiled in battle or attacked by soldiers?"

"Uh..."

The man could not muster a rebuttal.

"B-but still..."

"Gimme water!" another voice cried, cutting off the first man, who was haltingly trying to haggle for a bargain.

"You can pinch yer pennies all you want and die with those coins janglin' around in yer purse, but I'll gladly buy this water that these girls risked their lives to lug all the way here for our sakes! If five silver's all it takes to keep livin' then that's cheap as dirt, far as I see it!"

With that, the man slammed five silver pieces down upon the table.

"Of course! Coming right up!"

The girl went straight back to the barrels and drew a cup of water, which she handed to the man.

"Water! Glorious water..."

The soldier glugged the water down in a gallant fashion, not leaving a single drop behind in the cup. After drinking so joyously, he appeared reluctant to step away, muttering, "Wish I could have another cup, but it wouldn't be right for me to drink up all the water myself. There's limits, after all. I better let someone else get in here..."

Five more silver pieces were then smacked loudly down upon the table.

"Water!"

"M-me too!"

"A-ale for me!"

"Move, ya bastards! If ya ain't buyin', get outta the way!"

One after the other the men came rushing in, shoving aside the soldier who had complained about the prices.

"Of course, of course, don't you worry. I wasn't the only one carrying this water here, so we have more in stock. No rushing, no pushing! Just line up nicely, please. After all, if you push too much, the table's going to fall over, and all the water will spill!"

Truthfully, ale has diuretic properties, and so really, all it can do is cause further dehydration. However, the girls had no idea that this was the case and had included it in the options out of ignorance, not malice.

As the three girls busied themselves selling water, one of the soldiers looked up with a look of sudden realization. "Traveling

Restaurant, House of the Holy Maiden..." The man then turned to Pauline and asked, "S-say, if this is a 'restaurant,' that mean y'all are sellin' food, too?"

Upon hearing this question, the others around him stopped moving and fell silent. As a deafening quiet swept over the area, Pauline grinned and replied, "Well, naturally."

The silence seemed to crackle with excitement.

"Wh-whatcha got?" one soldier asked in a trembling voice.

"Um, rice porridge and hard tack, jerky, vegetable soup, and a few other things. One half-gold for everything."

*"That's expensive!!!"*

Both the food and drink flew off the figurative shelves. The men who had been walking behind the first group pitched forward as the men behind them stopped, and a non-commissioned officer, veins popping in his forehead, shoved past them to investigate. When he saw what was going on, however, he immediately took charge.

"Well, don't just stand there! Hurry up and buy your food, and then keep on walking! The guys behind you have gotta eat, too! Plus, the royal army's still hot on our tails. As soon as you can move, get going!"

With the officer's direction, the operation began to run much more smoothly.

Those who requested it could have their canteens filled, instead of drinking the water right there—that was easy enough to achieve with a funnel. Those who received porridge and soup were directed to make a big lap around the area of the tent while they ate, return the bowls, and proceed on, a gambit designed so as not to crowd up the table where the girls were selling. That was an NCO for you, always thinking on his feet. Naturally, those who carried their own cups had those filled up instead and then kept on walking.

"We can't thank you enough. Thanks to your help, most of these men will make it back home alive. You brave, brave girls have our eternal gratitude," said the officer. "It seems like you'll be out of stock pretty soon, so I suggest that you run away as fast as you can before the royal army finds you."

Pauline glanced behind her. Sure enough, most of the barrels and crates were nearly empty.

"Oh. You two, if you would?"

"On it!"

On cue, Reina and Mavis rushed into the tent and carried out more barrels and crates.

"Wh...?"

They traveled back and forth from the tent countless times, each time going away with an empty container and coming back with a full one.

"Don't worry, we still have plenty more food and water," said Pauline. "Wherever there are those suffering from hunger and thirst—whether it's on the battlefield or in the depths of Hell—all you have to do is call on us, and we'll be there in a flash! Because, we are..."

Reina and Mavis rushed to Pauline's sides, and the three of them struck a snappy pose, reciting as one, "The Traveling Restaurant: House of the Holy Maiden!!!"

There were no explosions or colored smoke bombs this time.

The flap of the tent, meanwhile, opened just an inch, and Mile peeked out from within, grinding her teeth. Thanks to the number of people to whom she had already revealed herself, she was relegated to the tent, assigned with retrieving enough goods from her inventory to fill the barrels and crates. Even if she were to wear a mask, it would still be too dangerous to let anyone see her face at this point. Still, she watched the other three with envy.

"S-sure..."

Meanwhile, the officer stood frozen and slack-jawed before the girls.

◇◆◇

"Those girls really were awfully brave," the officer muttered as he walked alongside his subordinates.

*Those wonderful girls, who provided our escaping soldiers with food and water yesterday at their traveling restaurant... Their prices were a bit steep, but considering how they risked their lives to carry those items all the way there, I can't complain. It's just like they said, really: it's supply and demand. No one would ever complain about the difference in price between buying something in the kingdom's capital versus buying the same thing out in a remote village, after all. This is the same principle.*

*They carried that food and water all the way there, just for us, while the royal army was pursuing us, risking their lives. Honestly, it's just like their shop name suggests—they may as well be holy maidens.*

*Are they girls of our nation who followed after our army? Or are they the daughters of former Albarnians who married into families here? Either way, they are allies of our soldiers, and treasured friends.*

With these thoughts in mind, the officer stopped suddenly as the men ahead of him came to a halt, the soldiers once again blocking the road.

"What are you all doing?! You're causing a traffic..."

The officer started to shout but trailed off. He could not believe what he was seeing.

It was a familiar tent, with a familiar table, three familiar girls, and a familiar sign...

*Traveling Restaurant – House of the Holy Maiden, Shop No. 2*

"You're kidding me!"

This time, however, ale and wine had disappeared from their menu. Apparently, they had not sold very much yesterday.

"Hey, can I ask you a couple of things?" the officer inquired, rushing up to the three familiar girls who sat at that familiar table before the familiar tent selling food and drink.

"My, you're that helpful fellow from yesterday. What is it, then?" asked the red-haired girl.

"Just how many of the men of our army did you girls get around to serving yesterday? Instead of selling to us again,

I'd rather you sell to the rest of the guys who didn't get a chance to buy anything yet, if you can..."

"Oh? But we kept selling until the end!"

The officer thought that the girl appeared to not quite be getting the point, so he clarified, "That's not what I meant. I'm asking how many of our men you managed to sell to before you ran out of stock."

After giving directions to increase the efficiency of sales and ordering the soldiers not to linger around the tent, the officer had gone ahead with his men and had not stayed behind to determine this answer for himself.

"I'm telling you," said the girl, "we kept selling until the end. We stayed open until the very last line of soldiers showed up."

"Wha...?"

The amount that these girls could have carried could not possibly have been sufficient to achieve such results. If they could do such a thing, then that meant that their entire army's supply units, wagons and all, could have been replaced with just a handful of "maidens."

The officer fell silent. There were so many things he wished to say and so many things he wished to ask. However, there was one, most burning question that he had for the trio.

"What is *that?*"

The officer was pointing to a fourth, girl-like form, which stood apart from the three girls selling at the table.

The reason that the form was "girl-*like*" was that the small figure wore upon its head a headdress of childish make, which resembled nothing so much as the head of an ass, on top of which were figures of a dog, a cat, and a chicken. They were singing an out-of-key tune and playing an instrument the likes of which the officer had never seen.

*Soo-soo-Sook! Ikhut-eigh!*

"Ah, that... Apparently, that's the song that you must sing if you're going to sell water—or so she says," said the redhead, seeming equally perplexed.

"Well then, what of those shabby clothes?" asked the officer.

The other three girls were properly dressed, so this clearly was not a matter of them lacking money.

The redhead, replied, looking troubled, "She said that you have to wear those kind of clothes if you're selling water outdoors. But I mean, that's something that she's gotten herself fixated on, so that's really none of our concern. She kept insisting that it was a 'stalesuit,' clothes that've gotten old that you don't plan on keeping much longer..."

This was making less and less sense by the minute.

"W-well then, what's up with that hat and those dolls on her head?"

"She kept going on about 'The Fremen Town Musicians'... Look, stop asking! Please don't ask me anything else! We have no idea what's going on here, either!"

Both the redhead and the other two girls, who had kept the line moving this whole time, looked rather concerned. Any more than this would be an impediment to their sales. That meant slowing down the army's pace of retreat. Plus, today it seemed that the line was moving smoothly from the outset, so there was no need for the officer's assistance. He couldn't continue interfering with their business just to satisfy his own curiosity. And so, he gave up, resigning himself to never having his questions answered.

"Thank you, then. We will never forget this kindness!" he said, bowing his head, before rushing back to his own men.

The other three turned to stare at the donkey-headed girl in exasperated silence.

The next day, as the army proceeded, the officer, walking in silence once more, looked ahead to see yet another incredible sight.

It was a familiar tent and a familiar table, with three familiar girls, a familiar wooden sign, and a familiar donkey-headed girl...

*Traveling Restaurant – House of the Holy Maiden, Shop No. 3*

"Yeah, I figured as much," the officer muttered with a weary slump.

"My! We're making a killing here! If we average about one half-gold per person, times 5,000 people, that's 500 gold pieces!"

In terms of modern Japanese money, that would be around 50 million yen.

"What a blessed act of mercy! A labor of love!!!"

The other three stared at Pauline in utter disbelief.

Meanwhile, Mile, wearing the same strange get-up as the day before, was, as usual, completely spacing out.

*This is a fantasy world*, she thought. *And this tent here is the temporary home for me, a donkey. A temporary home for a donkey... "Roba el Kaliyeh"?*

It was an absolutely splendid pun, but there was not a single person around who would understand it.

"Mile, why are you crawling around with your hands on the ground over there?"

Such a cruel, cruel, cruel, cruel, terribly cruel existence living in this world was...

Upon making their way out of Ascham and into the border fief of Cesdol, the imperial soldiers had found all of the villages along the highway devoid of life and empty of food, all of the wells having vanished as if by literal magic. At this discovery, they had fallen into a deep despair. Faced with few other options besides welcoming death with open arms, the soon-to-be starving, thirsty soldiers were sure to begin defecting one by one, turning to banditry and spreading disorder and chaos throughout the kingdom.

However, there was still the very small amount of water that the mages could produce, as well as the one half-gold and one silver they had been receiving once a day for provisions. Thanks to both of these, it now seemed that there might be a viable road to making it home alive, meaning that there was no longer any reason for the men to abandon their families and turn to a life of villainy. It would be difficult, but they would return home safely as valiant soldiers who had fought for the sake of their country.

Plus, there was no one who would dare act in any untoward manner or try to threaten the girls who had been providing for them. It would be one thing if they had no way to obtain the food and drink that the girls offered, but they could come by it easily just by parting with the small change they carried in their breast pockets as expedition allowance. Under such circumstances, no one would make the mistake of acting in an uncouth way in front of their comrades and superior officers.

Furthermore, their partners in survival were a group of brave young girls who had risked the odds to carry heavy provisions all the way into a war-zone, just for them. To harass such brave creatures would see them talked about behind their backs for the rest of their lives or even court martialed upon their return home. In fact, they likely wouldn't even make it that far; their fellow soldiers would probably slit their throats on the spot.

Anyone who did not have enough money on hand simply had to borrow it from their comrades or superiors. It was not especially rare to find those who were particularly well-off or, at least, who happened to have some spare coin or other squirreled away in the hems of their clothes for just such a rainy day.

And thus, somehow—just barely—the imperial soldiers were able to continue on with their honor and dignity still intact, and The Traveling Restaurant – The House of the Holy Maiden was able to continue selling food and water to the Albarnian army every day until they finally reached the national border and crossed back into their own homeland.

"Doing charitable work really is the best!"

"So, she really *was* Pauline, huh?"

"Looks like it was her the whole time."

"It couldn't be anyone else..."

# Didn't I Say
## to Make My Abilities
### *Average* in the
#### —— Next Life?!

# The Capital Once More

"**P**ARDON US," said Monika and Aureana as they entered Marcela's room, chairs in hand.

Marcela turned her chair away from her desk, facing it toward the other two.

"I wonder how the fight with the Albarn Empire is going..." Monika said worriedly.

Marcela replied in a soothing tone. "Well, our side is going at them with overwhelming military force, so I think they should be just fine."

Though she spoke to placate her friend, this was not a lie. Marcela had a number of connections in the palace, so any information she obtained was highly accurate. It was not as though she could find out every single detail, but in this case, she knew there was "a large-scale incident concerning the fiefdom of Ascham," and she had gotten her sources to inform her as best they could.

Plus, none of this was actually classified information, so there was no real trouble to be had.

One could not conceal a large-scale dispatch of military forces—nor was it something that needed to be hidden. After all, they were sending out all of these troops in order to defend territories in the borderlands who faced the threat of invasion; the event had been widely propagandized. Not only was it an opportunity to appeal to their subjects' goodwill and boast that they were a kingdom that did not abandon even its most far-flung citizens, but it was also a perfect chance to boost the name of the first prince, who had been assigned as commander of the men.

"But before we talk about that..." Marcela signaled a pause to the conversation and looked warily around the room. Then, she suddenly turned to the bed and thrust out her right arm.

"There you are!!!"

"Gaaaah!"

"Eeeeek!!!"

The air began to shimmer as a form appeared over the bed, and Monika, Aureana, and the mysterious shape all shrieked in turn.

"I thought you might be there!"

"H-h-h-h-how did you...?"

Mile trembled violently as Marcela seized her by the collar.

"I told you before, did I not?" Marcela replied, matter-of-factly, repeating the same words that she had said the last time. "Did you truly believe that yours truly would be unable to detect you, Miss Adele?"

"Aha... Aha, ahaha..."

Mile—no, Adele—began to laugh through tears.

Marcela, deep inside her heart, muttered softly. *Anyway, both this time and the time before, there was a weird, butt-shaped imprint on top of the duvet...*

After that, Adele and Marcela filled each other in on everything that had happened since their last meeting.

That said, Marcela's updates were mainly limited to academy life, so there was really not very much to tell. Naturally, it was Adele who dominated the conversation.

"And so, I ended up saying those same words to Sir Juno, the commander of the Ascham military," she continued.

"Are you a devil?!?!" the other three shrieked.

Adele, of course, abridged the part concerning her Goddess Formation exploits.

"And we sold them back the water at five silver a cup..."

*"You're all monsters!!!"*

"When we gave half of the 4,000 gold pieces we earned to the count whose lands had been the most devastated, and another half of the remainder to the people of Ascham, Pauline almost completely lost her mind!"

The other three burst out laughing.

Even though she too was a merchant's daughter, Monika had little attachment to money, but she knew that Pauline would have been scandalized at the mere mention of dividing things up in such a way, even if the money in question had not been hers.

"So then, what about the remaining 1,000?" Monika asked.

Suddenly, Adele averted her gaze.

The other three stared at her, silent.

"But yeah, anyway, so the imperial army made their retreat, without any of the soldiers deserting or turning to banditry or widespread looting to cause chaos in the kingdom. If they ever decide to commit other acts of aggression in the future, at the very least I think they'll probably avoid Ascham."

In her retelling, Adele explained away her transformation as "a simple disguise," and talked of "carrying the goods stealthily" rather than spiriting them away in her inventory. Marcela could guess at the truth. However, if one could not trust one's friends not to broach such topics, then what were friends for?

"I do suppose you're right. After the mysterious loss of their supplies, the appearance of the goddess, and the fact that they only barely made it home thanks to the benevolence of the holy maidens... If the goddess happened to get serious, or the maidens decided to abandon them, they would have been annihilated without even getting a chance to fight. Anyway, neither side took any damages, and Ascham is at peace again, so it sounds like all is well."

"I wonder about that..."

Marcela seemed convinced that the most favorable outcome had occurred, but Aureana appeared to think otherwise.

"The only way to be utterly certain of the fief's future safety would have been to wipe out the weakened imperial forces while they were down... Those soldiers who made it back safe may someday return to invade some other part of our kingdom, and we can't count on things ending without some more serious damages next time. There might be many soldiers and peasants who won't make it out alive..."

"So, are you saying we should have exterminated those 5,000 soldiers for the sake of decreasing the chance of future battles?"

"I-I didn't say *that!*"

Marcela did not seem willing to consider Aureana's line of thinking, but for a patriotic citizen—or even just a person considering the matter from a logical standpoint—Aureana was correct, and even Marcela could see that. Still, she could not countenance the notion of slaughtering thousands of fleeing men simply because they were soldiers.

"I think that the lives of a thousand soldiers and civilians from our own country are more important than the lives of 5,000 enemy soldiers," Monika said softly. "But if they're willing to buy the goods that our company sells, then *every* life is precious, no matter who they are!"

Infected by Monika's goofy smile, the others began to laugh as well.

*Monika's always able to break the tension between Aureana and Marcela when they get serious, just like this... It's been over a year and a half since I left them, but they haven't changed a bit. Oh, and come to think of it, they'll be graduating soon, won't they?*

The next time Adele saw the trio, they would no longer be students.

As she realized this, a strange loneliness welled up inside her heart.

The four of them chatted long into the night, but if they did not head out sooner rather than later, it would be a problem; not for Adele, but for the other three, who had lessons in the morning. She hated to leave them behind, but they would see each other again soon. Adele promised them this, and then once again left Marcela's room behind. With only herself to account for, it was easy enough for Adele to move swiftly and make a late night escape over the walls undetected.

That said, it would have been hardly any more trouble for Adele to do just the same with other people under her wing. In truth, the other members of the Crimson Vow did not want to intrude on some of the only time Adele had with her old friends.

And thus, as she vaulted over the walls of Eckland Academy, the young girl transformed once more, from Adele, back into Mile. She headed for the inn, keeping a light magic barrier up until she had made it back to their room—just in case.

Adele was the name that she used only with her classmates from the Academy.

It was that name she had received when she left her old world behind and was reborn into a new life. And then she had abandoned that name, and now she was Mile. She lived a new life in a new world with each new name.

Mile spread both of her arms wide and jumped up high.

*Butter...fly!*

No matter what, Mile could never take anything truly seriously.

Was that because that was truly the sort of person she was?

Or was it something else...?

As Mile gently opened the door to the room, she found a lamp still glowing over the other three who sat up talking.

"Oh, you all are still awake?"

"You would've been sad if we'd all been asleep when you got back, right?"

Mile could not reply.

*This* was the place where she belonged—where the girl named Mile belonged...

"Ah, hey! Don't squeeze me like that! That hurts!"

Reina tried to push Mile away, a bit red in the face.

"You're so shy, Reina," Pauline said softly, smiling.

Mavis, meanwhile, wrung her hands peevishly, wondering why it was that Reina always got hugs from Mile, but never her.

In truth, Mile avoided hugging Mavis, knowing that doing so would land her face or neck right in the middle of Mavis's bust. As a result, Mavis should not expect any hugs from Mile anytime soon, barring some extraordinary circumstance. It would not be until far, far later that Mavis gained any awareness of this fact.

"Time for sleep," said Reina.

"Yep! Good night!"

"I think we can stop by the Guild branch and scrub a request or two pretty easily. Mile, you have a lot of stuff in your storage. Pull out something that we can use to fill a daily request. That'll get us paid, anyway," Reina said to the others. They had just crossed back over the border from Mile's home country of Brandel to the country of Tils, from whence the others hailed.

"Wh...?"

"What? Don't look so surprised. We're still bound by a minimum term of duty in service to this country, in exchange for the free education we received at the Prep School. So we get some easy job out of the way to let everyone know that we're back in town, show some results, and get a bit of a head start on the, 'Hey look, we're working here,' thing."

"Ah..." said the other three.

That was Reina for you. The other three were aware of their unofficial contract with the kingdom, but they had not really given it much thought.

"Plus, if it's an extermination job, then just producing parts from monsters that we've hunted on the side as trophies for verification would count as fraud. The only thing we can give them in good faith would be herbs, raw materials, or edible meat."

"Y-you're actually pretty sharp, aren't you, Reina?"

"You little—!!"

A vein bulged in Reina's forehead.

"Mile, you're one to talk!" Pauline scolded.

There was no doubt Mile was in the wrong here. She quickly apologized.

At the first town with a guildhall that they came across, Mile produced five edible jackalopes from storage, and they turned them in, marking a safe and proper start to their return tour.

Incidentally, when one was on an escort mission upon leaving the country, all of the time spent until that job was completed counted as working within the country as well—even when you traveled beyond the country's borders. As a result, they were planning on inflating their completion time just a bit.

It was a bit underhanded, but if you piled up enough trash you could build a mountain. It was only natural for a hunter to want to free themselves from unnecessary obligations as quickly as they could. Of course, Tils was still home for Mavis and Pauline, and they both had families they loved and cherished there, so for as long as the two of them remained in the party, it only made sense for them to call Tils their home base. Because of that, their debt to the country didn't matter so much.

At any rate, now that they had made their presence within the country known once again, the Crimson Vow proceeded lazily towards the kingdom's capital.

They hunted small prey and gathered other raw materials along the way, but all of those things would fetch a better price in the capital, so there was no reason to sell them off piecemeal at every guildhall they passed. Since they wished to keep moving forward, they did not take on any extermination requests. There was no point in them hunting anything other than a monster that needed killing, no matter where they were in the kingdom.

With the heaps of goods that were already stored away within Mile's so-called "storage," they could easily deceive anyone they wished, but the four of them were not the type to take advantage of such a thing—not even Pauline.

Speaking of Pauline, she had been in something of a foul mood for the past several days. Or at the very least, there was something off about her.

This was, of course, because of their charity work—primarily the fact that they had given away the bulk of the money that they had swindled from the soldiers to the people of Ascham and Cesdole.

"Three thousand... Three *thousand* gold pieces..." she muttered deliriously every now and then.

"Ugh! Enough! Pauline, I know you're upset about the money, but for the four of us to keep that amount of cash all to ourselves would be utterly indecent! Taking even a thousand gold as our cut is plenty!"

One thousand gold pieces. For a citizen of modern Japan, that would be the same as having 100,000,000 yen. It was more than enough. Besides, to anyone else, it would look as though they had given away all of their money. Assuming that no one found out about the rest, of course.

Even so, Pauline was as good as heartbroken.

"You have to give it up already, Pauline," said Mavis. "It's not like we can go take back all the money that we gave away. Plus, thanks to Mile's weird storage magic, where the stuff inside never deteriorates, we have way more earning potential than other hunters. We'll make that money back before you know it, by honest means!"

"B-but *still*... With all that money, I would be one step closer to my goals..." Pauline muttered.

Reina raised an eyebrow. "*Your* goals? Don't you mean *our* goals?"

"Uh..." both Mavis and Pauline spoke without thinking. Mavis looked dumbfounded, and Pauline's face bore an expression that said, *Oh no.*

"Pauline, you—"

Pauline only averted her gaze, silent.

"Wh...?"

Beside them, Mile had her hand clapped over her mouth in shock. This time, however, it was not the childish, overly deliberate pose that she normally took—she appeared to be genuinely stunned.

"M-M-M-M-Mavis, what are you talking about? I have perfectly normal storage magic, I just use ice magic inside of it..." Mile babbled, desperately trying to play it off.

Reina, however, looked at her wearily, and then smugly replied, "Mile, are you still seriously trying to keep up that act? The jig is up. The meat that you say you're cooling down with ice magic isn't frozen when you take it out. It isn't even *cold*.

Vegetables in there never lose their flavor, and herbs keep all their potency. Do you really expect us to believe that you can achieve all that just by cooling things down with ice?"

"H-how long have you known?"

"Since around the time we first hunted the rock lizards, I think."

"That was about when I figured it out, too," said Mavis.

"Me too," agreed Pauline.

"So, pretty much since the *beginning?!?!*"

Mile, who had worked so hard to keep the trick of her storage a secret until now, hung her head in disbelief.

"A-all my pain and suffering...was for nothing..."

*Still, this means that now there's hardly any secrets that I have to keep from them—save for the story of my reincarnation, which no one is ever going to hear—and the secrets of the fundamentals of magic, including the nanos...*

*Well, I mean, I guess if you consider that I told Marcela and the others about the fundamentals of magic, but not the trick of my inventory, then both sides' knowledge about me are about at the same level now.*

On the one hand, Mile couldn't help but feel a bit bad. But on the other hand, she felt somewhat pleased as well.

*Well, it's all right...*

She wasn't going to let the little things bother her. In fact, not letting even the fairly big things bother her was just the Mile way.

*Next time, we're going to head in the opposite direction from the way we went this time, so I guess that means we'll be heading east.*

*Come to think of it, wasn't it something to the east that those men who kidnapped Faleel were talking about?*

Indeed, they had mentioned a country that lay far to the east. The men had said that was the place where their mysterious religion, and its mysterious teachings, originated. There was no rush to get there, of course, but Mile was dying to know what was out there that would give even the nanomachines pause...

If it was something that would disturb the nanomachines, who seemed to have no particular interest in the lives and deaths of most human beings, it had to be a matter of global proportions. Such harrowing phrases as, "this world has been destroyed and rebirthed numerous times," and "the cause of the destruction of civilization," came to mind. More than likely, it was something related to the elder dragons' mysterious actions, which was what had spurred Mile to go on a journey in the first place.

Mile thought deep and hard, and then...

"'While Mile still lived as Adele, to the east of the Kingdom of Tils, a mysteriously cultish religion began to take root...' Wait, is this the cult of the Golden Eye God?! Or could it be the Manji Clan, searching for the Diamond Bell?!?!"

As Mile carried on her one-woman comedy act, the other three looked on wearily.

"Oh, Capitaaal! We're hooome!" Mile shouted as they approached the city gates. The other party members, assuming

she was once again pulling a quote from some fairy tale, ignored her.

The first place they headed was their old inn. They could stop
by other places after, but if they didn't get into the inn straight
away it might get late before they knew it, and then, they'd end
up split between different rooms. Plus, if there was anywhere that
they should be showing their faces first, it was there.

"We're home!!!"

"Welcome ba—ohhhh! Oh my goodness, you're back!"

Lenny came flying out from behind the reception desk.

As always, there she was: Lenny, the ten-year-old—or perhaps
she was eleven now, as her birthday would have already passed—
poster child of the inn, full of pep, her hair in the familiar short
braids, her eyes looking a bit damp.

"I-I'm so glad you made it home safe!"

It was not strange for hunters to turn up dead, at any time,
in any place. As a result, even in her relatively few years, Lenny
had seen many patrons who, once they left on a journey, never
returned again. Whenever she said a word of parting to a guest
who was a departing for a trip, she prepared herself ahead of time
for just such an outcome.

This alone was enough to make Lenny overjoyed when there
were those who not only returned home safely but chose to frequent her inn again. Especially when those guests were ones that
she could put to great use…

And so, Lenny faced the four with a great smile, and said, "Welcome home!"

Such was Lenny the Penny-pincher for you.

Once the four had taken a room, they headed on to the Hunters' Guild—an obvious next stop, of course.

"We're back!" Mavis announced as they walked through the guildhall door.

The clerks and the other Guild staff all sat straight up and shouted, "It's the Storage Girls!!!"

"We're the *Crimson Vow!!!*" the party rebutted.

Apparently, the others had been giving them strange names behind their backs.

Truthfully though, Mile's storage magic—or at least the ability that she disguised as such—*was* the Crimson Vow's most distinct feature. They were fairly skilled in battle, but as far as anyone in the Guild was aware, they were certainly not A or S-rank level. By and large, the Guild's evaluation of the Crimson Vow as a C-rank party with abilities on par with B-ranks; the strength that they possessed was really not all that unusual. It certainly was not enough that they could have won against the Roaring Mithrils—if they were fighting at full strength, at any rate.

Of course, that would be the evaluation of someone who knew nothing about the fight against the elder dragons, or Mile's true power, or Mavis's doping exploits, or Pauline's hot magic...

And then, there was the fact that they were a group comprised entirely of cute, young girls. The fact that they possessed such abilities while still being beautiful young ladies, rather than wizened grandpas or old crones, granted them an unfathomable added value—and as they continued to grow from their experiences, opened up great prospects for the future, as well.

That said, the truth remained that what had most drawn the eye of all of the hunters and Guild affiliates within the capital was that (so-called) storage magic. With a power like that, you could carry several times—maybe even ten times—more when out hunting, or gathering, or delivering things. Really, the fact that Mile's chest measurements were still a bit lacking in their capacity was the only thing keeping some of the men in check.

Thus, at some point or other, their peculiar nickname had begun to spread.

"W-well I mean, that's really just another name for Mile, right? Th-that has nothing to do with the rest of us," said Mavis, not wishing to be affiliated with such an awkward title.

"What's *that* supposed to mean?!?!" Mile raged at the betrayal.

"N-now, now..."

"Oh, it really is you all!"

As Pauline attempted to comfort Mile, the guild master descended from the second floor, greeting them.

"You're back much sooner than I expected. Still, what's most important is that you're all safe. You'll be working in this country again for a little while now, I suspect? Well, I won't ask you to say.

I know that you young folks are always wanting to go here and there and everywhere. As long as you stay safe, and you remember to come back home, it's good to get out and broaden your horizons now and then. That's what being a hunter is all about, after all."

Compared to his treatment of them upon their departure, the guild master seemed quite a bit more understanding. Reina and Pauline eyed him a bit suspiciously, but Mavis and Mile were filled with a simple-hearted joy that someone seemed to understand their feelings.

The guild master had gone off on his own such journeys in his youth, and so it was not surprising that he would be able to understand them. Judging by his speech, they thought, it should be smooth sailing for them the next time they decided to travel.

"Until the next time you feel like setting out again, you all should work hard and focus on training yourselves, earning money, and racking up contribution points!"

With that, the guild master cheerfully returned to the second floor.

The members of the Crimson Vow watched him silently as he departed.

The guild master probably had no idea that they had over a thousand gold pieces in savings nor that they had already accumulated more than sufficient points for promotion and were merely waiting for the minimum required time spent as C-ranks to pass. Similarly, he would likely be surprised to learn that they already possessed skills on a level with B-rank hunters.

Of course, the reports of their achievements from the foreign Guild branches had probably already gone out in the Guild post, but such reports were only delivered once a month, and including travel time, it would be a few weeks at best, and possibly a month or more, before word traveled this far. Indeed, it might be some time still before this branch, where the Crimson Vow were registered, received word of their accomplishments abroad.

After greeting all of the Guild staff and the hunters who happened to be present, the members of the Crimson Vow retired to their inn once more.

"Has the Crimson Vow gone home yet?" asked the guild master.

"Ah, yes—just after you went back upstairs, sir," said the female clerk who had prepared his tea.

"All right, I'm going out for a few. I'm going to stop by the palace after I drop in at Count Christopher's, so I might be a little while."

With that, the guild master stood and began making preparations to go out. There was an unusually gleeful smile upon his face.

"The guild master seemed to be in a weirdly good mood. And he seemed to think that we would be staying in town for a little while..."

"Come to think of it, you're right. Even though we're only stopping by here for a little while because it happens to be on our way. There's no way we could finish a training journey that quickly, after all. Well, I guess we will be staying in town for about a week, at least."

As Pauline listened to Mile and Reina's exchange and thought back on the guild master's manner, a wicked grin spread across her face. Seeing this, a shiver ran suddenly down Mavis's spine...

"Oh, the Crimson Vow has returned, have they? They must have come to realize that our kingdom is the most comfortable place for them to live in, after all."

"They're back much sooner than I thought they would be. There are a lot of barriers to a party of four girls making a living in an unfamiliar land, after all. Without any men in the party, they must face a number of hardships..."

His Majesty the king was delighted at the thought that the Crimson Vow would have deemed their kingdom the easiest in which to live, a fact that he expressed to Count Christopher, master of the blade, the former-hunter-turned-noble who had himself gone on a lengthy training journey in his youth.

"Still, I am thankful that they made it home safely without getting caught up in some other country or entangled with any strange men. That ought to cool their cabin fevers for a bit, which will give them time to form all sorts of bonds here in this country—and perhaps even find themselves some worthy spouses..."

Seeing the king and Count Christopher smiling, the guild master, who had come to give his report, relaxed as well. If they could keep reinforcing the idea of expanding and improving the status of the Hunters' Prep School, it meant a bright future not only for the Hunters' Guild but for all hunters.

Plus, thanks to the influence of the Crimson Vow, the number of aspiring female hunters had begun to increase, meaning that the number of promising young hunters who quit the profession because their spouses begged them to do so would likely decrease accordingly. Yes, if two hunters married one another that it was likely that they would continue working as hunters even after the wedding, with far fewer partners pestering their spouses to find a safer job closer to home.

"Bwahaha..."

"Ahaha!""

"Wahahahahahahaha!"

The room was filled with hearty laughter. Each of the three men in the king's private offices were imagining the possibility that the futures they had envisioned only in their dreams might one day become a reality.

"So, you all are fine with us just staying here a week, right?"

"Yep."

"Uh-huh."

"Ten-four."

Sure enough, the members of the Vow had already completed more or less everything that they wished to do in the city. Really, the fact that they had stopped back here at all after departing on their westward journey was sheer coincidence, a result of their unexpected return to the neighboring Kingdom of Brandel. They had no intention of heading west again after this. Next, they would travel eastward.

When Reina had proposed this plan to the group, Mile had heartily approved, so it was decided then and there. At that time, Mile had also said, "It's a planned journey heading to the east... A *Touhou Project*!" but, as usual, she was the only one who was excited about this.

"Starting tomorrow, we'll stay in the capital for six days. We'll find some merchant caravan who needs an escort and leave on the morning of the seventh day. If there are no jobs that match what we're looking for on that day, we might leave a couple days before or after. That sound good?" Reina proposed.

"No objections here!" agreed the others.

Given that none of the group had any special attachment to this city, they could just as easily take it or leave it. As they really did not mind one way or the other, they had no reason to object to Reina's plan.

"All right then, from tomorrow until the day we leave, the Crimson Vow is officially on break! Everybody go and do whatever you need to do—and take it easy, all right?"

At that, the four girls nestled into bed, safe in their old, familiar inn.

At first, a week with nothing to do felt like an eternity, but in reality it passed in the blink of an eye.

Unfortunately, there was not enough time for Pauline to travel home to check in on her mother and brother. Even by carriage, the round trip would take eight days, and their stay did not line up with the days that the passenger carriages set out, meaning there was no way she could hope to manage the trip within the time allotted.

Mavis was in the same boat, and even if she were to travel back home alone, her family would probably try and force her into another arranged marriage situation—or find some other way to prevent her from returning to the capital.

And, of course, Reina, who had lost both her family and her former companions—and had no idea where her parents were even from—had no homeland to return to nor family, friends, or relatives to meet up with.

As a result, the three of them spent their days loitering about the inn and meeting up with the few acquaintances they had in town—chiefly the shopkeepers with whom they had grown friendly and their fellow classmates from the Prep School who were still around the city. They also spent time at the guildhall, petitioning more senior hunters for their advice and otherwise taking it easy. Mavis and Pauline did spend some of their nights penning letters to their families as well.

Naturally, there were times when the whole party went out together. Spending some time by themselves didn't mean that they were *required* to spend the entire week apart, after all.

Hunting was not typically a profession where one was expected to have one's nose to the grindstone every single day. Jobs that required a lot of exertion could leave you wiped out, and sickness and injury were always a consideration. Trying to work when you were not in peak condition was a foolish move that put not only your own life but also the lives of all of your fellow party members at risk. Therefore, it was only natural to take breaks between jobs, and even some prolonged holidays now and then.

In fact, for a party that had just returned from as long of a journey as theirs, a one-week break was probably on the short side. The Crimson Vow already did way more work than they ever needed to in the first place, considering how much more money they earned than other parties.

...And then, there was Mile.

"Long time no see!"

"Oh, Miss Satodele, you've returned from your travels! We really appreciate your continuing to send in manuscripts while you were out on your research trip. Your books are our shop's lifeblood, after all!"

"Oh, please, they aren't all that..."

Mile was in the office of Orpheus Publishing, the firm that held the monopoly on the comedic novels penned by popular author Miami Satodele. The man to whom she was speaking was Melsacus, the shrewd owner of the company, a young man still in his early thirties.

"Will you be settling down in the capital and focusing on your writing now?" asked Melsacus.

"No, I'm only here for six days. Then I'm heading out again."

"What?!" he cried unthinkingly but soon calmed down again. He had long since grown accustomed to authors' eccentricities—their drafting, and article writing, and travel journals, and horseback riding...

"So, where are my manuscripts?"

"They're with the Guild post, as always."

"And what of my royalties?"

"The standard percentage. All of your earnings so far have been deposited in your account at the Merchants' Guild—I've made sure of it."

"Ohoho! You Orpheus fellows are a wicked bunch..."

"As are you, Lady Satodele!"

"Bwahahahahaha!" they laughed.

For Mile, or rather, Miss Satodele, Melsacus, whom she could always count on to appreciate her "Fairy Tale Improv," was a valuable asset... He had read every single one of her works after all, and they had even planned some out together.

Mile was indeed happy to finally find someone who truly understood her.


After going to her favorite restaurant, Mile proceeded to the orphanage and the shacks where the orphans of the slums resided, where she handed out the food items that she had brought back

as souvenirs. Then, cloaking herself in light magic, Mile snuck into the academy.

August Academy, that was.

Just as the capital of Mile's home country of Brandel had two academies, Ardleigh and Eckland, the royal capital of Tils had two academies as well, of which August was one. And, just like Eckland, Mile's (or rather, Adele's) alma mater, August was attended by the children of lower-ranking nobles who were not in line for inheritance and by commoners. In other words, it was the lower-ranking school.

This boarding academy was the school attended by Mariette, the girl she had once tutored as a side gig on a previous party break. Worried about how Mariette might be doing now, she thought that she might slip in at least once to check in on her.

"I hope you're doing well, Miss Mariette..."

A few hours later, Mile exited the academy, still invisible, and utterly disappointed.

"I shouldn't have gone..."

In this world and any other, it was not advisable to overdo things.

This was something that Mile had come to realize.

"So, what are those girls doing now?"

"Well, it seems like they're taking a break after their journey.

They've been stopping in at the guildhall to check the information board but not taking jobs. Instead, they've been reuniting with old friends, going to the library, and making other outings, as well as loitering around the inn and idling about."

"Well, I suppose everyone needs to take some time for that, now and then."

In the king's private offices, his Majesty and Count Christopher carried on a pleasant conversation.

"So then, what of the search for a suitable suitor for Lady Mavis?"

"Well, we're currently considering the sons of counts, as well as the second and third sons of various marquis' lines. Should we find someone of good quality and character, we plan to introduce him to Lady Mavis directly."

"Very good. We can't force it upon her—we have to let them be introduced to one another naturally. Those sorts of people value things like destiny and romance, and revile being forced into anything, after all."

"By your will."

And yet, the pair were trying to decide on a suitable partner for Mavis, the girl's own opinions be damned!

"I've got it! Why don't we invite the girls to the palace? We can make up some reason for the marriage candidates to be present as well, and we can have them all mingle. If they at least know each other's faces, then next time, when they 'chance' to meet, they can say, 'Ah, you're that one from the palace...' and have a place to begin their conversation. Besides, I would love to meet her myself. If one had the chance to meet with one's ruler face-to-face, would that not elevate the love for one's own country beyond one's interest in any other?"

"I see... As the girls were previously involved in helping to unmask a certain lord's criminal actions, it wouldn't be so peculiar to use that as an excuse to invite them. I should certainly like to be present for that as well."

"Yes. You are, after all, their greatest role model as a hunter—the brave Count Christopher, living legend—the hunter who became a noble. I think your attendance should have just the right effect. That's it! I'll have my children attend also. There are two girls of about twelve or thirteen amongst the Crimson Vow, yes? The prince and princess are both close to them in age, and if they should all grow close, why that should raise their loyalty to and affinity for the royal family sevenfold—no doubt about it!"

"Oh, that's a splendid idea! I shall go drum up some candidates at once, and we'll send invitations to the girls a few days from now!"

And so, the king and the count set about their plans gleefully.

It is true, after all, that the days before one goes on a trip—when one spends one's time cooking up all sorts of different tricks, planning for this and that eventuality, can be some of the most enjoyable. Thus, the pair were currently having the time of their lives.

Regardless of how the day of the actual event might unfold...

"What? You're leaving again already?"

Lenny's eyes opened wide at the news of the Crimson Vow's sudden departure, only one short week after their return. Still, she had been the daughter of innkeepers since the day she was born. No matter how fond she grew of some of their guests, she was well accustomed to saying goodbye.

"I-I-I-I see," she stammered. "Well, since you dug that well for us, we're able to get the water for the baths, a-and I'm sure you'll be able to come back and see us again soon..."

Even so, being accustomed to goodbyes and being all right with them were two separate matters.

Last time, she had been prepared for the fact that the Crimson Vow might be leaving, and so she had been able to put on a brave face in front of them. This time, however, she had been struck by a surprise blow, thinking that they would be able to spend more time together now that the girls had finally returned. Much as she may have been a level-headed person, Lenny was still a child of ten—or rather, eleven—years old.

"Well, of course. Tils is where Mavis and Pauline were born, and where both of their families live, and we still have over four years left on our minimum term of service with the kingdom. We may leave the country from time to time, but I think this will always be our base of operations in the end... We'll never change our registrations to another country's Guild, anyway. Don't think of it as us leaving for another journey just as soon as we got back—consider this as a stopover, with us just popping in to say hello in the midst of our original journey. If we finished up our self-improvement trip and came running back home this quickly, we'd be the laughingstocks of the Guild, after all..."

Of course, all they had to do, if they wished to be exempt from their obligations, would be to pay back all the money that had gone towards their educations. But even though they were now in a position to pay back that money easily, they still intended to carry out their obligations dutifully—except, perhaps, if a situation arose that required them to get away immediately. Trying to pay back honor and kindness with money was against their policies.

Plus, there was one among their number who was firm in her insistence: "In any case, we have no plans to relocate to another country within the next five years, nor any reason to. It's a useless expenditure and a waste of money. I forbid it!!!"

Even if they did try to pay their way out of their obligations, people would suspect that it was because they intended to leave the country, and things would become bothersome as a result. In order to avoid such an outcome, the optimal choice was simply for them to maintain the status quo.

Hearing Mile's explanation, Lenny was a bit relieved. Normally when a group of hunters said that they were going off on such a journey, they usually came back in half a year at the earliest, and some of them took a few years or more. Of course, there were many among those who never came back at all. Perhaps they were still on their journeys, or had found a new place to call home along the way and settled down there, or else...

No, there was nothing at all strange about a hunter meeting a spouse and wishing to settle down in the place where that person lived. That was what happened to all of those who vanished, surely. There were plenty of other reasons why they wouldn't return, too, like if they had earned some great renown and been granted a title, or saved a village and won the hand of the village elder's daughter in marriage, or some such.

Little Lenny clung to such possibilities, even though deep in her heart she herself did not truly believe such fancies. However, without fantasies, the hardships of reality would be too much for a young girl to bear.

"Well then, next time you're back, please come stay with us again!"

"Hmm, I mean, I *guess* we could..."

"What?"

At Mile's reply, Lenny froze up. She had expected to hear an enthusiastic, "Of course!"

"Oh, um, I mean, it's not that we're unhappy here. It's just that I was thinking we might like to get an actual home of our own, sooner or later..."

"Ah..."

Hunters who were always traveling to hither and yon, only staying in the capital for a short while, naturally took rooms at inns. Renting a room or leasing a house was a waste of money, as they would be spending only a few nights there, and most of their time staying at inns or camping out in other locations... However, that was only the lifestyle of hunters who were single and hurting for money.

Anyone who was married would take a house. The same was true for those who were not strapped for coin, even if they lived alone. With a house, you could leave all of your belongings in one place, and there was no need to secure lodging every night, so there was no worry of finding a place to sleep if you returned to the city late. If you were alone, you might rent a room, or join forces with friends to rent a small house, which became the party's collective residence.

"Have you four been earning much money?"

"Well, a fair bit, at least..."

"It's that storage magic of yours!"

That was Lenny for you. As much as Mile had tried to deceive her, Lenny had seen right through her act. They always seemed to have some catch of theirs on hand as a souvenir, so she knew that Mile's storage capacity must be quite big. With acumen like Lenny's, such conclusions were not difficult to draw.

"B-but your ability to draw in customers..." Lenny began. However, the fact was that the inn was not hurting in that regard. After the Crimson Vow left town, other all-female parties had taken the fact that the Vow had stayed there as a good sign and begun frequenting the establishment.

Inevitably, as their reputation as an inn where female guests felt comfortable grew, other women who were not hunters began to stay, too. And then, once they became known as an inn that was popular with women—and an inn where you might be able to mingle with all-female parties, their male clientele began to increase in number as well. The whole thing had unfolded exactly according to Lenny's plans.

Of course, being an inn where female guests can feel safe, as well as an inn where male guests looking to find women gather was a clear contradiction, but the men were, for the most part, quite genuine in simply wishing to get to know the women guests—there was no rudeness or violence, and no attempts at anything untoward. If anyone *did* try such a thing, there was always *that*.

The perfect chance.

If a man wished to prove himself to a woman, there was no better opportunity than to be her gallant savior in such a time of need. Men who sought to show themselves as allies of justice, as heroes who defended women, would come flocking—some perhaps even forcing others aside.

If a man so much as began to bother a woman, a sudden glint would appear in the eyes of at least ten others, and they would surround the offender with glee...which was probably quite terrifying. Thus, all of the men who stopped by the inn were perfect gentlemen.

The members of the Crimson Vow had become aware of this on the first day that they returned to town. While none of the male hunters who knew of the Crimson Vow came around to make passes at them, they were vexed to find that the female hunters seemed to be following just a little too closely, poking or brushing past them now and then, "for good luck."

"We really do need to find our own place soon..." Reina grumbled, getting fed up with being lumped in with Mile and treated like a child as a result.

Lenny, however, protested, "Oh c-come on... You all are still greenhorns, aren't you? It's too soon for you to be settling down in a house!"

"Exactly!"

"P-Pauline!"

Reinforcements had appeared, from the most unexpected quarter.

"A house is a luxury that you shouldn't even consider until you have at least 80,000 gold pieces saved up!"

"Th-that's right! That's exactly right!!!" Lenny agreed, fired up by the support of her new ally.

Of course, if that amount were truly what was required to own a home, then there was not a single hunter in the entire world who would ever be able to afford it.

"Well, there's no point in us discussing this right now. We'll consider it when the time comes. We have no idea how our situation will change in the future."

"Y-yes, that's right!"

This time, it was Mile who backed up Reina, for even she seemed to have realized that it was her words that had so disturbed Lenny in the first place.

"Anyway, even if we didn't stay here anymore, you'll always be our friend, Lenny..."

"I-I already know that!" Lenny shouted, her cheeks going red as she promptly retreated to the kitchen.

Seeing this, Mile muttered down inside her heart,

*Ts-Tsunderenny...*

After a few more days in this vein, the Crimson Vow finally ended their short break by accepting a job: escorting a merchant caravan bound for the Kingdom of Marlane, which bordered Tils to the east. Brandel—Mile, or rather, Adele's home country, which lay to the west—was a kingdom with which Tils maintained typical, friendly political relations, but Marlane, to the east, was a kingdom with which Tils was on even closer terms.

The princess of one kingdom, popular among their people, had married into the other's family, and in times of famine they always sent supplies to one another's aid. Similarly, if either kingdom should be threatened with war, the other would send masses of their soldiers to the border in order to send the message that, "If you threaten a friend of our kingdom, you'll have to deal with us, too." In short, the two kingdoms were close allies.

Naturally, the flow of commerce between the two was great—which also meant that there were plenty of bandits to contend with. As a result, the route between the two kingdoms was also popular with hunters who were skilled in real combat. Though guard jobs often went in one direction, there were just as many that would take merchants back the opposite way, so there was no need to waste time on an unpaid return trip. To have such a steady source of income, rather than relying on the uncertainties of hunting or extermination jobs, was the stuff of most hunters' dreams.

Indeed, it was a perfect job for a C-rank party confident in their skills, a job with no twists or peculiarities. Thus, when the party went to the reception desk to accept their duties, even the clerk had no objections to raise.

"We already have permission to leave the country, and we were only stopping by for a little while along our way, so we don't need to stop in to say goodbye again before we leave, do we?" Reina asked, grinning.

"Oh, of course not. After all, it would be rude to take up any of the guild master's time unnecessarily." Pauline replied, a similarly broad smile on her face.

Mavis, however, grimaced and said, "I do wonder... Well, for better or worse, we're just going to quietly make our exit..."

"Ahaha..."

Then came the day of their departure.

"We baked you some puddings and pies as a snack. Please take them with you..." Lenny said when the party came to say their farewells, handing them two bundles.

"Did you make these, Lenny?"

"Yeah..."

The pudding referred to here was not the same as the sort of pudding sold in Japan, of course. It was a much more shelf-stable food, like the Christmas puddings that are sold in other countries on modern-day Earth. The pie was mincemeat, which, likewise, would not go bad too quickly... Though once it was stored within Mile's inventory, nothing would ever go bad at all.

"Thank you! We'll be heading out now!"

And thus the Vow departed to meet up with the merchant caravan.

Just then, however, Mile's head was in another place, another time.

*Pudding and pie...*

Unconsciously, she opened her mouth and out came a single phrase.

"...Kissed the girls and made them cry!"

Hearing this, the other three halted and stared at Mile.

"M-Mile, what are you...?"

"Hm? Oh, uh, that was just a line from a song in a story..."

"So, Miley, you really are into younger girls..."

"Th-th-th-th-that's not it! That's not it at all!!!"

"I swear, Mile..."

"I'm telling you, that's not it! I'm being framed, I tell you! Framed!!!"

Yes indeed, it was a typical day for the Crimson Vow...

"Are the Crimson Vow here?"

"Who's asking?"

"I'm looking for the members of the Crimson Vow."

"And I'm asking who *you* are."

No inn staffer worth their salt would ever willingly give up information about a female guest to a strange man who had suddenly appeared at their door, so Lenny stood firm.

"I'm the guild master of the Capital branch of the Hunters' Guild. I need to speak with..."

"And have you any proof of your position? I'm not just going to turn over information about a group of young ladies to some strange man."

Indeed, while there was no hunter in the capital to whom the guild master would be unfamiliar, it was not as though he had gone around making his name and face known to every little girl who worked at every inn in town.

"Er..."

The guild master knit his brows, but the girl did have a point. The children in town knew nothing about him, and in terms of business ethics, her argument was sound. The staff of the Guild and other young hunters could stand to follow her example.

"Hey, help me out here."

At the guild master's beckoning, a man who was waiting behind him came to the guild master's side.

"I am the submaster of the Hunters' Guild," the man said. "I can confirm for you that this man is most certainly the guild master of the Hunters' Guild branch of the royal capital of Tils. I give you my word."

The guild master looked smug, as though that solved everything, but Lenny grinned and replied, "Okay then, do you have any proof of *your* position?"

"Uh..."

Naturally, if most of the common folk of the town had no idea who the guild master was, then there was no reason that they would know who the submaster was, either.

"W-well then, you can ask any hunter who's staying here. They can tell you..."

"Okay, who would you like me to call? Even if you tell me that anyone will do, we won't be giving out the names of any of our guests, and even *then*, if we can prove that you *are* with the Guild, we don't intend to offer up information about the whereabouts or plans of a certain group of young ladies to two visitors who have no right to that information without the permission of those ladies themselves!"

"Er..."

Once more, she had a point.

They could not simply scream at a ten-year-old inn employee and get her to talk, either. Doing such a thing would drag the Guild's reputation through the mud. Furthermore, the girl was absolutely in the right. An inn could not simply give out information about its guests without having obtained permission from those guests beforehand, and if this young girl would not permit such a thing, then it was almost certain that the master and matron of the establishment would not permit it either.

That said, the Crimson Vow were not currently present—that much they knew. From what the girl implied, if they were to name a particular person with whom they wished to speak, she would call for that someone. Given that she had not done so, they could extrapolate that the Crimson Vow were not there.

"Might I leave a message?"

"If I relay it verbally something might get miscommunicated, so if it's important, you'd better write it down in a letter."

"I'll do that, then. Mind if I borrow a chair?"

With that, the guild master took a seat at one of the dining tables and began to write a letter. He was allowed to borrow a writing implement free of charge, but there was still a fee to deliver the message. The paper was not free, either, for while the paper used on this continent was not as costly as parchment, it was still fairly expensive.

"Please give this to those girls when they return."

"Very well, we shall. As soon as the Crimson Vow returns to this inn, I will hand over your letter to them."

Of course, she had no idea how many months it might be before she had a chance to do so, but Lenny was not about to tell the guild master that.

And so, the men headed back to the Guild.

Given that the Crimson Vow had just returned from a lengthy journey and were now resting up, the guild master assumed that they probably would not be taking any new jobs for a while. Furthermore, it had been so long since they had been in the capital that when they started working again, they were likely to take a job that was closer, rather than farther away, to allow them to get the lay of the land again. With this in mind, the guild master had not thought to confirm whether, in the several times that the Crimson Vow had stopped by the guildhall during their wanderings of the capital, they had taken on any escort requests. No matter how noteworthy a party they were, the clerk, who could not read the guild master's thoughts, could hardly be expected to inform him every single time a mere C-rank party took on some garden variety job.

And so, the result of all this was...

"Why hasn't the Crimson Vow shown up?!"

The next evening, the guild master appeared at the front door of the inn once again. This time, he seemed to be alone.

"I mean, I don't know what to tell you... And we're kind of busy with dinner right now, so..." Lenny replied, looking hassled.

The guests and diners all stared at the guild master. The guild master, who seemed to be in quite a foul mood, ignored their gazes and continued speaking. "You gave them the letter, didn't you?! The fact that I haven't seen them yet means..."

"Actually, I haven't given it to them yet."

"What?"

For a moment, the guild master stared dumbly, as though unable to comprehend Lenny's reply.

"Wh-what are you saying?! I told you to be sure to give it to them!"

"Yes, of course. You told me to give it to them when they came back to the inn, correct? Well, I still haven't had the chance to do so."

"Huh?"

"Is there something wrong?"

"What?! Then, what you're saying is..."

"Exactly. They haven't come back to the inn yet."

The guild master was getting flustered. "S-so, when are they coming back?!"

"I don't know. And even if I did know, that information is not mine to share. Even if you tried to torture it out of me, I'd bite my tongue before you could make me talk!"

**"Whooooooooooooaaaaa!!!"**

At Lenny's insistence in the face of the intimidating guild master, a cry of admiration rose from the inn patrons. Hearing these dangerous and biting words, Lenny's father also came running out from the kitchen—the knife that he had just been using to slice meat gripped in his hand.

This was bad.

The guild master could see that this situation was turning out incredibly poorly for him. He bore absolutely no ill intentions, and yet here he was, looking like a villain. In front of all of these hunters and traveling merchants... This was bad—very, very bad.

"Pardon me."

And with those words of parting, the guild master fled back home at top speed.

After the guild master left, the mood inside the inn was one of elation. The patrons fell all the more in love with the inn after seeing the dejection of the guild master, who was normally so self-assured, and the courage of a small girl willing to risk her own safety just to protect the inn's guests. As a result, the orders for food and drink began to roll in.

"Little Lenny, come over here a minute! You're such a brave girl—let your big sisters treat you to a feast!"

"No, no, come over here! I'll buy you the most expensive juice on the menu!"

That juice was something that was too expensive for her to even be allowed to drink on the job. Lenny's heart began to flutter.

"Come over here, Lenny! You can sit on my la...gwah!!"

Somewhere, a male patron was struck by a female guest and sent flying.

Out of nowhere, Lenny's mother appeared, advising her, "Don't you worry about keeping an eye on the desk, Lenny. Go ahead and enjoy yourself all you like."

Then, she said to her in a quiet voice, "And while you're at it, order the most expensive things you can. It'll be a huge help to us."

After all, she was Lenny's mother...

"Oy! What's the last job that the Crimson Vow accepted?!" the guild master roared at the night clerks the moment he returned to the guildhall.

One employee rushed to the register to confirm and then reported, "Well, it looks like they took a job guarding a merchant caravan headed for the Kingdom of Marlane. They've already departed."

"What?! Damn it, then that was all for nothing! That little girl should have just said so from the start!"

Guarding merchants heading for Marlane was a fairly standard job for this branch. If he just waited a bit, then would take a similar job from Marlane bound back for Tils, and they would be back in the capital. He had made a complete fool of himself for absolutely no reason.

That said, if he had just checked in with his staff before he had even gone to the inn, then this whole thing could have been avoided. He was the one who had assumed, of his own accord, that the Crimson Vow were still taking a break. The fact that he had failed to take even the simplest of steps to confirm whether or not this was true meant that he had been the agent of his own unmaking here. He had no one to blame but himself.

"Damn it."

Looking as though he had just swallowed a bug, the guild master scrunched up his face and stalked up to the second floor.

Thus, the day that the guild master and the scheming noble pair learned the truth came just a little too late.

"*Where* is the Crimson Vow?!"

A few days later, someone new appeared at the inn. This time, it was a young girl.

*Not again...*

Lenny was beginning to grow a bit fed up with this. The usual exchange unfolded.

"N-no way! I traveled all the way to Vanolark, in the west, before I lost their trail. Just when I thought I'd found them again, and I was certain they had turned around and were heading back to Brandel, I got all mixed up in the confusion of that invasion business, and after I found out that they were heading back here, I came all the way back myself. When will they be back, at least?"

The exchange proceeded in Lenny's usual manner.

"Come on, you can tell *me* at least! So untrusting!"

The last time they had met, Dr. Clairia had been quite moved at how splendidly Lenny comported herself in the presence of adults, but this time, the professor seemed to even forget that she was an adult herself, behaving instead like a spoiled child. Clearly, she was at the utter limits of her emotional stamina.

Yet Lenny would not be budged.

Seeing that this conversation would get her absolutely nowhere, Dr. Clairia dragged her feet off to the Hunters' Guild once more.

"Gosh, I mean, we'd heard rumors, but this is really..."

The merchants were in excellent spirits during their campground dinner, eating their fill of high-class cooking, the likes of which should have been impossible for any traveling merchant in the midst of a journey.

The drivers and other guards ate equally well. On the battle-field, when armies came together for meals, everyone ate the same things—officers and foot soldiers alike. It promoted a feeling of solidarity, above all else.

Yet on a journey such as this, where normally all one had to eat was easily preserved foods, like hardtack, dried meat, and re-hydrated vegetables, how was it that they were dining on such a luxurious meal?

"Now, now, this is only possible thanks to your allowing us to step away from our duties for a bit to hunt. It's thanks to your flexibility that we can enjoy a fresh, proper meal as well."

Indeed, as Mile said, the merchants who had hired the Crimson Vow had given them permission to leave the caravan behind for a short while in order to do a little bit of hunting and gathering...using Mile's location magic.

After a short while, they had returned, toting deer and veg-etables and fruit, as well as freshwater fish caught from a nearby stream. In terms of Japanese cuisine, these fish would have been equivalent to something like river salmon and char.

Mile and Mavis did the prepping, and then Mile and Pauline did the cooking, while Reina oversaw the process as a whole. In this way, a meal came to be, much to the pleasure of the entire assembly. It was still the usual rustic style of cooking favored by most hunters, but with a few extra touches inspired by the deli-cate presentation of Japanese cuisine. They used plenty of flavor-ing, and the cookware and tableware were of the kind that you might use at home—no leaf plates and twig forks in sight.

The merchants had offered to give them some extra pay in return for this service, but as always, they declined. It would have been one thing if the meal had been prepared from the ingredients that Mile already had in her inventory, but as everything they used had been caught while they were already on the job, it would feel wrong to accept twice the money for doing the same amount of work. Even Pauline insisted on this. Apparently, doing such a thing would sully the coin, or so she implied.

Of course, the merchants were more than aware of this. Even so, they had to at least make the offer. The merchants had their own code as well and prided themselves on the policy of rewarding extra work with extra pay.

Judging by what the merchants had said, it seemed word had begun to spread throughout the Guild that if you hired the Crimson Vow as guards, you got to eat delicious food along the way, so when the Vow had applied to work as their guard, they had leapt at the chance. Naturally, they knew of Mile's storage magic as well and had asked for her to store a few of their valuables and easily damaged items, too.

This time, the caravan was not the hodgepodge sort cobbled together from many different companies, but a mid-sized assemblage of twenty-six wagons, all in the employ of a single firm. The merchant in charge was not the head of the company, but the man who was in charge of the company's shipments. Along with him were several subordinates, the drivers, and sixteen guards, including the Crimson Vow, who made up the rest of the convoy.

Because this caravan had departed directly from the capital, there was not a hunter present who did not already know of the Crimson Vow. So rather than belittling them or trying to pull anything funny, they simply struck up random conversation with the girls. Even this was rather annoying. Reina and Pauline warded off the chattiest members of the group with their coldest gazes, and as a result, there were no injuries. However, the soft-hearted Mavis and chatty Mile had their ears talked off.

In truth, it wasn't that no one ever tried to start anything with them, but it was all in good humor, so Mavis seemed to put up with it, and Mile was positively chuffed.

Watching her, Reina was stunned. *Well, as long as she's having fun, I guess that's all right...*

There were few bandits or monsters who would ever attack a caravan of this scale, assuming that they had hired the appropriate number of guards. Here, with sixteen hunters on their payroll, this group had erred on the side of caution.

A few days later, the caravan safely arrived in the royal capital of the Kingdom of Marlane without incident.

"Oh, Capitaaal! We're hooome!" Mile announced, repeating her now-favored wording.

"Mile, we've never been here before," Mavis replied flatly.

"Not only is this the first time you've been to this city, it's the first time you've even been in this *country*."

"Or is this just some new catchphrase of yours, Mile?"

Reina and Pauline appeared equally dumbfounded.

"Anyway, we'll be staying here for a little while. Let's go introduce ourselves at the guildhall, check for information, and see if there are any interesting jobs on the boards."

Indeed, before they even found themselves an inn, it was always important to investigate these three questions. The chances were low, but it was always possible that there might be a job so enticing that they would wish to accept it on the spot and head back out immediately. When you arrived in town, you went to the Guild. That was the hunter's way.

*Ding-a-ling.*

*Turn...*

By this point, they were used to being met with intent, appraising stares of all the local hunters whenever they walked through the doors of a new Guild branch. It wouldn't be long before everyone's gazes returned to where they were before...*or not.*

*Stare...*

*Staaaaaaare...*

These were not gazes full of malice. These were bewildered gazes, as though they had all just seen something rare or surprising. While the members of the Crimson Vow felt a bit awkward, they were not angry—just bemused, looking around themselves as they moved toward the boards.

There was nothing particularly valuable on the information board. The buzz surrounding the invasion of Brandel by the

Albarn Empire seemed to have all but died down, with the only relevant posting being a Priority E notice that said "Due to some internal conflict within the Albarn Empire, those headed for the Empire should seek further information. All those heading westward are advised to travel via routes in the Kingdom of Brandel." At the moment, there was nothing more interesting on the job board than what they had left behind back in Tils, either.

"Same as always, huh? I guess just crossing a border isn't going to give us an especially different distribution of monsters... Should we head somewhere else?"

"Hmm, maybe. That's probably for the best."

"Our time as young maidens is short. We can't sit around frittering it away!"

"Ahaha..."

As the Crimson Vow conversed, a middle-aged man, who appeared to be the guild master, approached them. It seemed someone had summoned him.

"Oh, my! It really is you, the real Crimson Vow, in the flesh!"

"What?"

The four girls spoke in unison, suspicious of his tone.

"We've never met before. How do you know who we are?"

"And what do you mean by the 'real' Crimson Vow? Has someone been impersonating us?"

Reina and Pauline asked the obvious questions.

Now that they thought about it, the way that everyone had reacted when they walked through the door did give the girls the feeling that they knew something about them.

"Ah, well, the reason that I recognize y'all is that I've seen you four before—I was there at the graduation exam exhibition. I usually go and watch it whenever I have the time, and I can arrange my schedule to complete any other errands I have over in Tils."

"So what was with that reaction we got from everyone else? How do *they* all know us?"

"Aah... That's ah, well, perhaps you'd come meet with me for a few minutes? There's something I'd like y'all to see up in the reference library."

"What?" they all asked.

The members of the Crimson Vow caught the guild master's drift—that it was something they should see for themselves—and agreed to go with him. And so, they quietly followed him up the stairs and entered the library, only to see—

There, on display, were four very familiar items.

"*The Crimson Vow figures, half-gold discount for the full set!!!!!!*" they chorused.

"I've recounted the story of yer battles to the others again and again, while showing them these figures..."

"*No way!!!!*"

Promoting oneself was an important part of every rookie hunter's job. If someone else helped you out with that, then a thank you was in order. When the guild master of a foreign Guild branch was the one helping you, then really, the only proper thing to do would be to bow your head and grovel in gratitude.

So why was it that the Crimson Vow were raging at him instead?

The guild master, who had been expecting to find himself on the receiving end of the gratitude of four beautiful young girls, froze, mouth agape.

"Wh-why are you all so angry?"

The members of the Crimson Vow exchanged looks. Now that he mentioned it, why *were* they complaining? They had come up with, crafted, and sold those figures all on their own, for the sake of their first-ever earnings. And to have one's name promoted in such a way was a huge coup for any hunting party. So really, they ought to thank the guild master and perhaps even do him a favor or two...

*"Like heeeeeeellll!!!"*

"Eek!"

The guild master, who could not read the girls' train of thought, was stunned to be so suddenly and loudly redressed. He could not understand what was happening at all.

The Crimson Vow sullenly left the research library behind and headed back down to the first floor, not once offering the guild master even a simple thank you. Then, they continued to walk straight out of the guildhall.

"Wh-what in the world was all that about?"

The guild master truly could not grasp why the Crimson Vow had been so displeased.

"Well, if we can get such a promising newbie party, who made such a flashy debut, to stay here a while, that oughtta be good motivation for everybody... They didn't bother checking if there

were any escort jobs heading right back to Tils, so I'm guessing they do plan to hang around. This might even be the first time they've visited Marlane. Well, time to rustle up some of the boys and get them to at least keep coming into town... Geehee. Gyeeheeheehee!"

For the sake of his Guild, the guild master would do anything in his power, shy of breaking the rules.

...Including being rude to another country?

No matter how friendly relations might have been between the two, and no matter how good-natured the guild master normally was, under the circumstances, it wasn't out of the question.

"........."

The Crimson Vow walked down the avenue, silent and sulking.

Everyone looked as though they wished to speak, but no one dared say a word.

Finally, Mile decided to spark the flame.

"S-so, those figures..."

"P-please don't say it..."

Mavis hung her head, cheeks going red.

"I didn't think they'd really be that embarrassing... At the time, we all thought they were so cool!"

"Aaaaaagh, why did I tell you to give me such an embarrassing pose?! Idiot, idiot! I thought it was the greatest thing back then, but I couldn't have been more wrong!!!"

"Say Mile, I don't remember you emphasizing the bust on my figure *that* much..."

The three agonized fretfully.

As she listened, a thought occurred to Mile: *N-now's my chance! For one of the entries of the Phrases that I've Always Wanted to Try Saying collection!*

And so the words emerged from Mile's lips:

"Heh. Seems as though you all can't accept what you wrought in the follies of your own youth."

Silence then spread once more throughout the group.

Everyone had taken a grave blow and fell into a deep despair. Including Mile.

"Come to think of it, how many of those *did* we make?" Mavis asked.

Pauline replied. "One thousand figurines."

Once again, silence fell.

Three days later...

"The Crimson Vow should've about finished their sightseeing in the capital by now. Bet they'll come looking for a job soon."

Three days was more than plenty for resting-slash-sightseeing, the guild master thought with a grin.

"I've put a lotta good things on this board. Lots of interesting, unusual, and challenging jobs, the sort of things those young folks ought to like. I've made all the necessary arrangements with the staff to encourage them to take those jobs. Heheheh, I bet they'll have a lotta fun..."

Then came the fourth day.

"They still haven't come back, huh? Well, having fun's an important part of life for young folks..."

Then came the fifth day.

"Okay, all right, that's enough playing around for now! Oy, you! Go check on them!"

At the guild master's command, one of the clerks rushed out to go and investigate at the capital's various inns that were normally patronized by hunters. And yet...

"What? They haven't checked in *anywhere*? There's no trace of them having stayed at *any* inn? What's going on here?! They haven't taken an escort job heading back to Tils or any other jobs at all! Are they camping out to gather stuff for the daily requests or something?!"

Rage as the guild master might, there was nothing more he could do, and the clerks could only scratch their head in confusion at the guild master's fervor.

"We're pretty far from the capital now. I think this should be good," said Pauline.

"Sounds right. If we're this far away, there shouldn't be anyone around who's been into that library or who's heard the stories from the guild master. Let's stay a little while in the next town," Reina agreed.

Mile and Mavis nodded in approval.

After the incident at the hall, the party had departed the royal capital of Marlane immediately and not ceased walking down the highway until dusk. They made camp night after night and continued onward, not stopping in any town or village.

For this, there was one simple reason:

There was just no way that they could stay in any town inhabited by anyone who knew of the figures and the guild master's wild tales.

Yet at this point, they were far enough away from the capital that this should no longer be a problem. There might be those who had been to the capital—and perhaps even to the capital Guild branch—but it was unlikely that they had just so happened to go up into the library or to hear any of the guild master's yarns.

There was nothing saying they were required to stay in every capital or to even stay in every country during the course of their travels. If there was a boring city, or a country where nothing caught their interest, then they might as well keep straight on to the next city, or the next country. Even if it was no fault of that town or country—a result of nothing but their own folly.

"Given the fact that there are few people who have the time or the leisure to travel for days just to watch the graduation exams at the Hunters' Prep School in the capital of another country—and the fact that most of the figures were purchased by people who live in the capital, not a lot of them should have made it to other countries," said Pauline, hoping to comfort the others. However...

"But that means most of them are circulating around the capital of Tils, so..." Mile said, realization dawning.

*"Don't say it!!!"*

As always, Mile had failed to read the room.

*Ding-a-ling.*

The doorbell of the guildhall made the same sound as it did in every other branch, as though there was some standardized bell they were all required to use.

Again, the scene unfolded just as it always did when they entered a new guildhall in a new town: all of the gazes in the room turned to fix on the Crimson Vow. Some evaluated, some glared; some looked disdainful, some looked dumbstruck, some looked intrigued, and some looked as though they were already scheming to make trouble.

After a long moment, about half the hunters returned to whatever they had been doing previously. The other half watched the Crimson Vow carefully as they proceeded to the counter. Yes, it was just as it always went down at a new guildhall.

"We are the Crimson Vow, registered Guild members of the Capital branch of the Hunters' Guild in the Kingdom of Tils. We are currently on a training journey, and we will be staying in this town for a short while."

As usual, Mavis was the one to announce the group to the clerk at the counter. This was in part because she was the party leader but also because having Mavis do the talking always seemed to get the best reaction from the young ladies on the staff. This was not surprising. If a clerk were approached by a cheeky and youthful-looking pipsqueak—or a somewhat daft and equally youthful-looking pipsqueak—or a young woman whose assets were more prominent than their own—then they might grow a bit petty and say something curt. Until the party got to know the clerks, having Mavis do all the talking was the safest, surest bet.

"My, you've come far!" the clerk replied cheerily. "Welcome! We're glad to have you. Please pardon all the strange stares. It's almost unheard of to have a party of all young ladies around these parts. In fact, it's always like this when women come in. That's honestly a typical reaction for those fellows. Please forgive them, as they don't mean anything by it!"

"No problem! We don't mind at all!!!" the Crimson Vow chorused.

"C-come again?"

The clerk was baffled at their enthusiastic response.

Yes, when a party of strange women came in, that was the typical reaction.

*Typical. A typical* reaction...

*"Typical is just fine with us!!!"*

Suddenly, the entire party sounded an awful lot like Mile...

# Didn't I Say
## to Make My Abilities
## *Average* in the
## Next Life?!

## CHAPTER 65 |
# The Frontier City

THE CITY WAS a small frontier town in the eastern reaches of the Kingdom of Marlane. Though it was comparatively small, it was in fact a town of middling size, home to branches of both the Hunters' Guild and the Merchants' Guild. It was the sort of place that, while perhaps two or three ranks lower than a metropolis like the royal capital, would be referred to by the citizens of the countryside as a big city, the sort of place to which all the grandmas and grandpas of the countryside might go on a once-yearly outing with their sons and daughters and grandchildren.

For the common folk of these remote lands, who would never think to run off and forsake their home turf, the kingdom's capital was a place you might only visit once in a lifetime, unless you were a merchant or something of the like. So, in terms of the common person's reality, this place was as close to a city as one got.

Such was the nature of the frontier city, Mafan. If all you wanted was simple living—not too rural, not too metropolitan—alongside a river that never dried up even in the worst drought, then it was not at all a bad place to live. It was situated close to the border with the neighboring country, and while relations with that country were not especially good, they were not so bad that a war was likely to break out anytime soon, so this wasn't too much of a problem. In addition, Mafan offered an ideal stopping point for the trade routes that ran through the area, which was quite the advantage for a small city such as this.

"This seems like a town where you could really take it easy," Mile said cheerfully.

"We don't have time to 'take it easy' on a training mission!" Reina scolded.

Currently, the members of the Crimson Vow were in the room they had taken at one of the inns. As always, they had chosen their lodgings after first carefully investigating all the inns in town and asking around about them... Though of course, if they didn't like the place they first chose, they could just switch to another one.

The price, rooms, amenities, cleanliness, and the food and such were all all just fine...

Only, there was no catgirl.

This place had no catgirls...

There was the married couple who owned the place, a chef of about thirty, and a young woman of around seventeen who worked as a waitress and did odd jobs. All of the owners' children had married and moved off to the royal capital to make a name for themselves, so the chef and the waitress both appeared to be regular salaried employees.

When Mile asked whether the owners did any cooking at all, the two immediately looked at her askance.

Everyone in the world has one or two things that they don't ever wish to talk about. Therefore, when Mile saw their reaction, she enquired no further.

Even though there were no children here for Mile to fawn over, the waitress, Mitella, was a bit of a flirt. She was red-haired and freckled, with charming looks and a strong will...which was to say, she would have perfectly fit the part of a waitress in a saloon.

Perhaps because she was roughly the same age as Mavis—who, her birthday having passed, was now eighteen—she seemed to be fond of teasing her, though not in an ill-natured manner. Rather, she dragged her shopping on her days off or followed her around for no particular reason, all of which left Mavis nonplussed.

"Why does she only seem interested in *me?*" Mavis grumbled.

"That's obvious. She's using you as a substitute boyfriend," Reina replied without hesitation.

"Wh...?"

Terror spread across Mavis's face.

"I'm already pretty well set for red-headed, sassy, overbearing girls, thanks!"

"Wh-wh-wh-wh-wh-wh-wh-wha...?! Who?! Who are you talking about?!?!"

Apparently, even Mavis could be counted to turn up the heat once in a while when she was offended. Reina, though she herself was willing to talk about nearly anything, got easily riled up by others' words and switched to full-on rage mode.

"O-oh, come on! B-both of you, please calm down!!!" Mile said in a panic.

Pauline only gave a weary shrug of her shoulders...

"How does this one sound for our first job in town?"

There were nods all around as the Crimson Vow stood before the job board, selecting their very first professional outing in the Kingdom of Marlane.

"Well then, to the counter!"

"Hold it right there!"

Seeing Mavis and Pauline's nods, Reina had assumed that the matter was settled and began to head to the counter, when suddenly Mile raised an objection.

"Look at that one!"

"What?"

The other three looked where Mile was pointing, to a slip of paper that was posted to the side of the job board away from the others.

*EMERGENCY REQUEST:*
Exterminate the monsters flooding out from the forest.
Payment: 1 gold each.

"What is this?"

Reina's suspicion was warranted. Monsters flooding out from the forest? Such a thing rarely happened. At least, not without some extenuating circumstances. Plus, if the job were really all that urgent, it wouldn't have been posted nonchalantly on the wall like this. Instead, it would have been carried out by a specially recruited force of C-rank parties or higher. It didn't make any sense...

"Well, I guess we won't know until we ask."

The four proceeded to the counter to ask for an explanation. The clerk looked troubled and explained, "You all have come from another region, yes? The truth is, there are some peculiar circumstances surrounding that request..."

According to the clerk, part of the border—the border with the neighboring land, near which Mafan was situated—was surrounded by a dense forest. Apparently, the people on the other side of this border forest, i.e., the citizens of the other country, were known to periodically flush the monsters out of the forest—not to exterminate them, but to chase them away.

Naturally, any monster who was being chased down would go running in the opposite direction—and as a result, they were all fleeing into this country's side of the woods. Subsequently, turf wars had begun to break out between the fleeing monsters and the monsters that already lived on the Marlane side, and the monsters who lost then moved farther in Marlane's direction, the weaker ones fleeing the forest. As a result, the citizens were coming under attack, and their crops and livestock were being destroyed.

Therefore, while it was necessary to eliminate these monsters, if they were to put out a request every single time they needed help, the affected villagers would go bankrupt. The lord of this territory had sent out his own troops once already, but the fact was that the army was primarily in place to defend the land from external invaders, and while the men were practiced in fighting other humans, hunting monsters was a bit out of their wheelhouse. Consequently, they were not very good at it.

Plus, jobs like this were not good for soldier morale. It would have been one thing if they were fighting against other soldiers, risking their lives in defense of their country, but they were not too keen on dying or being injured and left unfit for service on account of a bunch of monsters. Once was bad enough, but to send them out again and again, and have the soldiers' numbers dwindle bit by bit, would be a huge blow to the fief's strength.

And so, it seemed that the lord had instead decided to bolster these numbers by hiring hunters, who were accustomed to fighting beasts. However...

"Let me guess," Reina ventured, "the soldiers and the hunters here don't get along very well, so fights have been breaking out, and the hunters have been having all of the most dangerous parts of the job pushed onto them, so the number of hunters who will accept this job is dwindling."

The clerk nodded.

"Yes. As much as the soldiers loathe this duty, they keep badmouthing the hunters, because having them involved hurts the soldiers' pride. They push them into all the most perilous roles, and they don't do anything to actively support them. Even if you had nine lives, that would still be too much to put up with, and certainly, no one would go out of their way to purposely have to deal with that kind of treatment. The result is that the only people who will take the job now are desperate for money, soft-hearted to a foolhardy degree, or simply idiots. And then..."

A look of rage twisted the clerk's face. "This is all just harassment by our neighbors!" she spat. "*They're* the ones who keep driving those monsters over to our side of the border!"

"Ah..." The Crimson Vow nodded.

It was a straightforward situation with an unsurprising outcome.

And then, of course, came the Crimson Vow's equally unsurprising reply:

"All right. We'll take it."

"What?"

The clerk froze. "N-no, I don't think you all heard me just now! Are you really *that* desperate for money?!" the clerk asked in alarm.

"We aren't," Reina said simply. "We're in the third category."

"Huh?"

Reina continued with a grin. "What I'm saying is, we're in the third category. The ones who would take this job because we're idiots. Is that not a good enough reason to accept?"

The clerk, along with all of the other Guild staff and hunters who had been listening in on the exchange, froze, and silence spread throughout the guildhall.

"So you're the hunters who accepted the job, huh?"

Two days later, the Crimson Vow, having officially taken on the aforementioned job, assembled at the garrison of the local army, their assigned rendezvous point. Upon arrival, their first move was to greet the captain in charge.

The participants in this sortie were a platoon of forty soldiers and three parties of hunters totaling fifteen all together—a combined fifty-five fighters. Yes, two other parties had also decided to join the Crimson Vow.

Truthfully, the other two parties had no interest in this job whatsoever, but when the clerk pulled them aside and told them what was going on, these men had begun to fear the possibility that a party of all young women, who had just arrived from another country, might be annihilated, or harassed or abused by the soldiers. For the sake of the Crimson Vow, these hunters had willingly put themselves in danger.

"If anything happens, you can rely on them. Both of them are trustworthy parties," the clerk had told the Vow, but rather than seeming relieved, as the clerk had imagined they might, the members of the Crimson Vow immediately grew tense. It seemed they were now being a bother for other hunters, and it would be terrible to see them injured or killed because of it.

"I'm glad to see so many of you here today. I'm sure you know that this isn't an easy task, but it's one that we must take on for the sake of our farmers and for all of the other people who rely on the crops and livestock that our farmers have raised with their blood, sweat, and tears. Let's grin and bear it, and do our best out there!"

Surprisingly, the captain of the extermination squad was a rather down-to-earth fellow. Whether you were in the army or the mob, it wasn't unusual for people with common sense to find their way into the upper ranks.

"We are the Crimson Vow. We've recently arrived from the Kingdom of Tils on a journey of training and self-discipline. Pleased to make your acquaintance!"

After introducing themselves to the captain, the members of the Crimson Vow moved to exchange introductions with the other two parties.

According to the clerk, both of these parties were made up of good people, and it seemed that they should properly express their thanks for the assistance. Even Reina gave the other hunters an uncharacteristically meek and modest greeting—with a brilliant smile no less. Apparently, even she remembered how to put on a bit of a show.

"Smiles and flattery don't cost a thing, after all." The words that emerged from Pauline's mouth were cynical as ever.

"I'm Wulf," said one man, "of the Devils' Paradise. Over there is Vegas, of the Fellowship of Flame."

At Wulf's introduction, one of the other men gently waved his right hand in greeting. The members of the Crimson Vow politely nodded their heads in reply.

"We're hunters—fighting monsters is what we do. So we can't let ourselves fall behind those army brats. If we don't kill at least two or three times the number that those guys do, it makes hunters everywhere look bad. Both the Devils' Paradise and the Fellowship of Flame are going to hit at least three times' their quota, and you all should try and aim for at least twice as much. That said, those lazy boys are gonna be pussyfooting around, not wanting to stub their little toes on unfamiliar turf, so if a few C-rank hunters can just do what they normally do, beating them should be a piece of cake!"

Collectively, the other two parties were comprised of a group of men in their early thirties to their forties, all in their prime—none of them of the age at which they would be interested in young women. In fact, the members of the Crimson Vow were probably all around the ages of these men's daughters. Anyway, as the clerk had made clear, there could really be only one reason why they had decided to accept this job—the only reason why one would accept a job not even worth its pay, for the sake of some strangers to whom they had no allegiance, when they likely had families of their own they should be protecting:

They were all idiots.

Of course, the Crimson Vow were in no position to talk about anyone else's foolishness, and really, they didn't even mind those sort of idiots. They just had to try and make sure that no one ended up hurt on their behalf.

*The Fellowship of the Flame! That definitely sounds like the name of the sort of party who'd get wiped out by a single monster,* thought Mavis. *We'd better look out for them...*

Meanwhile, Mile was thinking on something entirely unrelated, as usual.

*Why would they have a name like "The Devils' Paradise"...?*

The next day arrived: the day of the monster extermination.

Naturally, they knew the day on which their neighbors were going to drive the monsters out in order to harass them. The neighboring land hired hunters as reinforcements as well, so word got around. Information flowed freely between the Guilds on both sides, and the local lord was no dummy. He hired hunters who were registered to the other Guild in order to receive information from them. Thus, on the second day after the others began their scheduled campaign, the fighters on the Marlane side set out. Their goal was to drive the monsters back before they could even make it out of the forest. However...

"Shouldn't we just start at the same time as them and force all the monsters in towards the border?" asked Mile.

The captain replied, "We tried that before. All that happened was that the monsters got caught between the monsters coming from the other side ahead of them and the soldiers driving them forward behind them. They turned back on the soldiers, and a lot of men got hurt. It seems like the same thing happened on the other side with the same results. Since then, we've abandoned that gambit."

At this, Pauline looked stunned.

"In that case, why didn't they just give up on this whole harassment thing?"

The captain simply shrugged as though to say, "Why don't you ask them that?" There was no way that he could answer for them, after all.

Once the captain had finished giving out orders, they finally set out.

The captain's instructions consisted of three main points.

One: The number-one priority is your own safety. Always prioritize the lives of yourselves and your friends over defeating or driving off any monster.

Two: Do not touch any monster or animal that a huntsman could trap for his meal. The only creatures they should be focusing on dealing with were ogres and goblins and the like.

Three: Do not step over the border!

That was all.

It was no problem if a hunter crossed over a national border while hunting down monsters or beasts, but a soldier crossing over the border in the line of duty could cause quite the conundrum, for it might be viewed as an invasion of another kingdom or fief. Even if the other side had been the provocateurs, such a misstep was still bad news. Even Mile and the others could deduce that much.

The group was split into four teams.

First, the platoon of soldiers split up into four squads, numbered 1 through 4. Then, the Devils' Paradise joined up with squad number 1, the Crimson Vow with 2, and the Fellowship of the Flame with 4, while squad 3 assumed the command role, with the captain, his aide, and two high-ranking NCOs included.

The soldiers had been split into four groups of nine, so the numbers for each new team were 14, 13, 13, and 15, making up the 55 in total.

Unlike soldiers, who were trained to be able to fight smoothly alongside any combination of other soldiers, separating parties of hunters would be sheer folly. Likewise, there was no point in having the hunters, who had been hired on specifically to decrease the number of injuries amongst the soldiers, operate independently. Therefore, they were arranged so that the veteran hunters would be situated at the front and back, while the squad with the command staff would be placed in the middle. There was no one who would object to such an arrangement.

When it came time to fight, they would spread out side by side, but for marching they split into two columns. If they marched single file, the line would be too long, and they would be susceptible to surprise attacks, unable to easily change formation to adapt to changes in their circumstances. The Crimson Vow were in the middle of their line, with the second squad of soldiers at their front, and squad three, with the command staff, at their backs.

"Hmph. We waste all our money hiring hunters and all we get're these little girls, huh? Can't even use them as a shield..." a man walking in front of the Crimson Vow muttered bitterly.

Directly ahead of the Crimson Vow—in other words, at the tail end of the soldiers' formation—was the NCO serving as the leader of the second squad, the squad in which the Crimson Vow had been included. In one of Earth's militaries, he would have been around the rank of Sergeant.

When it came time to battle, the hunters would act under the direction of their own party leaders, but if the soldiers should give any orders, the chain of command went captain, aide, upper-ranking NCOs, and the leader of their squad, in turn. Even the hunters would be expected to follow orders.

Naturally, any particularly unreasonable instruction, such as, "I need you to hold back those enemies here to buy us some time, even if it costs you your life," would be in violation of their contracts and considered invalid as a result. However, orders such as "go strike those enemies to the right" or "go do some recon" would be considered instructions from their employer and dutifully obeyed.

In other words, were a leader so inclined, he could direct the hunters toward tasks with a high risk of fatality.

Of course, no employer could get away with not paying their agreed-upon wage simply because a hunter had died. Their deposit would have already been paid to the Guild, and that amount would be distributed to their remaining party members and their family. In the event that no one remained who was able to rightfully claim payment, the wages became the property of the Guild and were utilized for the good of all hunters.

Thus, the Crimson Vow had no reason to think that the squad leader would try to make them do anything truly perilous, just because he was acting a little surly. Still, the risk was such that both the Devils' Paradise and the Fellowship of the Flame had considered the Crimson Vow to be in need of protection.

With this thought in mind, the Crimson Vow steeled themselves all the more. And yet...

"Damn it! If we have to protect those little girls, they're as good as dead weight."

Apparently, the soldiers were just as worried about protecting them.

An ironic laughter rose up from the members of the Crimson Vow.

It had been a few hours now since they had entered the forest. Having taken only two breaks of average length and a number of shorter ones along the way, they were now reaching the end of the first day's travel. Breaking for lunch would have taken up too much of their time, so they had skipped it; everyone had eaten a hearty breakfast in preparation.

The monsters driven out from the neighboring lands had yet to reach this area, so they were able to proceed without incident. It would be the next day that they could expect to start encountering their foes.

Under normal circumstances, no monster would go out of its way to attack a group of soldiers or hunters of this size. They might have been fiends and wild beasts, but they weren't stupid.

For tonight, they would make camp where they were. The real job began tomorrow.

"It's about time we set up camp. No need to rush—let's just get set up before it gets dark and then take it easy to get ready for tomorrow."

The captain was right. They were already far enough into the forest that time was no longer of the essence in trying to meet up with the oncoming monsters. Learning the terrain of the place and having everyone in top condition for the fight should be their first priority. Plus, the place through which they were currently passing was a meadow that was fairly sparse with trees—the perfect place for camping.

"Company, halt! We'll make camp here!"

The upper-ranking NCOs shouted to the front and back, and everyone assembled.

No matter how loud their voices got here, it didn't matter. With such a large number of people traveling in a group, their movements would already be apparent to any monsters or beasts lingering in the vicinity, and none of them would be stupid enough to come pick a fight with a combat force of over fifty people. Besides, as soon as they started preparing to cook, their scent would get around pretty quick. It was pointless to even think of concealing their presence.

Though they were camping out, there was no reason for them to carry tents or the like. Their goal was to press through the forest with only the minimum personnel and equipment necessary for combat, which meant that everyone would either just trim down the grass and spread their cloaks down on top of it or wrap themselves up in their cloaks like a bedroll. If all went according to plan, the trip would be only four days and three nights—or five days and four nights at worst—so that was enough for them.

The soldiers all staked out their spots and began cutting the grass down. Several of them seemed to leave an unnatural amount of space around them, but it was likely that those men were guilty of tossing and turning, snoring or grinding their teeth, or some other unappealing habit.

Then, the hunters began to prepare their own camps.

Suddenly, the soldiers and two of the hunting parties ceased to move. Silence spread throughout the clearing.

"Wh-wh-wh-wh-what is that?" asked the captain, who was overseeing the operations and had left the preparations of his own sleeping space to his subordinates.

"Huh?" Mavis shrugged. "It's just a normal tent."

She pulled back the flap to show him quickly, not understanding the source of the captain's surprise. What he saw inside were four beds, a simple table with four chairs, and a small chest, which held all their changes of clothing. The beds were not the fluffy, canopy-adorned kind favored by young maidens; they were merely plain, simple beds.

"Y-you just pulled that out of nowhere..."

"Ah, yes, well, it's a huge pain to set it up and take it down every single time, so I always just store it like this."

***"That's absurd!!!"***

A chorus of voices echoed from all around them—the voices of the soldiers who had been listening in, accompanied by that of the captain himself.

"I-I mean, storage magic capacity is determined by a ratio of weight to volume, so..."

Storage magic users were few and far between. And storage magic, which relied more on aptitude than training, was not something that you could increase with age. As a result, it was not unusual for even someone young to be able to use it, provided they had the aptitude and ability. It *was* unusual to see such users, who were the darlings of merchants and nobles alike, take up such a dangerous profession as working as a hunter—but the captain thought, *To each their own.* That said...

"If you have that much space to waste in there, you should fold up the tent and put something else inside!!!" the captain shouted. All the surrounding soldiers nodded.

If they had known ahead of time that she was a talented storage magic user and that she was going to be wasting that much space in her storage, think of what they could have asked her to bring: blankets, meat, vegetables, and all sorts of other things. They wouldn't have been restricted to the minimal amount of drinking water produced by the two soldiers with enough practical magic aptitude to summon it—they could have even had enough for cooking. As they thought about this, a feeling of vexation began to bubble up inside the captain.

The members of the Crimson Vow were not bad people, he knew that much. As leader of the troops, he was merely ashamed at having let the chance to so greatly increase their provisions slip right out from under his nose.

"I do have more inside..." Mile said offhandedly.

"What?" the captain replied, in a hollow voice.

"I'm telling you, I've got more in here. A lot of other things!"

With these words, Mile began to produce a cook surface and stove and cookware and meat and vegetables, along with all other manner of things, one after another from her storage.

"And..."

*Slam!*

Finally, out came a large tank of water.

Everyone was speechless, their eyes wide, until Pauline broke the silence.

"Water is five copper per cup! Bread is five copper a piece. Meat and vegetable stew is five half-silver a serving!"

In truth, if the soldiers had shown themselves to have a bad attitude, then the Crimson Vow would have made only enough for themselves and the other hunters—or else they would have charged the soldiers an exorbitant rate to milk a profit out of them. Yet, despite their expectations, the soldiers had turned out to be decent people, so they decided to charge a more conscientious price.

Five copper pieces was the equivalent of about 50 yen, and five half-silver was roughly 500 yen, so besides the water, none of it was really all that expensive. It was about the same prices as you would find at a restaurant in town.

"You've gotta be kidding me..."

This had been a day full of surprises for the captain.

Less than an hour later, there was a throng of soldiers gathered around the tent where the Crimson Vow had set up their stove.

Already, from the time the cooking started, there had been a number of looky-loos. They watched as the stew pot was filled magically with water, and as Reina carefully sank in a fireball, bringing it to boil in an instant. Mavis chopped the dried wood with her sword in the blink of an eye. Then Reina once again summoned up her fire magic to set it ablaze. After that, they tossed in the ingredients that Mile had chopped and seasoned their food with spices pulled from her storage. The quantity of spices they used meant that the five half-silver for the soup was more than worth the cost. They were doing them a special favor here.

There was a strange silence, and suddenly Pauline realized that the soldiers and other hunters were all looking her way.

Mile, Reina, and Mavis had all performed their own little shows, so now, Pauline realized, the audience was expecting some kind of trick from her as well. Unfortunately, all of the cooking was now finished. Yet it would be rather dull of her not to do *something* to contribute to the group's earnings.

After hemming and hawing for a few moments, Pauline hit upon an idea.

"Get your healing magic! Five half-silver per injury! I'll heal you right up—all your scrapes, foot aches, and training injuries— you name it!"

Her price was ridiculously low.

It would be one thing if she were a magic user who was affiliated with their own group, but to get such healing at one of the infirmaries in town staffed by retired former hunters would be far more expensive. There was a limit to the amount of magic every mage could use, after all, so performing mass healing every single day was not possible, which drove up the demand and the price.

When traveling in remote areas, conserving precious energy stores was a necessity for mages. No mage would ever wish to waste their magic pointlessly. Thus, you normally waited to deal with everything other than the most serious injuries until you got back to town. For the soldiers of a rural fief, which could not be expected to have a healing mage to assign to every platoon, healing was just left to natural processes even after they returned home.

*"Seriously?!"*

The soldiers came running eagerly toward Pauline. Gaping, the hunters were just a beat behind them.

Though Mile had not imparted the fundamentals of magic to Pauline, she had taught her more efficient ways of using her healing powers to supplement her already existing abilities. Now it was possible for Pauline to continually use minor healing magic without expending too much energy. Plus, all they had to do tonight once they were finished eating was to go to sleep, so recovering that energy should be no problem.

With this many people present, including the rest of the

Crimson Vow, there was no reason to think that anything should go awry. The forest was wide, but it was not exactly uncharted territory. As far as everyone knew, there was nothing worse than ogres in these parts.

It would be one thing if this expedition were a more lengthy one, but as it stood, they were only scheduled to plumb the depths of the forest and come right back out. It was not as if there would be anywhere else for the soldiers to spend their money. Many of the men had thought of this, of course, and had left their purses at home, but now they scrambled to borrow coin from comrades who always kept their money on them rather than storing it back in their lodgings.

There was none among them who would be foolish enough to let the opportunity to get a good meal and healing for a pittance slip out from under their noses.

While all this was going on, the meat and veggie stew was completed under Mile's direction, and so the group was able to enjoy a proper meal in the wilderness—without having any supply wagons in tow. It was a feat that, up until that moment, no soldier or hunter could ever have imagined.

"Seriously, what was with that?"

"I couldn't believe my eyes!"

After the lively meal was finished and the members of the Crimson Vow retreated to their tent, the Devils' Paradise and the Fellowship of the Flame all sat in a huddle, discussing.

"First of all, having that much storage space is ridiculous! She's gotta have gotten calls from nobles and merchants—maybe even from a king himself! What's she doin' livin' out here as a hunter?"

"I mean, I dunno, everyone's got their own story. Maybe she wasn't suited to life in court or whatever. I mean, it's not like any of us is one to talk...but with a power like that there's no way there ain't B or even A-rank parties comin' for her! What's she doin' in a C-rank party?!"

Pearls before swine. Coins before a cat. There were phrases of equivalent meaning in this world as well.

"Still, I can see why those other girls are such a perfect match for her."

"Mm-hmm. There is that swordswoman. She chopped up that wood like it was toothpicks. And that attack mage—she has such exquisite control of her fire magic. And then there's that healing mage... She can use her healing spells so easily, and *so many times*. I bet they're all personal guards, hired to watch over that storage magic girl and heal her up just in case something happens. There's no way that many little firecrackers could've come together just by chance."

"You think she's a spy?"

"Doubt it. She's way too useful to be expendable, and if she were, she wouldn't have been taking on jobs like this. And anyway, I really can't see it, not with a face as stupid-loo—*ahem*, as, uh, pure and simple as hers."

"You've got a point," the others replied.

They were not a particularly courteous bunch.

Still, it was impressive how accurately they guessed at the extent of the girls' abilities, even without having seen anything flashy beyond the storage magic. That was veteran hunters for you.

Of course, the soldiers were not all fools, either.

"The hell was with that storage magic? She's like a demon!"

The commander's aide was focused on Mile's storage magic, but the commander himself had other things on his mind.

"Sure, there's that, but did you see that one with the sword?! She tossed those logs up in the air and cut them into kindling with no more than two or three swipes of her blade... You lads, could any one of you cut a log midair like that, nothing holding it up?"

The men toward whom the commander's question was directed all shook their heads.

"And then, there was that fireball the other one conjured up without even moving, with just enough power to get that pot boiling. She controlled it so easily, with just enough force so that it slipped into the water. Have any of you ever seen anyone who could use magic like *that?*"

Once more, the soldiers shook their heads.

"And I don't think I even need to tell you all about that healing magic... Yeah, sure, maybe it was mostly scrapes and bruises, but I know that every single one of you was in line, and she healed each of you without even breaking a sweat. I've never heard of any mage who'd let all their magic get used up while they were out in the wild. Let alone for little stuff like that, not even in a battle or an emergency situation. Looking at this logically, I'd wager she didn't use more than a half—no maybe even no more than a third—of her power to do all that. Though, hell, I don't even know what 'logic' means in this situation."

The commander was a bit befuddled.

At the very least, the unexpected powers that these girls— who they had thought would be nothing but dead weight—had shown them gave him a newfound respect for hunters as a whole.

The next day, when the camp awoke, a delicious smell was wafting through the air.

"What is it?"

When the soldiers roused themselves, they found before them a mountain of bread and a steaming stew pot, along with a platter of salad.

"Get your breakfast combos, five half-silver a plate!"

Today was the day of the big fight, and there would be no time for them to stop and have lunch.

It seemed they had two breakfast choices: hard tack, a few scraps of jerky, and some water—or this hot, delectable, and filling array.

There was not a man among them who had the slightest trouble deciding. No soldier would ever neglect his physical condition on such an important day just to save a few silver.

"G-gimme one!"

"Me too!"

"Can I have two portions?"

The soldiers came flooding over.

"All right, all right, no need to rush, there's plenty to go around! Everyone gets seconds for free today—our treat!"

"*All riiight!!!*"

Of course, it was not the best idea to fight on a full stomach, or really to have much food in your belly at all, but at least this time they were fighting against monsters and not people, so there was no chance of them being pierced in the gut by a spear or sword or arrow. Plus, given how far they still had to travel, it was equally important that they safeguard against fatigue and hunger in this case.

And so, the soldiers ate their fill—in moderation—and set off triumphantly from the camp.

*This is the first time I've ever seen these men so full of life on one of these jobs. I owe my thanks to the Crimson Vow.*

The commander looked ahead to where the Crimson Vow walked before him and silently nodded his head.

The group was about two hours out from their campsite when the commander shouted, "This is the place! Spread out and start patrolling!"

Where they now stood was the narrowest part of the forest, which was bordered on both sides by mountains. It was halfway between the national border and the outer edge of the forest on

Marlane's side, and it was the ideal place to ambush and drive away any monsters that might come running their way.

They would cut the beasts off here and let nothing get by them. That was their primary duty.

The head of the platoon, the commander of this expedition, split the group up into four teams again, spreading them out to the left and right at intervals. They formed an unbreakable line that crossed the expanse of the area between the mountains.

The moment that any monsters that came at them, no matter how many there were, they would be repelled in the opposite direction with no chance of slipping through between the patrols. As long as they were successful in getting all the monsters turned around here, all they would have to do afterward was keep driving them back all the way to the border.

Of course, in the process, all of the ogres and goblins on their side of the line would be driven away as well. There was no way of distinguishing between the native inhabitants and the invaders, and besides, if those other scoundrels were going to drive all their beasts over to Marlane, then what was the harm in the Marlanians doing the same?

Or so they figured, at least.

Of course, they did have to be very careful not to drive away the orcs, jackalopes, deer, and boar that the local huntsmen took as their quarries. Diminishing the number of edible beasts and monsters in the area would be incredibly detrimental, not only to the local huntsmen but also to the people of the nearby city, who relied upon such creatures for nourishment.

The neighboring country was apparently unconcerned about such matters, driving every creature in their woods, edible or not, indiscriminately towards Marlane. So when they were driving off the monsters, it was important not to lay a hand on the more valuable, edible creatures, allowing them to pass through unharmed.

It was roughly two hours after all of the teams had gotten into position that Mile, with her superhuman senses of sight and hearing, first spotted something.

"They're coming. There's a huge mass of monsters and beasts up ahead! But they aren't all in one group—they're spread out."

Hearing this, the other three members of the Crimson Vow gave a silent nod, while the soldiers looked on, perplexed.

"Mile's good at sensing these things," Mavis explained. "If Mile says they're coming, then they're coming. Get ready!"

The soldiers appeared to still be half in disbelief, but thinking back to the incredible feats they had seen performed the day before, they silently nodded and drew their swords. Apparently, they could find it in themselves to have a bit of faith in Mile.

"They're here!"

After a short while, the soldiers, too, began to pick up on the signs of the approaching monsters.

Reina gave a wicked grin, fangs bared.

"Let's do this!"

"All right!!!"

"Two o'clock, three orcs, two hundred meters ahead. Target irrelevant. No mark!"

"Roger that, no mark!"

"One o'clock, four goblins, three hundred meters ahead!"

"Mavis, dispatch the threat!"

"On it!"

"Eleven o'clock, six kobolds, 150 meters ahead!"

"Pauline, get 'em with a water spell!"

"Okay!"

Following the directions of Mile (or rather, her radar), Reina issued commands, and one after the other, the Crimson Vow flew forth to repel the monsters, jumping right back into place after each attack as the men stared on silently. Occasionally even Mile and Reina took their turns, landing the girls a number of kills apiece.

The soldiers of the second squad watched them, mouths agape.

"C-Captain..." started one man.

"What is it?" the captain replied.

"Th-this is kind of relaxing, huh?"

"It sure is, huh?"

The men fell silent again.

Meanwhile, having been told that it wouldn't hurt to take just a few of the orcs, jackalopes, deer, and boar, Mile busied herself sniping a selection of each and storing them away into her loot box. These were not for turning in to the Guild but for eating. There was no need to pay the inflated prices at the butcher's shop when they could hunt their own meat, after all. The soldiers made sure to take down a few for their own meals that evening and the following morning as well.

Of course, they only took two or three all told. With only around fifty people to feed, they wouldn't need much more than that, plus it would be difficult to carry home, and it would be bad form for a group of soldiers to go around masquerading as huntsmen. If they were to come back from battle hauling mountains of meat, the rumors would be absolutely scandalous.

Meat, shorn from the bone, comprises about 70 percent of a pig's weight, and a further 70 percent of that is typically considered edible. In other words, roughly 49 kilograms of a 100 kilogram pig can be consumed as meat. And of course, an orc weighed considerably more than 100 kilograms, so taking down just one should have been plenty. That said, when butchered by a layman, there were a lot of parts that would become inedible, and since typically only the good portions would be used and the rest discarded, they would actually need about two or three to make up for the lost portions.

(Incidentally, the edible parts of a steer account for only 27 percent of its weight.)

On the soldiers' request, Mile put away their kills in her storage as well. Without Mile there, they would have had to do all of their hunting right around the campsite, where the hunting conditions wouldn't be as favorable once they had driven all the monsters back—yet again, her presence was a huge help.

After about two or three hours had passed since the initial encounter with the vanguard of approaching monsters, they were already through the worst of it. There were still some beasts on the route of their initial approach, but when they collided with the now-retreating front of monsters, most of them would get turned around naturally, swept up in the retreating wave. Thus, the number of monsters still crossing the border toward them was in rapid decline. From here, they would keep driving the monsters onward, meaning that, if their neighbors were going to keep pushing the same monsters forward, they would receive their just desserts. Of course, much more than this would mean an increased possibility of casualties, so while the soldiers remained on their guard, they couldn't help but breath a collective sigh of relief at these developments.

"Captain, I was thinking it would be smart to have Mile and Pauline make rounds to some of the other squads. Might I ask your permission for them to do so?" Mavis queried.

The captain's face brightened up, and he gave a great nod.

"Yes, please, if you would."

Their squad had yet to take a single grave injury, but there were no such assurances for the others. Or rather, it was highly improbable that they would be in the same shape. After all, they did not have the members of the Crimson Vow at their disposal.

In truth, it was only natural to have their sole adept healer make rounds between all of the squads, an idea that the captain himself ought to agree to immediately. To fail to do so would be a lapse of judgment that would see him severely dressed down by the commander and the other captains after the fight.

It was a bit embarrassing that the likes of a rookie hunter was covering up for the captain's own delay in coming to this conclusion, but given the guileless sincerity of Mavis's manner, the captain felt not the slightest bit of shame in thanking her for her helpful words.

Of course, he assumed that Mile was being sent out as a guard for Pauline, the healer, though, in fact, that was not the case.

No one in the Crimson Vow would say it, but they all recognized the truth: Mile was stronger with a blade than Mavis, more skilled at combat magic than Reina, and more proficient at healing than Pauline. Really, this was only to be expected, since Mile was the one who had trained all of them into what they were today.

In circumstances like these, there was a possibility that some soldier or other would take an injury that left him on the brink of death. Pauline would never be able to address such a grave wound, so Mile was dispatched to assist her.

Since the squad to which they had been assigned was in the center of the forces, it only made sense for them to each go in a separate direction. Should it happen that there was someone too gravely injured on Pauline's side, she could simply do her best to stabilize them until Mile arrived.

And so, Mile and Pauline split up, running.

"You all did wonderfully out there today. We didn't lose a single man, and no one got injured enough to mess 'em up later. This is a truly momentous occasion. Obviously, I can't permit you to drink, but you all have my leave to eat your fill. Just not so much that you can't make the return trip tomorrow. From here on out, you're free to do as you like, lookouts excepted. But first, let's all work together to get that meat cooking!"

Everyone raised a great cheer at the commander's words.

Casualties: 0.

A number of men had gotten hurt, but thanks to the two healers, they were all fully recovered now. There had been a few in bad enough shape that it was unclear whether they would be able to withstand the return trip, but miraculously, even they had made a full recovery. To heal cuts and bruises was one thing, but Pauline and Mile had managed to erase even the most serious of injuries, ones that would have normally showed symptoms for many years—broken bones, ruptured organs, and deep cuts into tendons and arteries were cured without a trace. Truthfully, this was the sort of battle that normally would have seen one or two men D.O.A., and a few more forced to retire from the service, but in the end, their damages were a net zero.

Even healing magic had its limits. If too much time passed before the healing magic could be applied, and the natural healing process had already begun, the body would react accordingly, leaving the injured with wounds that could only heal in the natural manner. Under these circumstances, missing parts could not be restored. Certainly, no one had ever returned from death's door to full health as a result of healing magic alone. The fact that magic could not heal old wounds was related to this.

But here, they had healers with magic the likes of which could only be expected from the high priest of a temple—two of them, no less!

Furthermore, both of them had chosen to participate in this dangerous job for the measly sum of one gold apiece, and since healing in battle was technically part of their hired duties, it had come for free.

It was unthinkable. Where else in the world did one find such charity?! Even a clergyman would never work for such meager recompense.

The soldiers were overwhelmed with thanks for their good fortune and for the hunters' kindness.

After some time, everyone was treated to a nice barbecue.

Some of the grass had been cut away to minimize the risk of flames spreading, and a roaring bonfire was built up from fallen logs and branches. A little ways away, a pit was dug to discard the viscera, beside which the soldiers set to dealing with the orcs.

Naturally, these men had handled orcs before in the course of previous missions. However, they were still amateurs when it came to dissecting monsters and lacked any dedicated tools for cutting flesh or bone. As a result, it was a bit of an undertaking. While a short sword worked just fine in a battle, it was awkward for preparing food, and there were few soldiers who would risk chipping their beloved blade to chop through orc bones. And so, they all stood there looking at one another without even approaching the orcs.

"All right, I'll handle this," Mavis said.

There was a single flash of her blade, and the three orcs were freed of their heads and limbs, their bellies slit and their fat clipped away in a single breath before the sword went back in its scabbard.

"I'll leave it to you all to remove the entrails and dispose of them, if you don't mind."

The men were speechless.

If the orcs had been up on their feet, it would have been one thing, but she had brought her blade down on the corpses laid out on the ground without a moment's hesitation. Furthermore, she had not once stopped moving her blade, cleaving all the bones, the neck, and the limbs like she was cutting a hot knife through butter. Surely, an orc's flesh and bones could not be so tender.

The motion had not appeared to be an especially careful one, yet somehow, there was not a single nick on the organs inside of the split bellies, not a shred of meat tainted by the contents of the creatures' digestive tracts.

"She's on a completely different level..."

Magic, they could accept. They were swordsmen and lancers, after all—not mages. When they watched a skilled mage work, at best, they might think to themselves, *Wow, that's cool.*

This, however, was something they could judge.

All of them, in spite of their relatively mature ages, were no match for this woman of not even twenty years. Seeing the enormous gap between their skills and hers filled them with a deep sense of defeat. Today, they had won out against hordes of monsters...and lost to a group of young girls.

Still, none of them felt anger or ill will.

All they felt was regret—at their own weakness, at their own shortcomings.

"Damn it! Let's eat! Gut those carcasses! Cut that meat!"

"Yeah!!!"

Today they had their very own meat, more than they could eat. They could eat their fill without paying a single copper!

Reinvigorated, the soldiers began cutting the meat and roasting it over the bonfire, just as, from elsewhere, a terribly delicious smell began wafting toward them. It was not just the smell of cooking meat. There was something indescribable, something mouthwatering.

And then they heard it, a cry like the voice of the Devil himself.

"Barbecued orc sauce, two half-silver a pop! Salt and pepper, just two half-silver! And refreshing, ice-cold lemonade, the perfect complement to that greasy orc fat, just three half-silver a cup!"

"*Damn iiiiiiiiiiiiiiiiit!!!*" the soldiers roared.

And here they thought that today they would be able to eat to their heart's content, without parting with a single coin...

"*How are we supposed to pass that up?!?!*"


"So there really was no point in us coming along at all, was there?" muttered Wulf, leader of the Devils' Paradise, looking crestfallen.

"Yep. They're strong and sturdy. A party of all young'uns, half of them girls not even of age..." Vegas, of the Fellowship of Flame, was right down in the dumps with him.

"S-still, it was worthwhile! We earned money without anyone getting hurt, got in some good practice, and improved the
relations between hunters and locals," said another of the party
members.

However...

"The ones who made us hunters look good was a group of
little ladies who came from somewhere else—not us. We were
supposed to be saving them and making ourselves look good that
way, but we were about as useful as air..."

The men fell silent.

"Well, c'mon. Let's go get somethin' to eat. Can't work without a bit of meat in ya!"

"Y-yeah..."

Not a single one of the hunters was in high spirits.

While everyone but the lookouts slept, and silence fell over
the camp, there was movement in the Crimson Vow's tent.

"All right, I'll be back."

"Be careful out there. Of course, it's *you* we're talking about, so
I guess there's no point in worrying."

"Ahaha, I'll try my best!"

Mile slipped out from the tent and through the clearing,
cloaked in an invisibility field and sound barrier. This time, she
had made sure to tell her fellow party members what was going
on beforehand, so she did not have to sneak out.

And then, Mile crossed over the barrier and invaded the neighboring country.

Of course, given that she was a hunter and not a soldier, it was a harmless act that could not properly be called an "invasion." She was not acting as part of the military, and she had not received any orders from them.

As of now, Mile was merely a solitary hunter, going out in search of raw goods during her free time, outside of work duties. Yes, there was no problem with that at all.

She slipped through the forest at an inhuman speed, and soon, she came across an ogre.

"All right! Invisibility field, sound barrier, dismissed! Intimidation, full power!"

Normally, Mile's magical power—or spirit or aura or what have you, her general presence, which monsters and wild animals would sense as "the smell of danger"—was something that she fully suppressed, but now she released it in full force.

In other words, all of the creatures in the surrounding region suddenly sensed that there was a dangerous life form approaching, a life form with half the power of an elder dragon, dripping with wanton bloodlust.

And with such a presence around, what do you suppose might happen?


*KA-THUMP-KA-THUMP-KA-THUMP-KA-THUMP*


Indeed, a stampede broke out.

Ahead of her, all of the monsters from this side of the border, which had been driven toward Marlane earlier in the day, along with all of the monsters (the dangerous, inedible ones) that had been driven out from Marlane, began rushing at full speed toward the outskirts of the forest on the neighboring country's side. Meanwhile, behind her, all of the edible creatures prized by huntsmen began rushing at equal speed towards Marlane. Any useful prey that got caught up in the stampede, Mile carefully escorted out of the fray and sent back towards Marlane.

Mile then approached the tail end of the ranks of exiting "bad monsters" and drew in a deep breath, ready to release her powers of intimidation once more.

"*Hee-hee-hoo... Hee-hee-hoo...* No wait, that's all wrong!"

Even when she was all alone, Mile never failed to play both sides of the comedy duo...whether or not she intended to.

"Okay, let's try that again. All right, *grnnnnnnnnhh...* Er."

That time was a bit dangerous.

*It was important not to overstrain your muscles at times like this,* Mile thought.

It had been two days prior that the army of the enemy nation had approached the border between the lands, chasing down the monsters. However, just like on the Marlane side, they had settled down for an orc barbecue after finishing their duties. Furthermore, though they still had a fair distance to travel the following day, they had decided to make camp while there was a decent amount of light outside.

Of course, there was a reason for this. The possibility of Marlane driving the monsters back their way sooner than predicted, and their having to stay behind to block them in order to protect the huntsmen, farmers, and crops of their kingdom from harm, left the soldiers hesitant to make a premature exit from the woods. Plus, if they came back too early, people might think that they were *running*, which would hurt their reputation more than anything else.

That said, while both of those reasons were legitimate ones, their real motivation boiled down to something like, "We came all the way out here, so we may as well spend another night and enjoy a nice cookout."

The soldiers took their time on the retreat, moving only during the daylight hours at a normal human walking pace.

Now, the large monsters stampeded forth in a panic, no longer trying to maintain a safe distance between themselves and the men who had chased them down on foot. Behind them came Mile, and....

They were on them in an instant.

The following morning, the two enemy platoons had packed up their camp and were just starting to head out, when they heard a cry from the guards who had been positioned to the rear.

"A swarm of monsters coming in quick from behind! There are ogres and goblins and kobolds and others—all being herded by a dire wolf or something, approaching at top speed! There are at least fifty of them!"

"Wh-what the hell?!"

By the guard's report, there were "at least fifty," but in truth, their number was closer to seventy or eighty, at minimum. If luck was not on their side, there might be even more. In fact, in the worst-case scenario, there were possibly hundreds, or even thousands. There might be enemies that they could not even see, hidden in the trees or otherwise out of the line of sight—though it was just as possible that they might be imagining enemies that were not there. All they could tell was that the monsters were approaching—fast.

*I'm not sure we're gonna make it back from this one...*

Of course, one did not want to end up taking casualties when the goal was to harass one's enemy. Therefore, the enemy nation had assembled an avalanche of force for this mission, with 100 men in total between the two platoons, the hired mercenaries, and the hunters, all under the leadership of one captain, the company leader. Each of the two platoons that had joined in were further attended by their own lieutenants.

The remaining half of the company had been left out on the outskirts of the forest. Naturally, dragging 180 soldiers through the woods would be far too difficult, so they remained on guard at the fringes of the trees, prepared to put up defenses on the off chance that any monsters should escape.

It was worth noting that these soldiers were not the force of any regional army. It was unlikely that any singular fief would, on their own, harass another country in a blatant act of aggression—and though the injuries sustained each time were few, a small force could not afford to make that kind of strike again and again. Particularly if it was in the name of such a dishonorable act and not for the sake of protecting their homes or country.

Anyone who died in the name of such a shameful cause would never be welcomed into the gates of Valhalla. Every man, no matter his rank, knew that fact.

"A counterstrike! All troops in battle formation, about-face! Hurry!!!"

It was pointless trying to run away from an onslaught of monsters within the forest. They would never make it out in time, and if they were caught from behind, they would be annihilated, without even the chance to resist. Though they were fully aware of the futility of their task, they had no choice but to stand and fight.

If only they had a scattered enemy with just a few heads each to face.

If only they were in a more open place with fewer trees.

However, at this point, there was nothing to gain by wishing for such things. They were facing a horde of monsters in the middle of the forest, where humans were at a disadvantage. There were limits to how much they could move, or swing their swords, and more monsters could pop out at them at any second. Thanks to the sudden nature of the attack, and the direction from whence it came, there was not even time to assume proper battle formation.

*Iris, Teatelia, I'm sorry. Looks like I won't be coming home...*

The captain drew his own blade and turned to face the enemy horde. Just then—

"Bwahahahahahaha! I am the goddess, Visibiel!"

Above the trees, a strange form appeared.

There *she* floated, wearing an outfit that, should an Earthling have seen it, would cause them to remark, "Oh, a swimsuit!" Over that, she wore a translucent dress made of light, with ice wings and a halo already formed and attached.

Indeed, it was her usual look, just with a slight change in wardrobe.

Incidentally, now that her halo and wings had become more of a staple, she had improvised a few shortcuts. In other words, rather than issuing detailed instructions to the nanomachines each and every time, she now simply commanded them, "Goddess Formation!" and left them to figure out the rest on their own.

This strange form then thought to herself, *I mean, it's not a lie! Everyone can properly see me, and there's nothing unclear about my appearance, so it's fair to say I'm "visible." I'm telling the truth here!*

It was an assertion on par with, *I bought it from a little old lady who only drove it to church on Sundays.*

The two platoons were surrounded by a lattice barrier as the girl, Visibiel, descended from the treetops before them—not without some difficulty. The horde of monsters split around them, as though avoiding the soldiers, and continued running past. Apparently, they were unable to stop themselves in time and formed this pattern to instead put as much distance as possible

between themselves and a force that it was clear they should absolutely not be reckoning with.

"W-we've...been saved...?" the captain stammered, but it was still too soon to make such assumptions.

"You there! Why are you lot disturbing this forest? Depending how you answer, I may not be able to allow you to leave."

*Eeeeeeeeeeeeeeeeeeeeeeeeeeeeeeek!!!*

All of the soldiers cried out inside their hearts, looking to the captain.

This peculiar figure was clearly no ordinary person. They had initially been complacent, thinking her to be an ally, since she had referred to herself as goddess and saved them from the horde of monsters. But now, suddenly, she had turned on them. There would be no winning against a devil—nay, a deity. Their only hope now lay in the strength of the captain's wit.

"W-w-w-w-we were merely driving these dangerous monsters further into the forest, to ensure the safety of our farmers! They may be monsters, but they too are creatures who have received the blessings of life from Your Greatness! We would never think to do something so heinous as meddle in any innocent lives but for the sake of defending ourselves and feeding our families!"

It was a splendid reply. After all, the captain had earned his station.

"Oh, is that so? Then surely you were not, instead, driving those monsters into the neighboring land in order to harass your neighbors? Surely you would never do such a heinous thing!"

"Th-th-th-th-that is absurd!"

Sweat dripped down the captain's brow.

"Very well, then... Oh?"

Just then, Mile noticed that one of the soldiers had a limp left arm. Apparently, he had broken a bone while chasing the monsters. The rate of injury may have been much lower on their side than on that of those who had to drive the monsters back, but that did not mean that they escaped entirely without damage.

She slowly proceeded to the spot where the man stood, white with fear, and ran her hands across his broken arm.

"Hmm. It seems you've already had these bones set, yes? In that case..."

The soldier's broken arm began to glow, then at the very next moment—

"It doesn't hurt anymore!" cried the man, flabbergasted.

"It should not. It has been completely healed."

"Wh...?"

The man timidly flexed the limb and then swung it with more force.

"I-It *is* healed..."

Silent, instantaneous healing. Not only of bone, but of muscle, artery, and tendon as well, all fully. Not ever the master mages in the capital or the pontiffs in the greatest of temples could do that.

Silence unfolded across the company. No one made a sound.


"Now, I'll overlook this but once, so don't you dare cross me again. It would be a shame to have to sink this whole continent

beneath the waves, so I suppose I'd have to restrain myself enough
to destroy only this land..."

*Eeeeeeeeeeeeeeeeeeeek!!!*

The soldiers were shaking like leaves.

Meanwhile, the Visible Go—er, "Visibiel"—thought to
herself: Even if these soldiers believed her, there was no point
if their superiors, who would hear this report, did not believe
as well. She approached the men, who all immediately went
stiff as boards, and drew the sword from one of the soldiers'
scabbards.

"Take *that!*"

She kneaded the blade with her fingers until it was warped
into a metal spiral.

*Why didn't it break?!?!* The soldiers were flabbergasted—as
well they should have been. The sword *should* have broken. There
was no feasible way for it to take on such a peculiar shape.

Then she approached the next soldier, and drove holes into
his breastplate with her fingertips, as easily as though she were
pushing through a rice paper screen.

*Poke. Poke. Poke.*

After opening the three holes with her pointer finger, she
plunged all four of her fingers in at once.

"Eeeeeeeeeeeeek!"

The holes had not gone all the way through to his body, but
the soldier still cried out in anguish.

Finally, she turned to a rock that was a little ways away,
pointed her finger at it, and...

### KA-BOOM!

These men were the royal army, the pride of their country, and yet at this, a number of them simply collapsed on the spot. In truth, the fact that even more of them did not collapse was perhaps a testament to their spirit.

However, all they had really done was manage to stay on their feet.

Even those who had not collapsed merely stood there without moving a muscle. They appeared utterly shell-shocked.

"Go now, and tell of what happened here—tell your countrymen what will become of anyone who defies my will!"

Mile reversed the gravity beneath her and floated gently up into the air, flying in the direction of the herd, while the men watched, still and silent.

After another full minute, the soldiers slowly began to return to their senses. If they were to stand stock-still in the middle of the forest, monsters would fall upon them where they stood, and they would be annihilated...normally.

This time, however, there was no real worry of that. All of the monsters had just run away at full speed.

Finally, one of the more level-headed soldiers suddenly screamed, "Wait! Crap! All of those monsters are gonna rush right out of the forest! There are villages right outside the forest and towns beyond that! We were supposed to stay here to stop them, but the monsters all went right past us!!!"

Hoping to calm the men, the captain immediately replied, "It'll be fine. The other half of our company is waiting outside of the forest, prepared for just such an eventuality. They'll stop those monsters, I'm sure of it! Even if it means that those men will be wiped out... Our country was the one who started this thing, so we can't go crying to mama just because the tables have turned. Besides, I'm sure the local troops aren't out there just playing around. They should have all been making their own preparations while we were busy with our work.

"By the time that stampede reaches the outskirts of the forest, those monsters should've used up most of their energy, and they'll be separated from one another thanks to their differences in speed. Once separated, they should prove far less of a threat.

"Still, we need to follow them and participate in the defense, so there's no time to waste. Not if we want to protect our own men from casualties. Also—none of you need to worry about that goddess. Thinking about her, reporting to the Crown, being questioned, being hanged—no matter what happens, that's *my* job!"

As they looked upon the captain's weary visage, the slightest bit of composure began to return to the soldiers' own faces. Sure enough, none of them would have to give the report about the goddess. The only thing that would be expected of them was to have an amusing tale with which to regale their fellow soldiers and the serving maids at taverns. Such was the privilege of the rank and file.

"All right, let's get moving! Troops, roll out!"

Thus, the combined brigade of the two platoons, the mercenaries, and the hunters began their advance.

Their expressions were dark as they hurried home. Though they had all picked up on the captain's mood and nodded in agreement, most of the soldiers were aware of the grim truth: It would be impossible for the two platoons on the outskirts of the forest to repel that many monsters. Even after that, the monsters would not stop, and the villages beyond the reserve platoons, and the towns beyond those, would all be...

*Uh-oh, there's not much of a gap left before the forest ends, is there? At this rate, these monsters are all gonna go flooding out of the trees! Well, it's better to put the brakes on this before they overrun the villagers...*

Mile, who had been flying ahead of the stampede just in case, was now in a bit of a panic as she realized how close they were getting to the edge of the forest. She was not of the mind to see any innocent civilians suffer as a result of her attempt to punish the soldiers.

*Umm, it seems like there are soldiers on the outskirts of the forest, so I probably don't have to stop all of them. I still need to make them sweat a little bit... Okay!*

In the forest, it would be imprudent to use powerful fire magic, or any other magic with the chance of causing widespread natural disaster. Furthermore, any heavy-handed means of attack would just cause the monsters and beasts to turn back around again and start stampeding in the opposite direction. With this in mind, Mile, who had now overtaken the herd, turned back to the front of the stampede, began waving her arms, and shouted, "Ball Lightning!"

Ball lightning. A phenomenon infrequently seen in locations near active thunderstorms, where a bright ball of light streaks through the air near the ground. It is one of the myriad phenomena frequently mistaken for UFOs or the souls of the departed.

There are numerous cases where humans who have come into contact with such objects, which many theorize are made of naturally occurring plasma, have perished. Additionally, ball lightning vanishes as quickly as it appears, leaving no trace behind it.

In other words, it was a convenient little trick, one that would run through the air along the ground and dissipate fully into the first thing with which it came into contact without affecting the area around it in the slightest. By regulating its power appropriately, one might guarantee that the thing with which the ball came into contact would not be killed, but rather, stunned or startled into stopping—or at the very least, turning around. By adjusting the numbers here, she should be able to adjust the course of the stampede as well.

The phenomenon of ball lightning still had yet to be fully and accurately explained even on Earth, but whether or not it actually was plasmatic in nature mattered not. Mile hoped and prayed for "something like that," and so the nanomachines who received her thoughts brought something like that into existence. She got the result without having to question the process, and that was just fine with her.

Honestly, she had no intention of slaughtering a bunch of monsters en masse in the first place. There was nothing to be gained from leaving mountains of corpses to rot on the forest floor instead of putting them to some practical use like food or materials. In fact, doing so would upset the local ecosystem. As far as Mile was concerned, this was the only way to safely get everything taken care of.

*Gyek!*

*Ga-hwee!*

*Gnyarh!!!*

Various cries of terror and anger sounded as some monsters were felled, some collapsed, and some turned around, heading once more into the depths of the forest. Of course, some of them continued on as they were, unmolested, while others refused to change their course. These numbers were, of course, carefully calculated by Mile, who had determined the directions in which her lightning ball would fly.

"Looks about right."

She had culled the monsters' numbers by a sufficient amount, and those who were still proceeding had been greatly weakened. The rest? Well, the soldiers beyond the forest would have to do their best to deal with them. With that final thought, Mile retreated. If she didn't get back soon, she got the feeling that the commander would be quite cross with her.

"What? The storage girl's gone? Why? Where did she go?!"

The remaining three members of the Crimson Vow looked on, troubled, as the commander raged.

"Umm, well, she said that she wanted to go and chase those guys down just a little bit, so they wouldn't think of bothering you all again..."

"Bwuh?! You're telling me she crossed the border and invaded enemy lands, all by herself, in the middle of the night?! I told everyone, very clearly, *not to cross the border no matter what*. Was she even listening?!"

It was after breakfast the following morning, while the group was cleaning up camp, that Mile's absence came to light.

For breakfast, everyone had eaten the leftover meat from the previous day's roast, so the members of the Crimson Vow were able to sell the seasonings and beverages that Mile had left with them. This meant that they would have to discard the cask that contained the liquids, but they still had plenty left over from their previous sortie, so it was not something they were too concerned about.

Afterwards, however, when the soldiers thought that they might petition Mile for use of her storage magic to carry the rest of their still-uneaten meat to enjoy again that evening, the jig was up.

"Well, actually," Mavis explained, just as they had discussed the night before, "she's not a soldier, just a hunter, going out on her own time in pursuit of food for herself, which has no relation to this job or to national borders."

Hearing this, a light bulb seemed to turn on over the commander's head.

Now that he thought about it, it was just as Mavis said. Plus, given the report of the Crimson Vow's activities he had heard yesterday from their squadmates, he was aware that Mile possessed indeterminably more ability than the average soldier. However, no matter how strong she may have been, chasing down a herd of monsters alone was incredibly reckless. Besides, there was no telling what might happen to her in the time that she was gone, until she caught up with the other soldiers. It would be different if she at least had as much combat prowess as that swordswoman who was their leader, or the combat magic wielder...

The commander expressed as much, fretting over this reckless action he was permitting. However...

"What? Mile's better with a sword than I am, stronger at combat magic than Reina, and more skilled with healing magic than Pauline. She's the one who taught all of us, after all."

"What?" asked the commander, shocked.

"What???" chorused the other soldiers.

"I-Is that true?"

"It's true."

"So we don't need to wait for her?"

"She'll be fine. She's probably safer right now than we are."

The commander fell silent. He didn't wish to think about this anymore. He turned to his men and ordered, "Company, withdraw! We set off for home at once!"

Thanks to Mile, their food and water stores had scarcely gone down at all. They only had about a day and a half of travel left, but when traveling through the forest, where anything could happen at any time, it was simply common sense to try and economize or discard extraneous supplies. Thankfully, the soldiers had enough strength to carry a sufficient amount of the remaining meat to eat for dinner that night and breakfast the next morning. (They would not be taking lunch, which took too much time.)

"Sorry I'm late!"

"How did you catch up with us so quickly?!"

At some point around midday, Mile finally caught up with the group, approaching calmly, with no signs of fatigue. By now, the commander had already entirely given up on making sense of her.

"Oh, by the way, I picked up the casks and extra meat that got left behind at the campsite. My apologies—I should have just left you all enough for breakfast and packed up the rest beforehand. I really wasn't thinking. I can carry the rest of everyone's things, too, if you like!"

*Whatever she says,* the commander thought to himself. *I'm tired. I'm just so tired...*

"Time for a break!" he decreed to his men. "Give all your meat and your bags to the storage girl!"

Mile sputtered, "'S-storage Girl?!' Are you serious?!"

"Oh, sorry..."

Unintentionally, the commander had let their internal nickname for her slip. He immediately apologized.

That night...

"Well, it looks like there's salt and pepper and sauce here for the barbecue. And how about some ice-cold lemonade? We've got delicious apples to cleanse the palate, too. And some alcohol-free ale, nice and chilled, just five half-silver a cup!"

"Damn it, damn it, *damn iiit!!!*" the soldiers roared. "There goes all of our allowance moneeeeeey!!!"

Eventually, the soldiers of the neighboring kingdom—who were on pursuit duty—arrived back at the outskirts of the forest. When they got there, they found the other half of their company looking absolutely bedraggled.

However, bruised and beaten though they were, they were alive. And, as far as the soldiers could tell, it did not look as though a single man had been lost.

*Don't tell me they tried to protect themselves and let the monsters get past them—no, they would never do something so cowardly!*

"Your report?" the captain asked, directing his question at the commander of the third platoon, who had been left in charge of the outskirt forces.

"Yes, sir! Around noon yesterday, monsters began appearing from out of the forest. Though their groups were sporadic, their numbers kept increasing, occasionally coming in larger waves. Though our men were mostly able to hold them off, we grew fatigued, and while no one took any fatal wounds, there *were* an increasing number of injuries. However, thanks to the local army sending reinforcements, and the Hunters' Guild issuing an emergency request, we were able to fully protect the local farmers from harm beyond a few fields, which were destroyed.

"I was the one who made the decision to contact the army and the Guild, so I personally take full responsibility for any shame or expense the royal army may incur as a result of my actions. Please, let no harm come to the other men. I beg your consideration..."

"You stopped that stampede without losing a single man?!"

The captain was stunned. Despite what the man had reported, he had never suspected that they would truly be able to stop the monsters once they left the forest.

*Well, wait a minute... Which way had that "Goddess" gone? That's right! She went in the same direction as the monsters. We passed by a lot of monsters on the way back, too. We were able to ignore them or drive them off without any pointless fighting, though. But the numbers did seem a bit high for them all to have just broken off from the stampede on their own.*

*And then we get a miracle—lots of men hurt, but no one killed... Well I guess, not a miracle so much as an example of "divine balance"...*

*The wounded can be healed. We can spend a bit of money and request the services of skilled healing mages, or we can make a sizable donation to a temple and have their clerics take care of our men, as long as they aren't lacking in forces and the wounds aren't too serious... In other words, though we'll have to spend a bit of money on healing, the kingdom won't have to waste all of the money and time that it would take to train up new skilled soldiers. I'm sure that the Goddess must have realized at least that much...*

The captain patted the man on the shoulder.

"You idiot! That's my job. You did well. Let's get to the nearest town and contract as many healing mages as we can. We'll have them work until their power or our coin runs out, whichever comes first. We'll borrow the money if we have to. We need to get back to the capital as quickly as possible. If we don't want the kingdom to be destroyed, that is..."

"Wh...?"

It seemed that there were hardships yet to come for these men.

"Brilliant work back there, everyone. It is a great blessing that we were able to complete our duty perfectly without having a single person seriously wounded or killed. Honestly, we didn't even have any light wounds by the time we made our way back. The accomplishments of the ladies and gentlemen of the Hunters' Guild are an example that we should all strive to emulate. We extend to you our deepest thanks and look forward to working alongside you all in the future. I now declare this special alliance dissolved. Dismissed!"

There was a great cheer at the captain's decree.

Everyone had made it back safe and unharmed.

The soldiers were overjoyed at this unprecedented achievement. The hunters, however, did not participate in the rejoicing. Unlike the soldiers, who were constantly asked to face down death, regardless of their own wishes, a hunter's life was one that was guided entirely by one's own free will. It was perfectly normal for them to make it home alive. After all, they only chose jobs that were suitable to their own skill sets.

Thus, the hunters never lost their cool and unaffected manner, though on the inside they were thrilled as well.

"I'm sorry. We would love to pay you a bonus, but I don't have the authority to do so. I'd give you my pocket change, but I still have to buy a drink for these soldiers, whose special allowances you all enticed them to spend. There's forty of them, so it's probably going to take at least three or four gold pieces. Those guys don't really know the meaning of holding back…

"So, I apologize! We'll pay the agreed fee for the hunters' help, no question. If all goes well, we can probably get them to raise the pay for next time, too! Please forgive me!" said the captain, bowing humbly.

The Crimson Vow smiled wryly.

"I wonder if there will be a next time," said Mile.

"There won't," said Reina.

"Doubt it," agreed Mavis.

"I don't think so," added Pauline.

One might imagine that not much had been accomplished during that short outing of Mile's. Considering how quickly she had caught back up with them, she couldn't have gone very far, nor even caught up with the tail end of the fleeing monsters. So, what could she have possibly achieved?

However, her triumphant pose suggested that she had set *something* in motion. Still, she appeared to have no intention of asking for any additional pay.

In any event, none of this changed the fact that more than sufficient support had been provided by the Crimson Vow to the army, by transporting goods, providing them with provisions, aiding them in battle, and healing their wounds. Furthermore, while the other two parties had fallen short of these girls, they were still far more skilled than any of the other hunters who had aided the army to date and provided far more help than any groups of soldiers ever could.

All of the hunters who had participated in this endeavor had hit home runs, and each and every one of them was instrumental to the fact that not a single soldier—nay, not a single member of their special task force as a whole—had been lost in the line of duty. The captain readily recognized this fact, along with the fact that without having the same members once more, there was no way that they would be able to achieve the same result in the future.

"We have some light food and drinks prepared over there for the hunters, too. After you've got a bit in your bellies, please feel free to head back to the Guild. We'll send a report of your job completion. I'm guessing that you didn't have much of a chance to converse with the other hunters while we were marching or camping, right? You were split up between the squads while we marched, and the Crimson Vow retreated right back into their tent after our meals. It would be good for you all to spend a little time together, right?"

The hunters headed towards the indicated building, gladly accepting the captain's kind consideration. It was as he said; they hadn't had much chance to mingle, after all.

"I'm so sorry..."

When they arrived at the spot where the food and drink had been set out, Wulf, leader of the Devils' Paradise, suddenly bowed his head.

"To tell you the truth, we were all underestimating the four of you. 'Our two parties are gonna do three times what those guys do, so you all should try and aim for at least two times.' Augh! What was I saying? I'm embarrassed to recall..." he said, covering his face in his hands. "Anyway, I really am sorry. And also, thank you. You already took our money for the food, so that's its own thing, but you really saved us with that healing magic, and you've improved the reputation of all hunters in the eyes of those soldiers. The fact that you all were here was just one of the reasons why the army had a much better attitude towards us than they usually do—as well as why this job went as well as it did—but it certainly was a major reason. That captain always was pretty favorable as far as soldiers go, but still—normally things would go much more poorly than this."

Vegas, the leader of the Fellowship of Flame, as well as all the other party members, nodded in agreement.

"Still, I mean, both of your parties did take this job that you otherwise had no interest in just because you were worried about us, right?" asked Reina.

"Hm? How did you—? Leutessy, that little..."

Wulf immediately guessed the offender. Apparently, the clerk they had spoken to was named Leutessy.

"Well, everyone was able to avoid injury, and we all made a little money off of it, so that's all that really matters!" piped in Pauline.

*A little?!* At her words, the two other parties exchanged exasperated looks. *You made a killing!*

Of course, all the money that they had taken went into the pockets of the whole party, not just Pauline, but from the wicked grin on her face, the other hunters could not help but see who held the purse strings.

Still, based on the payment of one gold each specified in the original job posting, the Devils' Paradise had earned five gold, and the Fellowship of the Flame six. Not bad at all for just four short days of work. Of course, when one considered the high probability that they might have just been used as a shield for the soldiers—and the possibility of them being greatly injured or killed—it was not a particularly generous amount of pay for a veteran hunter. But compared to other jobs of similar length, it really was not half bad.

The Crimson Vow, meanwhile, had four people, which meant four gold. In terms of Japanese money, this amounted to earnings of roughly 400,000 yen. In four short days—only one-ninth of the thirty-six day month—they had earned that amount. And then, factoring in the food that they had sold to the other hunters and soldiers, they had taken in nearly double that.

They had earned much higher wages than this, many times before—such as when hunting down the bandits or dealing with the wyvern. Still, for an average C-rank hunter, this would be a spectacular reward...assuming that all of the party members came back unharmed, anyway.

The three parties snacked on the provided food and made small talk, exchanged information, and generally got to know one another better. Then they went to give the soldiers their thanks and headed, as one, back to the guildhall.

*Clapclapclapclapclap!*
Upon entering the guildhall, they were greeted by the sounds of applause.

"Wh-what?"

The three parties stood stunned, confused as to what was going on. Through the cacophony, Leutessy, the clerk, called out to them.

"That was amazing, you all! You really did splendidly out there! The army captain himself came here earlier to sing your praises. The guild master extends his gratitude as well. And also..."

She glanced at the Crimson Vow, confirming that they were all completely unharmed.

"You were a great help to our friends who came from so far away. You're the pride of our branch!"

Applause broke out once again from the Guild staff and hunters.

However, the Devils' Paradise and the Fellowship of Flame wore muddled expressions as they took in said applause. Clearly, these were men in deep conflict.

It was understandable, of course. The ones who had flourished were these young rookie girls, whose abilities they had failed to recognize, looking down on them with the haughty assumption that they would be the saviors of such innocents. And yet, here they were being praised, everyone thinking that the accomplishments of those girls—who had, on the contrary, saved *them* in many ways—were their accomplishments. There were few other things in life that could possibly cause a man such anguish.

However, this was not something that they could explain to any of the others. That would require them to speak of the girls' special skills and combat methods, as well as their exceptional abilities. For a hunter, sharing information about other hunters they had met in the line of duty was the greatest of taboos. Such a thing could affect a hunter's livelihood and safety, after all.

In other words, they could not give even the slightest hint of the girls' abilities or strength. Besides, even if they were to insist that the members of the Crimson Vow had been the ones saving lives out there, no one would believe them. At most, some might think that they were just joking around or trying to pull some kind of prank.

Furthermore, back while they were eating, the girls had drilled it into them: "We don't intend to keep the fact of Mile's storage magic a secret, but don't tell anyone about her storage capacity, or our combat styles, or anything else. Just let everyone know that all three parties worked hard and contributed to the success of this mission."

*Ugh! This is so awkward!!!* The two parties screamed internally in agony as the other hunters congratulated them and clapped them on the shoulders as offers to treat them to ale came flooding in.

Meanwhile Mavis, who, unlike her three teammates, could relate far too well to the hunters' feelings, watched over them piteously.

"Thanks for everything out there. Hope we can do it again sometime!" said Wulf.

"Of course! We'll be looking forward to it, too. Thanks for all your help!" Mavis replied as each of the parties retreated to their respective homes.

Apparently, as veteran hunters, they did not stay at an inn but at their own home base. Of course, even while they called it a base, it was really more of a typical, rented domicile, set up for shared living.

Everyone had already received their completion marks along with their pay. The Devils' Paradise and the Fellowship of Flame had excused themselves soon after, claiming that they were exhausted—probably on an emotional level from having to drink in everyone's praise.

As for the Crimson Vow...

"More than anything, I'm glad you all are safe. From now on, I hope that you will choose jobs that are a little more suited to your abilities," Leutessy, the clerk, said cuttingly.

Apparently, Leutessy assumed that the fact that the Crimson Vow had made it back safely was thanks to the Devils' Paradise and the Fellowship of Flame, and, having been the one who informed these two kindly parties about the girls' plight and persuaded them to participate, she felt that she had indirectly been responsible for saving the girls herself.

It would seem that when giving his praise of the parties, the army captain had not named any individuals, but rather, offered his thanks to the hunters as a whole. Indeed, most soldiers were generally aware of the hunters' "greatest taboo," and thus, they did not offer any concrete praise regarding the Crimson Vow's actions. It wasn't surprising, then, that Leutessy should think that the words of congratulations were meant primarily for the two veteran parties.

"Ahahahaha..."

Able to plainly guess all of these facts, the members of the Crimson Vow could do nothing but laugh.

"Let's take it easy for the next couple days," Reina proposed.

The other three nodded. In a regional capital, three half-gold per day was about sufficient to cover food and lodging for four people. Including their sales, they had taken in about seven or eight gold pieces, so it was only right that they take a few days to themselves. Even if they were not hurt or exhausted, those who work themselves to the bone every single day without stopping to rest never live very long lives.

Plus, what was the point of working nonstop to the point of death or injury when you were already doing a job that put you in the line of danger for the sake of enjoying yourself and living a happy life? No matter how quickly they were aiming for a promotion, to rush like that would only detour them with injuries and failed jobs.

Outside of sleeping at inns, the Crimson Vow had barely been using their money.

They didn't use arrows or throwing knives, which would require them to replenish ammunition for their weapons, and they had two experts in healing magic on hand, which meant that they never wanted for bandages or medicine. When it came to food, Mile's storage was already chock-full of meat, herbs, and vegetables acquired from hunting and foraging, and they even had a stock of fish as well.

They had already collectively agreed that they would not eat into their savings except in extraordinary circumstances, but really, it was almost impossible for them to even spend what they earned.

So they spent their time sightseeing around the town, which they had not yet seen very much of, trying the local cuisine, and purchasing souvenirs for Little Lenny.

Normally, one did not purchase souvenirs until right before returning home, as it just made more luggage to carry, but for Mile, with her storage magic and her pseudo-inventory disguised as storage magic, this was no concern. They could buy anything they liked the moment they laid eyes on it. They were absurdly handy, these tricks of hers...

Four days later, the girls of the Crimson Vow stood in the hall of the Hunters' Guild in Mafan, capital city of a fief in the frontier region of the Kingdom of Marlane.

"Hmm. Not really anything interesting here..." Reina muttered, but that was more or less the norm.

There weren't a lot of "interesting," well-paying jobs that a rookie hunter would find exciting in a remote place such as this, and if there were, they would be snatched from the board the moment they were posted.

The world was a harsh place, after all.

"Ah well. Wanna do some dailies or an escort job? If we do some daily requests, we can study the spread of plants and monsters in this area, and if we do a guard job we can familiarize ourselves with the local geography and get cozy with the other parties who come on the journey. Then, they can tell us more about how things work around here. And either way, we'll be earning a bit of coin," said Mavis.

Reina, who wished to earn a promotion as quickly as possible; Pauline, who wanted to save up money to support the dream of establishing her own company; and Mile, who just wanted to live a carefree life, all nodded enthusiastically.

"A round-trip guard duty, bound for Glademarl?"

The request slip Reina had come across mentioned an unfamiliar-sounding name. The fact that they had never heard of the place meant that it was probably located somewhere that they had not been yet, and that the job was a round trip meant that they would not have to travel unpaid for the return. Besides, most merchants were unlikely to turn around the moment they had arrived somewhere, so they would probably have a bit of time to explore this new town when they got there.

The real question was just how far this Glademarl or whatever was from Mafan.

At times like this, it was best to ask the clerk. The Crimson Vow walked up to the desk to see Leutessy, who was fast becoming a familiar face.

"Um, about this guard request, the job bound for Glademarl..."

"What?!"

Leutessy appeared shocked. "What is it with you all and wanting to take these jobs?"

"What?!"

This time, it was the members of the Crimson Vow's turn to raise their voices in surprise. They had no idea what she meant.

Guarding a merchant caravan was a perfectly normal job for a group of C-rank hunters, no matter who they were—even bottom of the barrel, fresh off of a promotion from D-rank. Therefore, it was a natural choice for a party like the Crimson Vow, who had embarked on this journey specifically for the sake of self-improvement. In fact, they actively sought guard missions that would take them in the same direction they already wanted to travel, and even if the employer had already filled up their slots and was no longer taking applications from hunters, they would worm their way in somehow or other, offering reduced rates or the like.

They could choose to walk on foot, carrying all their own things, or ride in a wagon and get paid for the privilege. There was no hunter who would ever go on such a journey without taking guard jobs. As a result, they could not understand why Leutessy should doubt them.

"Ah, you all don't know anything about that area, do you? Glademarl is about three days from here, each way. They'll be staying for two days, which means that the trip will be eight days, seven nights. The village itself is a lovely place, peaceful and quiet."

The four found themselves slightly surprised. The destination was not a town but a village. And it was not a peddler who was heading to this tiny village but a whole merchant caravan. This was unusual, to say the least—assuming there was not some exceptional reason.

"However, the route to the village traverses a rather steep mountain road, and there are a lot of monsters, as well as bandits."

"Awesome!!!" the four cried.

"What?"

It was not every day that you heard a prospective guard cheer at the possibility of bandits.

But by now, Leutessy and the Crimson Vow were only exchanging interjections, and the conversation ground to a halt.

"A-anyway, merchants regularly travel between here and the dwarven village of Glademarl in order to sell daily necessities and purchase the metalwork they manufacture there, but this route is more dangerous than the others, so it's not very popular. There aren't a lot of bonuses given out, either. The veteran hunters usually take it half out of charity."

"In that case, that's the perfect job for us to take!"

"Huh?"

Reina's unexpected reply set the clerk straight back to stammering.

"Well, I mean, we're just overflowing with volunteer spirit!" Pauline continued with a grin.

At that, Leutessy resigned herself, no longer knowing what else to do.

"Fine, fine. I guess you should take it then."

Meanwhile, Mile was practically vibrating with excitement.

*Dwarves... Dwarves! I finally get to meet some dwarves!!!*

Indeed, by now Mile had met almost all the races of this world: elves, beastfolk, faeries, demons, elder dragons, and more. The one race she had still yet to encounter, however, were dwarves. If she really put her mind to it, she probably could have found some in one of the royal capitals, but she had yet to chance across any. After all, back in the capital, they had spent most of their time either at home or working.

"Yes! Finally, a complete set!"

"Complete set???"

As usual, no one had any idea what she was talking about. The other three members of the Crimson Vow and Leutessy all stared at her silently.

"I think something like this ought to do it..."

The evening after they accepted the job, the Crimson Vow received word that their departure would be in two days, so the next day, each went about town individually, making her own preparations for their vacation-slash-journey. Though Mile had more than enough food for all of them already stored away, buying luxury items, books for entertainment, and changes of clothing was still important in preparation for such a lengthy sortie.

Normally, no one would bring expensive books on a journey where they were sure to end up tattered—and likewise, few would think to bring along any luxury goods, which would just be more for them to carry. However, the Crimson Vow had Mile, along with her absurd amount of storage space. With that in mind, the other three party members went about buying whatever they pleased, not caring a jot about transportation or storage.

That really was no good. Whatever happened to their vow that they would work harder, so that they could survive even without Mile? It was no good, no good at all...

Following Pauline's lead, Mile decided that she would try her hand at a bit of commerce. Indeed, if there was one thing that she knew dwarves liked, it was booze! Or at least, that was common knowledge in all of the books she had read in her previous life.

"Say, little miss, is it really okay for you to be buying those? The alcohol's pretty potent. And anyway, how're you gonna carry them all?"

Yes, Mile had taken it upon herself to travel to all of the breweries in town and pick up the strongest spirits she could find. She had asked around with folks who had been to the dwarven village before. According to her investigation, while there were breweries around the village, their product did not compare to the high-class liquors sold in Mafan, and there were in fact many dwarves who enjoyed a stiff drink.

Then again, that wasn't true only of dwarves. In a world such as this one, where amusements were few and delicious foodstuffs hard to come by, it was not at all bizarre that there were many folks who were fond of a good drink. In fact, even amongst humans, who were, after all, brethren to the dwarves, there was many a soul who was fond of the bottle, far more so than in modern day Japan.

That said, this did not change the fact that there were many dwarves who enjoyed drinking, so Mile's assumption was not totally off the mark.

"I'll be fine! Store!"

With that, all of the casks and jugs that Mile had just purchased vanished in the blink of an eye.

"You've got storage skill, do ya?! And such a large amount—I'm jealous."

After a momentary shock, the old shopkeeper looked upon her with deep envy. It was normal for any merchant to be covetous of such a skill, but for a brewer, being able to transport goods safely and securely was a gift all the more longed for. And that was the purpose for which Mile was using her skill right now.

The route they were going to travel was a mountain road, rarely maintained, and it was full of monsters and bandits. Would anyone ever risk transporting alcohol, which was stored in heavy, easily breakable containers, along this route? It wasn't a daily necessity, and even the most rough, backwater villages produced their own booze. Factoring in the cost of transportation time and labor and hiring guards would cause the sales price to skyrocket. And then there was the fact that, no matter how high quality if was, if it didn't knock you off your feet the way the local stuff could, it would never sell.

Therefore, there were few merchants who would bother transporting alcohol for sale, or so Mile judged.

The day of their departure, the Crimson Vow arrived bright and early in the square before the Merchants' Guild. Other parties had been hired as well, and they couldn't keep their employers waiting. It was only to be expected that a group of low-ranking rookie C-rank hunters should be the first to arrive at the meeting place. They waited for a short while, until finally...

"I-It's you all!"

"So you're the other party who took this job, huh?"

Two sets of familiar faces had appeared: the Devils' Paradise and the Fellowship of Flame.

"That minx, Leutessy! She came all the way to our house to tell us, 'Oh, this poor caravan, if they don't hire more guards soon they won't be able to leave on time!' and we just had to take on the job."

"She came to us, too..."

The two party leaders, Wulf and Vegas, began to grumble.

*Oh dear...* thought the members of the Crimson Vow. It was obvious that the clerk had once again acted on their behalf.

It was something of a mixed blessing for them, though surely, as far as the other two parties were concerned, there was nothing "blessed" about it.

"We're sorry!"

Even though it was no fault of their own, the Crimson Vow felt compelled to bow their heads in apology.

"It's fine—we know it's not your fault. On the contrary, it feels bad to say it, but we'll probably just be a burden on you."

Despite Wulf's words, as far as the members of the Crimson Vow were concerned, having all of these capable hunters present meant that no one would bother messing with their party; traveling with two such trustworthy-seeming parties at their side put them all a bit more at ease. Nothing ill would come of this trip.

"We're looking forward to spending yet another mission alongside you all!" Mavis said cheerfully, and the two other parties nodded in reply.

They made their introductions to the merchants and drivers who had finally arrived, and the caravan set out soon after. They only planned on moving during the daylight hours, so they would have plenty of time for talking during breaks or at night. Only a fool would waste good travel time on chitchat.

The merchants were a bit wary upon seeing the Crimson Vow, an unfamiliar party comprised entirely of young women of questionable age. But once Wulf and Vegas, who sensed this, gave the party a ringing endorsement, the merchants, who were already acquainted with their two other parties, seemed a bit more at ease.

Of course, having them along was a blessing. Not only could they use attack and healing magic, but they could summon drinking water with magic as well. This meant that their chances of survival were greatly increased in the event of any unexpected incidents.

As important as water might be, there was no merchant alive who would dare cut into the amount of goods they needed to transport for sale just to bring along large stores of water. Most merchants carried only the minimal necessary amount, with only the slightest reserves. It was difficult to resupply water in the mountains, and horses required a lot of it. Thus, in the event of an emergency, having access to extra water supplies could mean the difference between life and death.

With that, the merchant caravan—which was rather small in the grand scheme of things, while simultaneously being rather large for a caravan that traveled only between a regional city and a small village—proceeded steadily into the mountains. There were seven wagons and fifteen guards, resulting in quite a high ratio of guards to wagons.

At the head wagon was the Devils' Paradise. At the tail was the Fellowship of Flame. And with the very center wagon was the Crimson Vow. Reinforcements shored up the front and back, while the mages and the nimble-seeming fighter were at the middle, able to protect the caravan from attack on both sides, as well as quickly lend support to either end of the caravan. It was a formation that any of them might have come up with, which made it a logical layout to which no one had any objections.

In each of the parties, half of the hunters rode in the wagons, while the other half proceeded on foot. There were two reasons for this: First, having the guards make an active show of their presence would ward off bandits and well as intelligent monsters, and second, the more people there were riding in the wagons, the less space there was to carry goods.

The movement speed of a fully laden merchant wagon was much less than that of a stagecoach, both due to the weight and the need for caution—no merchant wanted to arrive at their destination with damaged goods. So walking alongside at a normal pace wasn't taxing for a hunter. The fact that they changed shifts now and then made things even easier.

"All right, everyone! Let's take a break! Time for lunch!"

The transport manager, who was the leader of the seven-wagon caravan, shouted to the wagons ahead of and behind him, just loud enough so as not to startle the horses. He was the mediator for the three merchants who were participating in this expedition, and the driver of the central wagon.

This merchant was of the ilk who would proudly decree, "Hiring a driver when I can drive the damn wagon myself's nothing more than a waste of money! Sheer folly! What good's a merchant who can't drive his own cart?! Sure, you might be doin' real well for yourself now, but what happens when your money all goes down the gutter and you're left with nothing but yourself and a single wagon?! If you can't make your own wagon move, then you're gonna end up nothing but a peddler, carrying your little pack of wares on your own back!"

Perhaps because they had such a person in their midst, the other two merchants were each at the reins of a wagon as well. Thus, there were only three hired drivers, with a clerk from the leader's shop at the reins of the final cart.

When it came to the caravan's general operations, the transport manager was in charge, but if it came to a decision of whether to fight against, surrender to, or run away from any attacking bandits or monsters, the merchants would defer to Wulf, the combat leader. The merchants were more than welcome to refuse a recommendation by the combat leader that they should abandon their goods, but doing so would mean that running away was off the table, leaving the combat leader with only the option to surrender.

Such a scenario would likely conclude with the hunters turning over any money and weapons they had on hand, though there was also the possibility of the merchants being taken for ransom.

Most often, those who surrendered were not killed. To inflict such a thing on a group would mean that travelers in the area would begin to give up on the idea of surrendering, which would only serve to increase the losses that the bandits took. As such, there was no merit in putting together a large-scale subjugation force to hunt down bandits unless the problem got very serious.

They were not yet very far from town, so the highway itself was still fairly smooth. They pulled into a clearing a short distance from the road and stopped so that the merchants could begin to prepare a simple lunch.

For such a job, it was the employers' responsibility to provide food and libations while they were on the road. It would be a huge burden on the hunters for each of them to have to carry their own foodstuffs and water on their backs; to individually prepare their meals would be a greater burden still. So unless the conditions of a contract were particularly bad, or a merchant's means particularly paltry, this was the normal course of things.

However, the meals provided were the sort in which hunters could expect to be treated to the Three Sacred Treasures: the familiar travel standbys of hardtack, dried meat, and reconstituted vegetable soup. Once in a while they might be treated to dried fruit, for a real treat.

As the merchants set about assembling a simple stove with which to boil water for their meal, the Devils' Paradise and the Fellowship of Flame looked to the Crimson Vow expectantly.

"Ah, well, I think we should enjoy this meal that the merchants have provided for us, just for now. They're working so hard to put it together for us, after all. I'll put something together for dinner, though," said Mile.

Everyone's shoulders slumped in disappointment.

The first day came to an end without incident. The caravan was still close to town, so they had not yet entered the region that was plagued with bandits and monsters.

"Why don't we make camp here for the night?"

The merchants seemed to already have a predetermined set of locations for taking breaks and camping, having traveled this route many times before—assuming, of course, that there were no major changes of plan due to weather, wagon malfunctions, or attacks.

Once more, they pulled a short distance off the highway and made a circle enclosed by the wagons. In the event that any attacks came during the night, the wagons would serve as their shield. It was quite futile to try driving a wagon in the dead of night, and the merchants could not possibly bear to bring themselves to abandon their fully laden carts if they came under attack. Even abandoning the wagons themselves and riding away on the horses would prove difficult.

They would either have to fight, or they would have to surrender. There were no other options.

That said, surrender was only a viable option if it was bandits they were up against. In the event that their opponents were monsters... Well, in that case, they would just have to hang their hopes on the strength of the guards they had hired.

"Um, do you mind if I step away for a bit?" Mile made her usual request, seeking the merchants' permission.

There would be no need for her to seek permission if she was just stepping away to pick flowers or something nearby, so this meant she was probably hoping to go a little farther. That said, she could only go *so* far in a place like this, so permission was quickly granted.

Seeing this, the other hunters' eyes glittered with anticipation.

After Mile stepped away, Reina said to the merchants, "Don't worry about preparing dinner for me tonight."

The members of the other two parties cut in one after the other, while the merchants looked on, perplexed.

"Me neither."

"Nor me!"

"Nor me..."

"What?" the merchants cried.

What were these hunters thinking, going without dinner? The merchants were flummoxed, but, as requested, they prepared an evening meal for themselves alone.

"I'm back!"

A short while later, Mile returned. She appeared to be empty-handed, but the other hunters did not seem disappointed to see this was the case.

"All right! Here we are."

As planned, Mile pulled her spoils out of storage.

Deer.

Some fruits resembling persimmons.

And the old standard, a cask. Inside was fruit juice, and beside it were drinking bowls filled magically with water.

Seeing this spread, the other hunters hurriedly grabbed for their wallets.

"Ah, there's no need to pay for anything that I hunted while on the job here. The only thing I'll need payment for is the juice that I bought ahead of time, and the sauce, salt and pepper, and other seasonings. The juice is two half-silver a cup, and as a special bargain, for just five half-silver, you can use as much of the sauce and seasoning you like while we're on this trip!"

Obviously it would be a bit much to keep spending silvers here and there the entire time they were on the road, which would be six days of their eight day venture—excluding the two days they would spend in the village. It would be a particularly piteous thing to inflict upon them after the two parties had once again let themselves get screwed over for the sake of the Crimson Vow. And so, Mile decided to provide this special service.

"Whoa! Seriously?!"

"N-now that's some thinking I can get behind. Hope you don't mind if we take you up on that offer!"

Granted, it was not as though career hunters such as these were truly hurting for money. Still, having to shell out every single time they wanted to eat a steak was sure to lead to a lot of unfortunate feelings, including a sense that they were being used. Even though it was so tasty! Even though they were so glad to have it! Even though they were full of gratitude!

But if everything except the drinks and the seasonings were free, and they could use the seasonings as much as they liked, they certainly weren't going to complain.

*We're gonna eat. We're gonna eat until we burst!!!*

Hunters took a good meal very seriously.

As always, the Crimson Vow set off like busy bees. Reina began preparing the stove that Mile had produced, while Mavis chopped the dried wood that she had collected while Mile was gone into kindling. Then, she began butchering the deer carcasses, while Pauline helped out, cutting the meat into portions of appropriate size.

Mile began bringing out cookware and sauce and seasonings, placing them on the table that she had produced beforehand.

The merchants and their hired drivers only stared on in awe.

"Y-you've got...storage magic...?" one of the merchants asked Mile, in a voice full of disbelief.

Of course, as he had just seen, there were more things to question than just the storage, but it was the absurd capacity of her storage that shocked him the most.

Deer. Not fawns, but fully grown deer. And a table, chairs, a stove, cookware and tableware, a cask, and much, much more. Plus, just to put a cherry on top, behind Mile was a fully assembled and furnished tent.

The merchants had heard that the Crimson Vow could use attack and healing magic, and produce water with magic, too, but judging by how they were outfitted, they had assumed that the party only had two mages, with the other two being sword wielders.

As the three parties had already fought alongside one another previously, there was no need to inform each other about their strengths or battle styles, and so there had been no opportunity for the merchants to learn more about the Crimson Vow. Furthermore, Mile had not bothered to disclose the fact of her storage to the merchants, as it had nothing to do with her combat abilities.

"Ah, yes. It's quite handy."

"Handy" was certainly one word for it! The merchants stared at her like wolves looking at a plump sheep, unable to suppress the feeling that they would snatch her right up if the chance should arise and milk that ability for all it was worth...

"All right, eat up, everyone!"

The merchants and drivers looked at the deer meat roasting on the spit and the soup that Pauline was making on the stove—not reconstituted powdered vegetables, but an honest-to-goodness stew filled with real ingredients—and then turned back to look at their own table, where the hardtack and jerky were laid out.

Then, they all replied in unison: "Please and thank you!!!"

After dinner, the group miraculously managed to avoid a scene in which the merchants pulled Mile limb from limb in the hope of winning her favor. On the contrary, she turned the tables on them, asking the merchants a number of questions about the merchandise they were carrying.

As Mile had gathered, thanks to her investigation back in Mafan, the merchants did not appear to be carrying any alcohol to sell for profit, given the many drawbacks associated with transporting it. At most, they had a few bottles that they might offer as gifts to the village chief or any skilled blacksmiths.

*Yes! Jackpot!*

If she wanted to curry favor in the village, then liquor, particularly high-class, expensive liquor, was an obvious choice. There would be nothing in the village that could compare. Now, the only question would be the selling price.

"Um, so, about how expensive is that liquor you brought as gifts?"

When you didn't know something, it was best to ask the experts.

"Ah, well, there's wine, which is about three silver a bottle, and some distilled spirits, which run about eight silver each. They're both pretty pricey, of course. The wine's a bit cheaper because they don't make their own there, so it doesn't have to be quite as good. However, the spirits have to be the real deal."

*I see, I see. They came to the same conclusion I did. Plus, as I don't have to give my stock away for free, I brought more expensive stuff. I should be able to cut a good profit on this...*

Mile's windfall—and her win—was assured.

Bandits often appeared on the way to the village.

This leg of the journey was when the caravans were still fully loaded with daily necessities and luxury goods for sale, as well as money that would be used for stocking up. On the return trip, they would only be stocked with metalwork that had been purchased for later sale, goods that would be less appealing to bandits, who operated largely without horses so as not to rely on the main road. Such items were hard to carry, and if they tried to sell them off anywhere in the immediate area, they would be easily tracked and discovered. Anyone who would buy them knowing that they were stolen goods would be sure to bargain the price down to such a pittance that it would hardly have been worth the bandits' trouble.

Additionally, by their return, the merchants would have spent all of their investment money, and the money earned from selling the goods they brought would have already been invested into new stock. As a result, they would have very little actual coin on hand, and so, it was rare for bandits to bother targeting anyone leaving the village.

Even monsters with any sort of intelligence realized that attacking the caravans when they were traveling uphill instead of down was to their advantage, as they would find plenty of things to eat on the wagons in addition to the humans.

And so, the attack came right on schedule.

*Fweeeeeeeeeeee!*

At the telltale sound of a whistle from the front, all of the wagons immediately stopped, and Pauline and Mile, who had been taking the resting shift in the central wagon, leapt out. Sure enough, it was the signal of an impending attack. The members of the other two parties who had been resting in the front and back wagons jumped out as well.

Now, when the guards had all descended and everyone would be in position to hear, a voice rang out.

"Ambush! Four ogres, straight ahead!"

The five members of the Devils' Paradise were in charge of protecting the front of the caravan. For C-rank hunters, they were reasonably skilled, but in the grand scheme of things they were really only around the middle ranking for C-ranks, or perhaps a little lower. Five men against four ogres would be a tough battle. The Crimson Vow immediately rushed to the front.

Meanwhile, the Fellowship of Flame split up, leaving two men at the rear, while one each moved to flank the left and right sides of the central section of the caravan, and the final two rushed to the front to lend their support. They were seasoned guards who would never be so foolish as to send all their forces to the front line while leaving the rear and flanks of the caravan vulnerable to attack.

As formidable a foe as four ogres might be, they would be no match for eleven C-rank hunters. However...

There came a sudden, harried cry from the two Flames who had remained in position at the rear.

"Three more ogres coming from behind!"

Apparently, despite the fact that the enemies were ogres, they were intelligent enough to think of attacking from multiple directions simultaneously. That said, the fact that there had been a delay before the ones at the rear had appeared was probably sheer chance and not a result of any mindful planning to strike after the defense was already concentrated at the front.

"Flames, to the rear!"

At Wulf's direction, the Flames who had come up to the front and sides rushed back to their original position. That left nine hunters to face the four ogres at the front, and six to face the three at the rear. At first glance, this was just about sufficient balance, and yet...

"I'll go to the back, too!" Mile declared.

"Go for it!" replied Wulf, granting her permission. Like Mile, he had realized that, numbers aside, the rear team was at a disadvantage in terms of objective combat strength.

Mile headed immediately to the back, as fighting broke out on both sides almost simultaneously.

"Flare!"

There was no need for a mage to wait until an enemy came into striking range. Their incantations were finished before the approach even began. Before both sides got into the thick of things, leaving it harder to distinguish friend from foe, Pauline let off a full-strength Flare attack.

The ogres were fully consumed in flame, but since the area of the attack was wide, the actual power behind it dropped accordingly, meaning that it was not enough to fell an ogre at full health. Of course, Pauline had already fully accepted this from the get-go. Even if she could not manage to fell any monsters, the fire was at least enough to slow their approach and wound them somewhat. Pauline wasn't the only one here with combat abilities, after all.

Up next was...

"Firebomb!"

*Ka-boom!*

With a sudden explosion of flame, one of the ogres sank to the ground. Obviously, this attack had come from Reina.

With the one ogre down, Mavis, beside Reina, turned to face the ogre for which Wulf was aiming. The other two ogres were attended by two of the Paradise apiece.

The ogres stopped moving. There were now three groups of two against one. Normally, these would be dangerous circumstances for lower-ranking C-rank hunters, but for this group, it was no issue. Reina and Pauline had already finished incanting their next spells, which were to be held on the off chance that they were needed. For the rest, they trusted the sword fighters to do their thing. It wasn't good to hog all the glory, after all.

Meanwhile, of the Flames, only the two who had been at the flanking positions made it to the back in time for the start of the battle, leaving them at four-versus-three. The members of the Fellowship were slightly more skilled than those of the Paradise, but they were up against three ogres with a third of their membership missing. It was a dangerous situation—indeed, a battle that could not possibly be won without casualties.

Realizing this, the remaining two hunters rushed toward them at full tilt, but it did not seem as though they would be able to make it in time.

As the two Flames ran, praying to the heavens that their companions' injuries would be mild enough that they would heal without any long-term effects, something went whizzing past them. Suddenly, from behind the four at the rear, who were brandishing their swords desperately, doing all that they could to hold back the ogres and protect the carts and the merchants, a single tiny girl launched up from the ground, flying over both the pivoting Flames and the three ogres to touch down behind the monsters.

In a single move she drew her blade and cut down the ogre who had been slowest to react.

With Mile and the Flames surrounding the ogres, it was five against two, and shortly after, seven against two. The ogres did not stand a chance. Before much longer, all the ogres lay lifeless on the ground.

Apparently, the Flames had been in rather dire straits before Mile's arrival. One of them had a cut in his left arm, and another had taken a blow to the flank, hard enough that while he probably did not have any broken ribs, it was likely that he had at least sustained fractures.

At first, Mile thought to start applying healing magic straight away, but for the most part, the healing role in the Crimson Vow was left to Pauline. They were not in any great rush, so she was not about to steal Pauline's thunder on that front.

Yes, even Mile could remember to have consideration for others and "read the room" sometimes. At least, every once in a while...

By the time the battle finished at the rear, the front had already cleaned up as well. The ogres' numbers had been reduced to three with Reina's firebomb, and their strength weakened and pace slowed by Pauline's flare. At that point, against six melee fighters, the ogres had about a snowball's chance in Hell.

The whole group gathered beside the central wagon—guards, merchants, drivers, and all—to confirm everyone's status and discuss their next moves.

"The only injuries sustained were the two Fellowship members. They've both already had healing done, so they're fit as fiddles and feeling fine."

The non-hunters were agog to see the first man's arm healed without so much as a scab, thanks to Pauline's magic. They were not as impressed by the wound on the other man, as blunt internal trauma was not something judged easily from the outside—though of course, to completely heal the fractured bones, bruised organs, and ruptured blood vessels that lie underneath a wound was, particularly in this world, no mean feat.

It was hard to picture in the mind's eye things that one could not see, especially for those not well versed in the internal construction of the human body.

"Let's take the ogres with us. This area is outside of the bounds of any extermination requests, and no one would bother eating ogre meat except in a famine. Still, their hides and tusks can sometimes be used in making armor, so I bet we could get some of the dwarves to buy them from us," said Mile.

"Yeah," Wulf agreed. "I bet those guys in the village will be happy to know that we took care of some of their local ogre problem, so it'll be a nice show of strength as well. Once they know that there's no risk of the fruits of their labor falling into the hands of ruffians and humanoid monsters, they should be less reluctant to part with some of their more impressive stuff."

"What? But the carts are full... Oh right, storage magic!"

Given that Mile would choose to store as huge a waste of space as that tent—which was spacious but largely empty inside— just because it was too inconvenient to take it down and put it back up every single night, one could conjecture that she still had a reasonable surplus of storage space. Anyone who could not guess at least that much was not fit to be a merchant.

If only they could use magic like that themselves. If only they could convince that girl to work for them. Or better yet, to become their wife. Or mistress. Or lover...

At that thought, a series of rose-colored visions that they knew would never come true floated through the merchants' heads.

Everyone had the right to dream. It was an unalienable freedom which no one could take away from them.

Underneath the concentrated heat of their covetous gazes, Mile felt a shiver go down her spine...

# Didn't I Say to Make My Abilities *Average* in the Next Life?!

CHAPTER 66 |

# The Dwarven Village

"THERE SHE IS! The village of Glademarl!"

On the morning of the fourth day, the driver of the first wagon, who had the highest vantage point in the caravan, turned and called out to the others behind him.

This particular driver was not one of the merchants but a professional who had been hired on for the expedition. No matter the industry, being at the forefront was always a position requiring the utmost skill.

They had managed to arrive having taken only the one ogre attack. Of course, one was plenty. Had their guard been fewer in number, or had there been any parties of lesser rank in the mix, someone might have been seriously injured or killed, not to mention the damages that the caravan might have taken. Being attacked by seven ogres at once was not exactly a commonplace occurrence.

Regardless, they had now safely arrived at the gates of Glademarl.

They were only able to arrive so early in the morning because they had made camp quite near the village the night before. Getting in late at night would have caused trouble for the villagers, the merchants deemed, and it was an unnecessary expense. Of course, the hunters, who typically stayed in inns whenever it was possible, could not understand this logic.

It was not that they could not grasp the merchants' explanation, but still—they had to wonder why they could not have just made camp in some empty corner of the village, or the village square, if expense was their only concern. It would be far more convenient, if only in terms of them obtaining water. The members of the Crimson Vow pondered this question, but the other two parties did not even seem to pause, as though this had been the pattern on every journey.

"Oh, is it already that time again? Welcome to the village of Glademarl, merchants and friends!"

Just shy of the village, they were greeted by a young girl who looked to be no more than ten years old.

*Oh my goodness, my very first dwarf! She's so little and cute! Wait, no, I won't be deceived! She might look like a primary schooler, but she might well be a mother of three! Her speech patterns are definitely adult-like, no doubt about it!*

Adjusting her own first impression, Mile piped up, addressing the youthful-looking dwarf.

"Pardon me, but this is our party's first time here. We're pleased to meet you. And I hope you'll forgive my rudeness, but—how old are you?"

*Oh my gods!* thought the others.

It was a straight pitch, right down the middle. Or really, a beanball. The group was flabbergasted at Mile's candor.

"You said it yourself, kid—you are pretty darn rude. But whatever. If you wanna know, I'm ten!"

"She's a straight shooter, too!!!" the group chorused.

*What a two-faced trick! I thought she was an auntie masquerading as a child, but she really is a child! Dwarves are formidable!*

The first round was a loss for Mile—not that she had any idea who or what she was fighting against.

The dwarven girl did not have a beard, and her body was not the short, stout figure you would expect of most dwarves. She was a bit shorter than the 144 centimeters that was the average height for ten-year-old girls across the humanoid races, and a little bit pudgy, giving her somewhat of a roly-poly appearance.

Apparently, dwarven growth rates were the same as those of any other humanoid race during their formative years. It was just that their heights topped out a bit sooner than the others. Elves worked much the same way.

If, as per her previous conjecture, Mile's height was the average of the heights of all the humanoid races—humans, elves, dwarves, and such—then it would be fortunate if she ended up just a slightly short human, with the soaring heights and elegant features of elves canceling out most of the dwarven features.

Except for the areas where the combination of their features only amplified her lack of certain *other* parts...

The caravan passed by the girl and headed for the square in the center of the village. The first order of business was to begin selling off all of the goods they had brought. For dinner, they hoped to make a meal out of fresh fish and vegetables purchased from the villagers. There was no time for that in the middle of the day, so for lunch they would eat the food they had brought with them.

As travelers rarely stopped by this village, situated as it was in the middle of the mountains, there were no inns or anything of the sort. There was a small eatery, or rather, a tavern, but it could not be expected to host a sudden influx of twenty-plus people in addition to its usual crowd. They would need to have stocked up and prepared extra food ahead of time. Therefore, the caravan had no choice but to take care of their own amenities.

The Crimson Vow initially presumed that they would simply cook their meals using the ingredients that Mile already had in storage, as they did when they were camping, but they were informed that they ought to drop a bit of money in the village while they were there. If they did not buy some foodstuffs from the locals, as the merchants typically did, the villagers might take offense.

In a tiny village like this, the huntsmen and butchers and food sellers might all be friends or relatives of the smiths, or the village chief. Meaning that there were quite a few potential pitfalls...

The leader of the caravan went to give his regards to the village chief, while the other merchants began unloading their wares from their carts, setting up an open-air market.

"Hm? What are you doing there, Mile?" Pauline asked, watching curiously as Mile brought out a long table and began lining up various bottles and jugs upon it. Behind Mile was one particularly large bottle.

"Oh, well, I brought some liquor with me. I thought that the dwarves might like it. It's strong, high-quality stuff…"

*Mutter mutter.*

A growing din rose up from the dwarves, who were standing nearby watching the merchants work, all hoping to be the first to snap up the best goods for themselves.

"High quality, huh?"

"There's no reason she'd have brought it all the way here if it were cheap stuff. Wonder if I should be intrigued?"

A gaggle of dwarves, all short and stout and fully bearded—very much the sort you could point to and say, "Yep! Now those are the kind of dwarves you hear about in fairy tales!"—slowly began to approach.

"Yes, of course! Hmm, I suppose I can let you have a little sample. Only one sample of each, though. If I let everyone have as much as they wanted, you'd drink up all my stock!"

The dwarves gave a wry laugh, as if to say, "She's not wrong!"

Out of fairness, they chose eight trustworthy individuals from amongst themselves, each serving as a representative of one of the three varieties of wine and five types of spirits. Each was handed a sample. Among the spirits there were those similar to whiskey, distilled from corn and wheat, and those similar to brandy, distilled from fruits. Things like sugarcane and molasses were expensive, so one did not often see rum-type products on the market.

The representatives each took one cup from the table and then passed it down the line so that each person could taste a tiny bit—after they had taken the first sip, of course. They all drank from the same cups; there was no one here who would be bothered by a thing like that.

They each smelled the cup, took a bit into their mouths, appeared to roll it around on their tongues, and then drank it down, all with very serious looks upon their faces.

*This is kinda creepy*, thought Mile, and one could not really blame her. It was a bit creepy to see this many bearded old-timers all in one place, looking so serious about anything.

"I'll take 'em! One of each!"

"I'll take two each of the spirits!"

"Now wait a minute! Don't just run off with 'em while everyone else is still tasting!"

"I've just gotta run home and get my money, I'll be right back. Three of each, can you hold 'em for me? You better not sell out while I'm gone, okay?!"

The crowd was split into two: those who wished to buy on the spot and those who were worried that everything would sell out before they had a chance to. There were also those who did not have enough money on hand and had to rush home for more and those who rushed in to purchase without even tasting, based on the reactions of the eight representative dwarfs.

"She really nailed this one, huh? Well, I guess I'm not surprised, if they can buy these from her for only twice what you'd pay in town..."

The other merchants were stunned to see how Mile's stall was flourishing. Of course, as much as everyone was running to her now, they would still have to buy salt and other staples, and any luxury items they wanted, so the others would begin to turn a profit too once the hype had died down. As a result, the merchants were not especially bothered.

They were still stunned, however, both at what an incredible trick it was that she would have so much storage space and at the bargain prices for which she was selling her stock.

Including the round-trip travel and the stay in the village, this expedition would take 8 days in total. There were 15 guards and 7 in the merchant party. Totaling that, you got 176 man-days. The average expected allowance to support one person per day, when factoring in the danger, was 2 half-gold per day, which totaled up to 352 half-gold. In terms of Japanese money, that was 3.52 million yen.

When further considering the necessary expenditures for a business and matters such as the wear and tear to carts and horses, it was necessary to add in about 600 half-gold in order to turn a sufficient profit.

That number was for gross profit, however, not a net return.

In other words, it included the seed funds to purchase goods from the village for resale. It was important to allow for additional funds here, so that they did not lose everything in the event of a bandit or monster attack. Even if they were able to make a safe escape, moving too hastily would leave the horses and carts and a portion of their goods ruined.

And yet, here Mile was, selling such a heavy, easily breakable, unnecessarily high-risk item such as liquor, for a mere 100 percent markup. Such a thing would be utterly impossible without that ability of hers...

Envy overflowing, the merchants could not but heave a sigh at the thought of this most rare and precious blossom, who would never be theirs to hold.

"So then, Miley, how much profit did you bring in for us?" Pauline asked with a grin.

"Huh? This was my business. I bought the goods on my own time and sold them on my own time. It has absolutely nothing to do with the job that we accepted, so... *Eeek!*"

Pauline continued to beam. However, the feeling her expression conveyed was a complete 180 from what it had been moments prior.

"So then. Miley. How much profit did you bring in for us?"

"Uhh, oh ah, uhm, aaah..."

Mile blanched as she sensed the black aura emanating from Pauline's entire body.

"Guess even the little lady's got it rough..."

The merchants who had been watching Mile with envy could not help but gaze upon her with pity now.

"Pauline, that's a little..."

"The last time Mile made any money on the side, carrying the goods for those merchants who hired us, it was something we all agreed was 'part of the job,' right? As guards, our job is to protect the caravan, and that includes both the people and their property. This time is a little different, though. I'm sure even you can see that, Pauline."

"Grngh..." Pauline grumbled at Mavis and Reina's chiding.

Unlike Pauline, Mile had little attachment to money. However, even though the other members of the Crimson Vow were her friends—or rather, *because* they were her friends—she wished to remain a bit independent when it came to matters of cash flow. After all, there were plenty of stories the world over of friendships torn asunder on account of money.

She never borrowed money from anywhere but the bank. More importantly, she never lent or deposited money anywhere but the bank. Even if threatened, she never handed over money without reason. If she did so even once, she'd have people nipping at her heels for the rest of eternity.

This was a lesson that her father had instilled into her and her younger sister time after time in her previous life, and reborn or not, it was a teaching she intended to uphold.

And so, Mile continued peddling her wares. Once the dwarves realized that she had a practically endless supply, those who had only purchased a few bottles at the beginning, out of consideration for others, came back for more. Those who did not have enough money on hand rushed back to their homes yet again. Until, finally...

"That's all of it!!!"

Mile stood up and stretched, finally having reached a stopping point. Behind her, Pauline gnawed furiously on her handkerchief.

Somehow she had sold out of the massive amount of liquor she had brought with her, and all before noon. After that, business began to boom for the other merchants as well. Given that they had visited this village many times before, they already knew exactly how much of which items they would be able to sell. To have a large amount of stock left over would be a big loss for any merchant.

While this village aimed to be as self-sufficient as possible, there were still certain things that they could only import from other places, such as salt and medicine and other specialized items. Then there were those items that, while they were not absolutely necessary for survival, were still something of a necessity. Paper, soap, and other such items always sold well. And because they were not bulky or easily damaged, they did not need to be sold at an absurd price.

Finally, there were the so-called luxury items, such as spices and high-quality fabrics.

There were clothes and furs produced within the village as well, but they were of poor quality. Rough and tumble as they might be, even dwarven women liked to have nice things to dress up in for special occasions, like festivals and weddings—outfits that you might call their Sunday best.

Glademarl was a mountaintop village, so naturally the journey had been an ascent. The merchants prioritized keeping their loads light for speed and safety of travel over carrying goods that would not turn much of a profit. They needed to sell plenty in order to restock, for keeping too much cash during their journey could be a danger.

And of course, however much the villagers might request something, there were still some things that they could not carry. So, folks normally had to forgive the fact that they could not stock alcohol, which was not only heavy and easily damaged by bad roads, but also exclusively a luxury item. For a regular merchant, it was not possible to sell the bottles for a price that offset the effort involved in transporting them—so all they brought were a few select samples to be given as gifts for the sake of currying favor.

That said, there were ale and crude spirits produced even in the village, and most people drank just to get drunk—another reason there was no real need for the merchants to shoulder the risk of supplying alcohol.

"What? I understand that you all face dangers to transport necessities here for the sake of the village, but shouldn't you be selling your goods at prices that properly reflect the danger, effort, and expense of getting those goods here? Why are you allowing yourselves to take in such a narrow profit? If those goods are really items that they truly need, wouldn't the villagers be willing to pay a higher price for them? And if they won't pay, then they must not be items that they really need, in which case there's no reason for you all to add to your own burden by carrying those unnecessary items up here!" Pauline said indignantly, having heard the whole explanation from the merchants while they camped. Even if it concerned someone else's affairs, Pauline had a low boiling point when it came to any mercantile practices that she deemed to be irrational.

"A merchant's life comes with a lot of difficulties," one of them replied, shifting uncomfortably. Of course, this comment was not directed at Pauline, but at someone else entirely...

Just as Mile was in the process of packing up her empty stall, the caravan leader, who had headed off to the village chief's house immediately upon their arrival, returned to the village square. While he was gone, apparently to take care of various negotiations, the clerk from his shop who had accompanied him had handled his sales. It was for this reason that he had been the only one to bring along an employee.

Upon his return, the leader's expression was not a happy one.

"I know it's a bit early, but why don't we have lunch? Everyone, close up shop for now!"

Though he had directed them to close up, this was still but an open air market. All they had to do was place a little sign saying, *Out to Lunch*, which had apparently been prepared ahead of time, on their register—the whole process was over in a matter of seconds.

The villagers were all well aware that the merchants typically took a break for lunch at midday, so they had already purchased anything that they desperately needed. Afterwards they could window shop at their leisure, so there was no real hurry. For now, the villagers all returned to their homes. There were many places out in the countryside where folks ate only two meals a day, but a large percentage of the population here were involved in heavy physical labor, so they made sure to get their three squares.

With the wagons lined up at their backs, the caravan parties gnawed away at their travel meals.

While they were within the village, all of the food tucked away in Mile's storage was off-limits, and any of the ingredients purchased from the villagers were meant for dinner. For the sake of saving money and time, lunch would be a simple affair. The food sellers and their dependents in the village could not complain about that much.

As he chewed on his hardtack, one of the merchants turned to the leader. "So, what's the bad news?"

Having known each other for a long time, he could guess that something had gone awry just based on the air around the leader on his return. The third merchant, of course, looked as though he had come to the same conclusion.

It was not yet noon, but the leader had gathered them all together the moment he returned. He had directed them to sit with their backs to the wagons in such a way that they could easily survey their surroundings and guard against any eavesdroppers. From these clues, the situation had become clear to everyone.

(Of course, by "everyone," we mean the merchants, and the Devils' Paradise, and the Fellowship of Flame. The three hired drivers and the four members of the Crimson Vow had not picked up on this at all.)

The leader replied in a low voice, "Only half of the metalwork we were promised is ready for us. And yet, the total price is the same as it always is."

"What?!" the other three merchants, including the leader's employee, cried.

Their shock was understandable—the price of the goods they had come to purchase for resale had just doubled. And since they only were getting half of what they had been promised for the same cost, they would have to double their usual markup just to turn a profit. In other words, they would have to raise their sales price in town to twice what it normally was or never be able to recoup their costs.

And yet, that was never going to fly with their customers.

They were being charged double the previous price for the same goods—for goods that were non-perishable, unaffected by the vagaries of the weather or season. There was no customer who would buy at that price. There was no set market value for metalwork, after all.

Everyone would just buy their goods from other shops, who obtained their stock by other routes—or hold off on buying until the prices returned to normal.

"Showing their true colors, huh?"

At prices like that, the smithed goods alone would put them into the red. Moreover, continuing to provide the service of carrying necessities all the way into town and selling them at a reasonable price was out of the question without the profits from the metalwork.

Consequently, there was not going to be a next time. This was the last time that this caravan would ever travel to Glademarl, and they would not be making any purchases while they were here, either.

This poor mountain village, atop a road overrun by monsters and brigands, had just lost its revenue stream, along with its only means of obtaining necessities.

It was over for them.

"B-but none of the villagers seem like they would do anything like that," said Mile.

"*Those guys forget about everything else when you put some good booze in front of them,*" the merchants retorted in unison.

*That's weird though,* thought Mile. *Why would they purposefully do something so suicidal?*

Finding this suspicious, Mile asked the leader, "This is obviously pretty weird, right? For them to pull something like this so suddenly. There must be something going on..."

"Yeah, I think so, too. There has to be a reason that they couldn't fulfill our order. I don't think they'd tell us that unless they had no other choice in the matter. However..."

"However?" Mile interjected.

The leader continued, "Even if something is going on, they're the ones who decided, 'Well, even if we only made half of what they asked, we can still give it to 'em and just request the same price.' It would be one thing if they had actually discussed it with us, but instead, they're treating us like idiots!"

*Ah...*

Finally, Mile understood why there had been such an eerie feeling in the air—and the reason they had camped just outside of the village rather than inside. And even now, why none of them seemed enraged or even frantic about the chief's sudden demands. And why none of them were the least bit concerned about the village's well-being.

*None of them actually like this village very much...*

She then pitched a straight ball right over the plate. With gusto.

"Do you all hate the villagers here?"

"M-Mile, what are you saying?!" asked Mavis, but she was the only one who appeared to be surprised.

Apparently Pauline and Reina had already picked up on this fact.

"That would be correct. We put a good face on for them because we're merchants, but to tell you the truth, these villagers have always taken us for idiots. So, as far as we're concerned, the folks here aren't anything more than trade partners who can help us increase our profits. They certainly aren't valued customers or anything like that. So, if they lose value to us as trade partners, then we're outta here. That's all there is to it.

"The fact that we accept all the risk of coming here and bringing them their necessities to sell at a completely unprofitable rate isn't because we care about them or anything. We only bother because they demanded that we do so if we want to buy their stuff. But if they're gonna gouge us on the one thing we come here for, then there's no point in us even coming. We're merchants. We aren't idiots or saints."

All the usual warmth had vanished from the merchants' faces. It seemed their plans were already set in stone. They were going to abandon this village, or rather, withdraw from any future dealings.

It made sense. There was not a single reason that any merchant would continue to make a dangerous eight-day round-trip journey to a village of surly customers who did nothing but put them in the red.

Even so, Mile still found something suspicious about this whole thing.

"Um, but as far as I could see, none of the villagers really looked like bad people..."

Indeed, Mile had seen the villagers who had stopped by to shop from them as nothing but smiling, friendly dwarves.

"You're right, they aren't bad people."

"What?"

The members of the Crimson Vow, save for Pauline, appeared shocked at the merchant's unexpected reply. They looked frantically around, but as far as they could tell, none of the villagers still in the square were paying them any mind. It would be difficult to overhear a conversation that was spoken in such hushed tones, and none of them would have any interest in the internal affairs of merchants, anyway. The members of the Devils' Paradise and the Fellowship of Flame, who had been listening silently this whole time, continued chewing on their provisions as though they were not affected at all.

They had known this all from the start. That was what their attitude conveyed.

"These villagers are, by and large, craftspeople by trade. There are plenty of farmers and lumberjacks, too, but the ones we deal with are the blacksmiths, who are really the heart and soul of this village, a fact with which I'm sure most folks would agree. They have a strong sense of dignity and are incredibly proud of their skills and techniques.

"Their smithing is number one amongst the humanoid races. Far better than anything that a human or elf could produce. So, they 'allow' the other races to purchase and use what they create. That's what they believe, from the bottom of their hearts.

"So, it's not that they harbor ill will towards us, or hate us, or wish death on us, or resent us, or anything like that. They're skilled craftspeople who enjoy good booze with good friends. It's just that they're prideful and look down on the other races when it comes to smithing. They feel that anyone who desires what they make should grovel before them and do anything they say. But no, they aren't exactly *bad* people."

"*That sounds plenty bad to us!!!*"

As they often did, the four members of the Crimson Vow spoke together.

"At any rate, everyone, let's keep selling this afternoon, just as we planned. I'll head over to the blacksmith's shop and try to find out what's going on. If it seems like we can work something out, we'll continue selling tomorrow and leave the day after next. If it's no good, then we might just head out at some point tomorrow. If there's anything in town that you can still buy at the normal price, then we can probably go ahead and buy just that. Any objections?"

The other two merchants shook their heads. The third was employed by the leader, so his opinion did not have much additional weight. He himself was aware of this, and as a result, did not even bother reacting.

Meanwhile, the members of the Crimson Vow were silent, still puzzled at this turn of events. Though the other two parties were already aware of the situation with the villagers, they too looked a bit stumped.

Later, Reina would ask them, "Why didn't you tell us about the villagers beforehand?"

Her question was met with the following reply: "There wasn't any need to tell you any unfavorable information about people who you hadn't even met. We figured it was best that you meet them and decide for yourselves, rather than unnecessarily biasing you against them."

It was a fair explanation that Reina could not help but accept.

"Now then, I think it's about time we got back to our stalls.

I'll head over to see the smiths, as a representative of the caravan. There's no point in even talking to the chief anymore."

Apparently, the reason that the leader had not come back right after going to give the chief his regards was because he had been trying to press the man for more information. Yet ultimately, he had come up empty-handed.

Just as the leader stood to leave...

"I'd like to come, too!" Mile declared, standing up with him.

"Hm?"

The other members of the Crimson Vow stood as well, looking exasperated.

The leader was momentarily taken aback, but once he considered the fact of Mile's storage magic, he nodded. There were really no drawbacks to bringing the Crimson Vow with him, and if they could use Mile's magic as leverage, that might make negotiations a bit smoother, or so he hoped.

Everyone finished their pitiful lunches of water and bread, and then dispersed to their various tasks.

"This is one of the blacksmiths we usually purchase from," said the leader, as the five of them stood before a shop.

The other hunters had not accompanied them, instead splintering off to tend to their own affairs. There was no real reason for them to come, and having that many rough-looking hunters all in one place would probably look like intimidation, which would certainly be bad for negotiations. The Crimson Vow gave off no such impressions, so bringing them along was much safer.

"Is the master in?" the leader called into the doorway of the workshop, and a youth who was probably an employee or apprentice went to summon the master smith from further inside... Though of course, judging by the beard on him, he was not a very young-looking youth...

Everyone in the village knew that the caravan had arrived this morning, so the dwarf did not bother asking the leader's name. At the same time, there was no doubt that the folks from this shop had all been lined up at Mile's little stand, the master smith included.

Indeed, the man who appeared to be the master smith shortly appeared. He had rosy cheeks, perhaps due to the fact that they were warmed every day by the flames of the smithy.

"Well, I'll be! The little lady booze-seller is here! If you've got any left, I'll take all of it!!!"

Ah, yes. The reason that his cheeks were so red was that he had been drinking like a fish since morning.

"What? You're tellin' me you weren't goin' door to door to sell your leftover liquor stock...?"

The smith slumped in disappointment.

"Liquor? Oh, pardon me!" said the leader. "This is just the usual little extra we have with us, but here, have this!"

He took out one of the gift bottles he had prepared and handed it to the master smith.

*Oh...*

Finally, Mile realized exactly what it was that she had done.

"Oh, liquor, huh? Say, what is this...?" said the smith, clearly disappointed, as the leader began to fret.

There were, of course, breweries in town, and being that this was a village of blacksmiths, they possessed the equipment with which to distill their own spirits. However, they were usually unable to temper their own appetites long enough to let the spirits age, drinking them all up as soon as they finished producing them. Thus, on a practical level they lacked the means to make their own high-quality drink. And to be honest, their most basic productions were nothing to write home about.

So, the brands that the merchants always brought with them as gifts had been received with a warm welcome...up until now.

The master smith normally felt it was unfair to drink it all on his own, so he usually let his workers have a nip here and there, too. However, he now looked upon the merchant leader's gift without much interest. It was inevitable that the merchant leader should be perplexed by this, wondering what about the circumstances had changed.

This was especially true because Mile had not set up her temporary stall until after the leader had headed to the chief's house, and by the time he got back, she was sold out of her stock and had more or less packed everything away. He knew that she had been selling something, as she had sought his permission to try opening up shop with something that she had brought along in her storage. He had given his permission but not thought to pay the slightest attention to exactly what kind of wares she was offering. He had assumed she was just playing a little game to pass the time, selling something that she had bought along her travels: some items she no longer needed or perhaps some fresh herbs that would not keep for very long.

At any rate, a delicate set of negotiations then began, though it seemed that the leader and the master were a pair who had had such exchanges many times before. This time, with the lady liquor-monger, who might have more of her high-quality stock by the merchant's side, the master smith was inclined to be a bit more receptive.

"You'll get half of what you asked for, but the price is gonna be the same."

Unfortunately, this talk was not going well for the merchant's side. Hearing the same thing from the smith as he had from the chief, the leader looked troubled.

"Your chief told me the same thing. However, I know for certain that the chief would never make a decision like that on his own. The fact that it seemed like it was a done deal for him means that what he told me was in agreement with what your people must have told him. What we wish to know is the reason that you came to this decision out of the blue and whether there is any way we can get you to change your minds. Apparently, you did not tell the village chief the truth, so I was hoping you might tell us the reasoning behind the change in prices.

"All I'm asking you to tell me is the facts. If you cannot give me any reason for this change, then we will not be purchasing anything, and we will likely never return to this village again. I feel that we've built up a mutually beneficial relationship. It would be unfortunate to tear down everything that we've built up over the years simply because you refuse to be honest with us, wouldn't it?"

From the leader's stern wording, the smith could tell that he was serious and that refusing to talk could become a problem for the village's longevity. So, with a solemn expression, he opened his mouth.

"Very well. Apparently, the chief didn't think it was his position to say, but I guess it's a problem if I can't tell ya. Tell ya the truth, it's a matter of pride. Of course, ya can't blame him. He's gotta act as our representative, and this is a matter of honor for us dwarves. We might all be the same types of people, but we can't just go lettin' humans or elves see us in a moment of weakness when it comes to our smithin'. Please don't think bad of 'im...

"Anyway, if the caravans stop coming here, then we won't have anyone to sell our works to, and that just can't happen. We'd have to get our own carts and guards, and go around from village to village, sellin' our wares on foot. T'think of it..."

For the dwarves, who were craftsmen and not merchants by nature, the thought of spending their lives going around peddling instead of making things was unbearable. Plus, even at twice the price as before, they could not hope to turn much of a profit that way considering the cost of wagons and guards and such. Whether or not the others would admit it, the master smith was ready to acknowledge that much.

Apparently, orcs and ogres had begun taking up residence on the mountain where the dwarves mined iron ore. They could get the wood that they used to fuel the flames of their forges from elsewhere, but that mountain was the only place from which they could source their raw materials.

The fact that that mountain was nearby was the reason why the dwarves had even built this village where they had in the first place. Without it, there was no reason why they would settle in such an inconvenient location, deep in the mountains.

At this, the merchant leader replied directly. "Well then, why don't you just eliminate them?" It was, of course, the logical solution.

Dwarves possessed both physical strength and stalwart forms. On top of their solid bodies, this village could easily produce the necessary weapons and armor. All of this meant that they were in a good position to take out these monsters all on their own. In fact, there was a certain subset of dwarven youths who left such villages as this one favor of moving to human settlements to become hunters.

So, if the villagers were to put together a band of young fellows in their prime, hardened by their daily labors of mining and smithing, the likes of orcs and ogres would never stand a chance.

Indeed, living in a little village in the middle of the mountains meant that they had to drive away the local monsters themselves, and in between the times when the merchant caravan arrived, they had to carry their own goods to other settlements to sell them, and to purchase their daily necessities. Surely, they could kick about an ogre or two.

"We could, with a lot of damages."

"Hm?"

Yes, they were dwarves: strong, healthy, able to forge skilled goods and make their living in the direst of environments, a proud race.

With their pride on the line, they had set out to quash the monsters that had settled in near their precious mines. The village poured their all into the battle, putting their faith in a collection of brave, skilled volunteers—of which they lost six, while many more were injured. They had failed their mission, and at great cost to themselves. Alas, it was unlikely that there would be any skilled healing mages in a village populated by dwarves, who lacked an aptitude for magic. Even piling on all of the healing herbs in the village was only enough to dull their pain, not cure the fighters.

With so much of the village's battle strength lost, they could no longer afford to break up the capable fighters into two groups: one to defend the village, and the other to protect the mines. Left with no option but to sneak into the mines with just a few miners and a few guards so that the monsters would not catch wind of them, the acquisition of new iron ore had sharply decreased. Furthermore, there were many craftsmen, smiths and apprentices alike, who were injured badly enough that they were in no shape to do their work. Losing even two skilled smiths from a single shop was enough to grind production to a halt.

Thus, even though they could only provide half of the usual stock, they could not afford to sell it for half of the usual pay. They had intended to send a representative of the village back to town along with the caravan, earnings in hand, and use it to buy a stock of medicine, as well as hired a skilled healing mage, if possible. To accomplish this would require a lot of money.

"A healing mage? What? No, you should hire some hunters to get rid of those monsters, first! The way things are going, more and more of your miners are going to get hurt. And if things get worse, the village might even end up overrun! You need to contact the Hunters' Guild immediately!!!" the merchant leader cried.

The smith, however, shook his head.

"For us dwarves to go cryin' to a bunch of humans because we can't protect our precious mines with our own hands would be a disgrace to our whole race! We'd be the laughingstock of the continent, and our village's reputation would be in shambles. No one would ever want to buy anything we make ever again!"

*These guys are a pain in the neck!!!* the humans silently screamed.

Truly, these dwarves did place just a little too much worth on their own pride...

"Well, at least now I understand the situation. My heart's a bit more at ease knowing all this—and that you aren't just arbitrarily holding some absurd price over our heads," said the leader.

"Oh, so you understand!" the smith replied, with a smile of relief.

"Still, no matter what the circumstances may be, we can't make any transactions that will put us in the red. We have a responsibility to ourselves, our allies, our families and employees, and of course, our valued customers. It's one thing to make charitable contributions in more prosperous times, but to accept such unfavorable terms in the line of our main business would be truly idiotic. We'd lose credibility, and be made fun of, looked down upon. People would start provoking us, saying, 'You bought at a higher price from those guys! Why are you trying to pull the rug out from under us?!' and we'd never be able to negotiate for a good price ever again.

"These monster problems are your problems, not ours. They are by no means a compelling reason for us to complete any questionable transactions and risk both our fortunes and our reputations. Honestly, this is an awful lot like how the chief imposed his arbitrary conditions on us in the first place. He doesn't care about our circumstances at all!"

The smith fell silent, his face clouded. He did not appear to have been expecting such a vehement refusal.

He may have been a fool for his work, and a man of hubris, but he was not truly a fool. He seemed to be aware that they were asking something absurd of the merchants, and so he could not bring himself to rebuke or rage at the now-unhappy merchant he had done business with so many times before. He could only look on, his face vacant and bitter...

"Well, I guess we should go and take care of those monsters then, huh?" Reina abruptly proposed, breaking the silence.

"Wh-what are you—?"

The smith was lost for words at how simply she had said this. The merchant leader looked surprised as well. The other three, however, chimed in, hot on her heels.

"If you don't have medicine, why not just use healing spells?"

*Who is she, Marie Antoinette?!?! Well, honestly, Marie never actually said that famous line. When the book that quote was written in first came out, Marie was only nine years old, and definitely was not yet on the throne...*

Pauline's words had apparently sent Mile down one of her usual rabbit holes.

"That's right," Mavis added, "If you failed once, you just have to come back stronger. Get more forces and fight for those mines!"

*W-wait, is this a Chrome-Shelled Regios situation?!?!*

As always, a thought floated through Mile's head that no one else would understand, but it got her fired up nevertheless.

"Have you all even been listening?! Like I said, our village's fighters are in shambles, and we're not gonna go crawling to the humans for help!" the smith shouted, forgetting his position.

Mile looked at him, dumbfounded, and said, "What? You don't have to go all the way to town to put in an extermination request. If you want to go for a second round, all you have to do is make use of the hunters who just happened to be in town along with a merchant caravan—hunters, who might join in for a little extra pay? It's nothing but a little bit of work for a little bit of coin. That shouldn't be a burden on your dwarven pride, right?"

"Uh..."

She was right. It might wound their pride, down in the depths of their hearts, but they were no longer in any position to have the luxury of worrying about that. However...

"A-are you sure? Those monsters are really strong! We haven't been living up on this mountain for centuries just for show. We never thought we'd fall so easily to some measly orcs or ogres. Honestly, how did it come to this...? You humans in this country, you're adults at fifteen, right? Sure, those other hunters are one thing, but some of you girls are barely out of the nursery! You might be really hurt—hell, you might not even make it back alive! You shouldn't be risking your lives!!"

The smith tried to refuse the Crimson Vow's proposal and urge them to reconsider.

"Hah!" Reina said with a sneer. "Don't underestimate a C-rank mage!"

"Nor a C-rank swordfighter!" added Mavis.

"And don't underestimate us humans!!!" they said as one.

Ignoring the master smith, who was now at a loss for words, Mile asked the merchant leader, "We're only employed as your guards during the travel portion of the trip, yes? While we're staying in town, we're free to do whatever we like with our time, regardless of our employers' wishes. That is what our contract says, correct?"

"Yes, that is true, but..."

"But?"

"If you don't come back in good enough shape to complete your guard duties on the journey home, that would count as a breach of contract."

There was no malice in the merchant's words. It was merely a very merchant-like way of praying that they would return home safe.

To a merchant, contracts were everything. If there was any danger of a promise being broken, the fury a merchant could summon would transform them into an army of one. This merchant was doing everything within his power to confront the Crimson Vow's reckless proposal.

"We'll come back safe, I promise," said Pauline. "I swear it in the name of the gods of commerce."

The leader was stunned to suddenly be addressed as a fellow merchant. The other three followed her lead.

"I stake my honor on this, as a future knight," said Mavis.

"And I stake my reputation as a C-rank hunter," chimed Reina.

"And I swear on the name of the little old lady who runs the candy store!" added Mile, at which all the others asked:

*"And who the hell is that?!?!?!"*

"Still, in my opinion... At the very least, we need to propose this to the chief, and then get the approval of two-thirds of the smiths. If we make an extermination attempt and end up with that many more smiths injured, it's gonna be a problem for the village's future. I'm sure that most of the other smiths feel the same way I do, but they might agree, if I explain it to 'em. As for the chief... The chief ain't hardheaded or crazy, but he has got the weight of the whole village on his shoulders, so he's always gonna pick the village's safety over anything else. Even if I as an individual think you've got the right idea, there's still a chance the chief might have to say no. We can't put this to him bluntly.

If we just go bargin' into the chief's house like this, our little talk's never gonna get anywhere..."

The others were at a loss for a reply, but they understood what he was saying. Understanding this, and knowing that they could not simply march straight up to the chief's house and demand his approval, the members of the Crimson Vow looked troubled.

Just then—

"*Youuu bashtaaards!!!* What'sh the big idea shellin' yer fancy-schmancy highfalutin shpiritsh t'everyone but me?!?! Y'think ya can messh with me like that?! Why you little...!!!"

"Oh! It's the chief!"

The chief was angry. He had been in talks with the merchant leader the whole time Mile was selling her liquor, and so he had no idea that the sale was even going on, only hearing about it after the fact from those who'd been lucky enough to purchase something and let him try a tiny nip. Apparently he had tracked them down on the report of the other merchants.

"Give it t' me! Give me shome right now!!!"

At first glance, Mile was a thoughtless idiot, and while that was in some ways true, she was also an unexpectedly anxious in-dividual, who always put safety first. Therefore, she always had a backup plan, a "just in case" contingency that allowed her to live by the philosophy that one should always be prepared. Pauline knew as much from the way that Mile always spoke and acted, and from the morals in a number of the Japanese Folktales Mile told. So, she looked subtly over to Mile's face to confirm, and...

*Nod nod.*

Mile nodded, with a warm smile.

Seeing this, Pauline smiled as well, the grin on her face a wicked one...

CHAPTER 67 |

# Monsters

"SO ANYWAY, it looks like we'll be going monster hunting tomorrow."

"*Hang on, hang on, now hang right on!!!*"

The Devils' Paradise and the Fellowship of Flame were momentarily shocked at this sudden change of plans, but they were not truly all that taken aback. Including the Crimson Vow, they had fifteen C-rank hunters, enough that ten or even twenty orcs or ogres would not pose too much of a threat. Add some powerful dwarves into the mix, and there would be hardly any danger at all. Thinking about it that way, this really was no big deal.

The merchants, meanwhile, were fairly well aware of the extent of the abilities that the Crimson Vow possessed—with Mile, who was a hunter despite her ridiculous storage magic; Mavis, who could wield her sword like a hatchet; and Reina, who was a master magical tea kettle—having observed them at the campgrounds and during the battle with the ogres. They were none too surprised by this news, either.

"Phew! I guess we're in this then. All right, we'll come with you. When do we head out?" asked Wulf, of the Devils' Paradise, a tired look upon his face. Vegas, of the Flames, nodded in agreement.

"Huh?" Mile cocked her head curiously. "We're going to be the only ones accompanying the villagers, actually. We need you all to stay here to guard the village while we're gone. If all of the dwarves who are capable of fighting ogres are out on the mission, along with all of the hunters, it would mean the literal destruction of the village if some monsters decided to come here while we were all gone."

"Wh...?"

The other hunters paused in disbelief, but as they paused to consider the idea, a group of orcs and ogres that had only recently settled in could not be particularly sizable in number. With the Crimson Vow in tow, the dwarfs really should be able to take out the monsters in one go. This in mind, the other two parties understood that it probably was best for them to stay behind to protect the village, just in case.

Naturally, protecting the village also meant protecting the merchants. It was all just a part of the job.

"Oh, and of course, since you'll be protecting the village, you'll get some extra pay from the village for that job as well."

Neither Mile nor Pauline would ever neglect to mention such a crucial item.

The village chief was not the sort of person to change his mind merely because he wanted alcohol. He had come to realize, how-ever, that with all of the damages they had taken, their current forces were not enough to escape from their current predicament. His hesitation was due mostly to the fact that he still lacked the resolve to go and petition the humans for help, fearing that, should they take any more damages, there would be no coming back. However, a single offer from Mile had changed everything.

"If we accept your extermination request, then we will also heal all of your people who are currently injured. We have two very skilled healing mages in our group, and we can recover all of our magic quickly with a good night's sleep. It's for the sake of strengthening our forces and preparing for the upcoming battle, so it won't cost you another copper. Naturally, we can provide the same guarantee for any injuries incurred in the battle tomorrow as well."

This was the first that chief was hearing about the Crimson Vow's healing magic. With two healing magic users, any serious injuries—short of death or the loss of limbs—could be repaired. Given that the opponents they were facing were not people armed with blades or magic, and could not go chopping or blast-ing off anyone's arms or legs, most injuries would be easily dealt with. Granted, if anyone's limbs or fingers or toes were smashed or torn off, no magic could fix them, and if they had their heads bashed in or their bones or organs twisted up, they would surely die. However, there was nothing to be done about that.

At any rate, the chief would never be foolish enough to pass up on the chance to have access to skilled healing mages and added combat strength to bolster up the forces protecting the village—along with the chance to bring the already injured villagers back to fighting shape.

Why would he go and pay just for healing if he could get it included as part of their extermination services entirely for free? They would have to deal with the monsters either way, for the sake of the village's future.

Indeed, once he had heard Mile's offer, the chief had no other choice.

Of course, that "just in case" item that Mile had pulled from her inventory hadn't hurt. Just a few bottles of spirits she had set aside, pressed into the chief's hands, had been enough to get the conversation rolling.

Once they were alone, Mile said to the other members of the Crimson Vow, "Okay, guys. We can't let our guard down on this one. The villagers honestly should have been successful in eliminating those monsters last time, so there must be some reason why they ended up so badly hurt. I'm pretty sure this isn't a case of the villagers just slipping up or having bad luck. If they could sustain injuries like on a fluke, then there's no way that this village would have been able to stand in this spot for centuries. In any situation, it's always important to try and imagine the worst-case scenario. Then, you can prepare yourself for an eventuality three times worse and come at it from every angle. That is the nature of reality."

Silence fell following Mile's words of warning.

"You have my thanks."

The battle leader of the dwarves, head of the Mine Recovery Operation Force, Part 2, bowed his head toward the members of the Crimson Vow. Previously, he had been one of the individuals laid up with an injury, but now his broken left leg and the deep wound on his side had been completely healed, allowing him to return to the front lines.

Dwarves were not often ones to show such deference to other races, particularly not to humans or elves. Unaware of this, the Crimson Vow politely waved their hands and shook off his thanks, but the eyes of the members of the other two parties were wide with shock.

"Roll out!" the battle leader decreed, and the operation was underway.

There were twenty-eight dwarves and four members of the Crimson Vow—a force of thirty-two in total.

The first extermination force had apparently consisted of exactly thirty men. Of those thirty, six were never to be heard from again, and three lost fingers or limbs and were no longer able to return to the battlefield.

If Mile really pulled out all the stops, she might have even been able to do something about the missing body parts. However, that was beyond the bounds of what the people of this world considered to be healing magic. Obviously, she had no intention of displaying such unimaginable skills to outsiders, unless it were under the most extreme circumstances. No matter how much anguish a person was in, it was impossible to save absolutely *everyone*, and even Mile could guess what might happen if a person of influence were to find out that such an ability existed.

At any rate, with seven volunteers to replace the missing nine, and with the Crimson Vow in tow, they had thirty-two people.

They moved out, thinking of those who had lost their lives, and those who had lost their limbs, and with them, any hope of a future as a craftsmen. This time, the villagers were giving it their all, the lost hopes of those fallen nine carried on their shoulders.

Soon after they departed, Reina issued a complaint: "Why are we right in the middle?!"

"I mean, it should be obvious," answered a dwarven youth, "You always put the women and the weaklings in the very middle."

"Just what do you mean by 'weakling'?!" Reina raged. "Besides," she added, as the lad began to look troubled, "it makes way more sense to put Mile at the front—she has location magic!"

Here, the combat leader interjected. "If anything happened to the little lady booze-seller, every one of us here plus that old geezer would be slaughtered! Now settle down and stick to your positions!"

The other dwarves desperately entreated them to stay put, fully in agreement with their leader. This arrangement was, first and foremost, meant to protect the one who had supplied their booze.

If anything were to happen to Mile, they would never be able to get in another shipment of high-quality liquor the way they had this time. And, if this were to happen because of this mission, and the others in the village determined that it was due to some mismanagement on the part of the extermination team, none of the men involved would ever have standing in the village again—even if they were successful in today's mission.

Reina was taken aback, unable to say anything in reply in the face of such desperation.

"It's fine, Reina," said Mile. "My magic will still have enough of a range from this position."

"Plus, from here, we can jump in to help no matter which way an attack comes from—front, back, or flanks. It's really not such a bad spot at all," Mavis added.

Reina, who was fairly skilled at striking opponents with her staff, had forgotten this—mages were normally stationed at the back in smaller groups, and in the center in larger groups, to protect them from ambushes or close-range attacks.

None of these dwarves had any idea of the Crimson Vow's combat abilities, and even though they knew that they were C-rank hunters, as far as any of the dwarves could see, they did not appear to be anything more than a bunch of children. Moreover, compared to dwarven girls, who were round and healthy, these girls were clearly emaciated, all skin and bones, gangling, frail, and sickly.

As such, the dwarves intended to relegate the Crimson Vow to the position of healers, leaving Mavis the swordswoman and Reina the magical fighter to protect Mile and Pauline, while the dwarves handled all of the actual fighting. There was no one amongst them who doubted that this was the righteous decision...except for the Crimson Vow, the Devils' Paradise, and the Fellowship of Flame, of course.

"We should be reaching the monsters' lairs soon. Be careful."

"I've picked up on something, three hundred meters ahead!"

Before the leader could even finish his sentence, Mile announced her radar finding to the group.

Three hundred meters was still a bit too far to actively enter into combat stance. And besides, three hundred meters carried a far different meaning on a mountain or in a forest than it did in an open field with no obstacles. So here, on this steep terrain, dotted with thick groves of trees, three hundred meters was still quite a distance.

"How many, and what type?"

Rather than wasting time on the usual reaction of, "How do you know that?!" the combat leader merely asked for clarification, using the minimal amount of words. Apparently, he was a very capable sort.

Yet Mile's response was unusually tepid.

"Um, well... Normally, I could tell you that, but there's something weird about them... Are there any rare monsters in this area?"

"Nope, just your garden-variety, run-of-the-mill monsters around here. We've got orcs and ogres and goblins and kobolds, jackalopes and vampire bats, giant worms and mountain wolves..."

All of the monster types that the leader had just tossed out, Mile knew well. Furthermore, her radar had already been attuned to the reactions that each of those types would give...

"That's really weird. Oh, okay—there are eight of them."

Finally, she was able to report something more.

Because Mile knew these to be larger monsters, if describing them in Japanese, she would have used the counter for large animals, "-*tou*," instead of that for small animals, "-*hiki*." By Mile's calculations, anything that a human could hold was "small," and anything that a human could not hold was "large." Of course, the reason that she defaulted to what a human could do, and not what *she* could do, was that Mile was fairly certain that she could lift a horse, so there was no way that anyone in the world would accept a system where Mile was the baseline.

This time, they were aiming to eliminate. They had no intention of avoiding the monsters or running from them. Therefore, they would continue straight forward. With Mile counting down the distance, there was no reason to draw their swords and get on guard prematurely. The dwarves felt blessed to be able to make it through this mission with as little damage to their pride as they had so far.

For a while now, everyone had been on edge, not knowing whether they might suddenly stumble upon or be ambushed by monsters, but with someone who could use surveillance magic among them, they could be a bit more at ease.

Though Reina had told them ahead of time about Mile's abilities, they had assumed that, given that Mile appeared primarily to be a swordswoman, her search abilities just meant that she could vaguely sense the life signs of nearby monsters. They certainly did not think that she had the ability to pick up on monsters that were as far as three hundred meters ahead.

Thus, the reclamation team faced down the eight monsters, standing ready, with perfect form.

"I see them! Orcs—eight of them!" the dwarf at the head of the line reported to the others in a low voice, signaling with his hand for everyone behind him to stop.

They were still downwind, so the orcs appeared not to have noticed them yet. The leader spoke quietly, gesturing for everyone to get in formation to strike the orcs head-on. With the difference in number, there was no worry of the orcs getting away right from the start, so there was no need to surround them.

Mile, however, was racking her brain.

*Orcs? But that feeling I got...*

"What are you standing around for?! Let's go!" Reina said, clapping her on the shoulder.

Mile hurriedly drew her sword.

For this rush, the Crimson Vow were positioned only on the second line of the attack. This was a battle that rightfully belonged to the dwarves; they were there only to assist. Besides, from back here, they were in far better position to rush to the aid of someone in trouble or heal someone who was hurt.

It was some comfort that it was only orcs that they were up against. With ogres, things might be different, but there was no reason that a group of stalwart dwarves, who had protected their village and mines for ages, should have anything to fear from a couple of orcs. Plus, they did not seem to be underestimating their opponents nor giving them any quarter. So, the members of the Crimson Vow watched the battle with no great worry, prepared to launch a healing or attack spell as needed should any unexpected turns arise. Yet to their surprise...

*Ka-fwump!*
*Ker-smack!*
*Ka-thud!!!*

With a cry, three of the dwarves were sent flying the moment the battle started.

"Wh—?! Th-they're so weak!" shouted Reina.

"I guess dwarves aren't as strong as they look!!!" Pauline cried, a second jeer to smash straight through the dwarves' pride.

Hearing this, Mavis shouted, "You dummies! Why would you go and lower your own allies' morale?! And the people of this village *aren't* weak!"

"They aren't!" Mile followed up. "The monsters are too strong! These guys aren't at the level of normal orcs! I got a different reaction from them with my search magic than from normal orcs, too. They don't look anything like the normal, muscular, rotund orcs we've seen. If we don't come at this like we're fighting ogres—or maybe something even stronger—even we won't eliminate them. Instead, *we'll* be the ones annihilated!!!"

It was then that Mile finally realized why these dwarves, who had protected their own lands from monsters for so many years, would suddenly suffer such heavy losses.

"Well, if they weren't normal monsters, then why didn't these guys figure that out the last time?!" Reina shouted angrily.

However, a different, much scarier thought was floating through Mile and Mavis's heads.

*If the orcs are this much stronger, then I wonder if the same goes for the ogres...*

"Pauline, use your healing! After that, start using your attack spells! Right now, we need to prioritize making sure that no one ends up seriously injured or killed! Reina, please start attacking. We're in an all-out battle now, so just keep it to simple rapid fire. Be careful of allies, and make sure it's nothing that'll kill anyone if you miss! Mavis, be mindful of the time limit, but use your True Godspeed Blade! Let's go!!"

For once, it was Mile, not Reina, who was giving the battle directions—quickly and forcefully. However, the directions she was giving were logical ones, so everyone reflexively obeyed.

Pauline rushed toward the three dwarves who had been knocked back, approaching the most injured of the three, not wishing to waste the healing spell that she had already been holding in wait. Then, she began rapidly incanting an attack spell. It was monsters they were up against this time, so there was no need for her to conceal the nature of her spell by performing the incantation silently.

After releasing the spell that she had likewise been holding, Reina began a simple attack spell as well. She made sure to limit it to something that would not injure someone to the point that healing magic would be ineffective should she accidentally strike one of her allies. Of course, it would not do anything to the orcs if it was *too* weak, so she still had to put a little *oomph* behind it.

Mavis had not thought there would be any reason to break out her ultimate technique in a battle against orcs, of all creatures. However, heeding Mile's judgment, she began using her True Godspeed Blade. Even Mavis knew that her normal Godspeed Blade would not be enough to get them through this, and her body could only stand up to the power of the EX version for a few short moments, lest she self-destruct. Truthfully, she could not use the True Godspeed blade for much longer, but at least it was much more bearable than EX.

The moment Pauline and Reina released their held spells and began casting again, Mavis and Mile flew forth together, plunging into the thick of the battle, each swinging their beloved swords in tandem.

In a frantic melee, where both enemies and allies were close at hand, it was much easier to strike with a blade...at least when there was a clear difference in strength between you and your enemy.

Thankfully, that was an advantage that Mile and Mavis had.

The two blades danced through the battlefield. Rapid fire bursts of magic struck again and again.

If the Crimson Vow had not been present, this would have been a battle of twenty-eight on eight, and the dwarves would have ended up with several major casualties. It was possible that they might even be wiped out—against an opponent that they could normally clean up with nothing more than a few minor injuries...

However, with Mavis and Mile now in the fray, the dwarves were able to hold out, and with the assistance of Reina and Pauline's magic, they were able to successfully exterminate the orcs without the dwarven side sustaining any major injuries.

"So, what's the deal here?"

While Mile and Pauline tended to any men with minor injuries, beside them, Reina questioned the combat leader.

"What deal?"

"Don't play with me! I'm clearly asking you why those orcs are so strong and why you didn't tell us about it!" she screamed, but the leader looked dumbfounded.

"I mean, I thought we did tell you that the monsters were strong..."

"Well, we thought that was just a threat, or a warning, so that we didn't let our guards down!! Why didn't you explain the situation more clearly?! Did you really think you had any chance of winning against monsters like that in the first place?!"

The leader, however, coolly replied, "Whether we have a chance or not, we will win. On that we stake our dwarven pride. That's all there is to it."

"But last time you lost and came running home in shambles, didn't you?!?!"

"So, what do we do?" asked Mile.

"What should we do?" echoed Mavis.

"We already had the merchants draft up a formal contract, and we received payment beforehand so that there would be no disputes later," Pauline replied.

"There's nothing that we can do!" Reina cried.

Indeed, there was nothing they could do.

The Crimson Vow had already received their pay for the job ahead of time, requesting the aid of the merchants, who were pros in the field of contracts, in writing up theirs. When taking independent jobs, where the agreement was made directly between employer and employee and not through the Guild, disputes were a frequent occurrence. In order to prevent against this, they had prepared a contract and gotten their money up front. However, there was a downside to this, by which the Crimson Vow were now bound.

If a client's report of a situation were found to be untrue or incomplete, typically, the contract was to be torn up immediately and the fee confiscated. However, there were no lies or deficiencies in the report that the dwarves had given them. The opponents they were to fight were monsters in general, orcs or possibly ogres, to be specific. The dwarves had tried to take them out before, but the monsters were too strong and so they lost. In order to try at driving them out a second time, they had requested backup.

In truth, there was absolutely nothing amiss here.

"We did tell you that the monsters were a lot stronger than normal. I'm sure that the chief told you that much before you finalized the contract. So, what are you so upset about?" the battle leader interjected, having overheard the exchange.

"No loser is ever going to tell you that their enemy was weak!" Reina roared. "Obviously, you would say that they were strong! No one would ever assume that was true!!!"

Reina continued gnashing her teeth, Mavis consoling her with a soft "there, there."

"Well, whatever we think about it, there's nothing to be done now. It's not like monsters have special training camps, and this wasn't some elite band of orcs. Every once in a while some stronger individuals appear, but that's only on a case-by-case basis."

As Mile said, none of them had ever heard of monsters forming any special elite units. The fact that these orcs were strong was just a fact. That was all there was to it.

"They had the strength of high orcs, but otherwise they were still pretty much like normal orcs..."

Mavis was correct as well.

Back when the Crimson Vow were first starting out, they had gone out into the hills, packing their own lunches and water in order to save money. Their grand aim was to hunt the fabled "high orc and goblin king." In other words, they went out *high-king.* Thanks to that, they were very familiar with high orcs.

"Plus, there shouldn't be any orc hordes made up only of high orcs. That's like having a single army squad made up of nine generals. Who would want a squad like that?" Reina added, and Mavis nodded in agreement.

"There's a saying in my country, though," said Mile. "'With enough boatmen at the helm, a boat can climb a mountain.' It means that with enough powerful people on hand, you can achieve the impossible"

"Mile, I'm pretty sure you've said the same thing before, and I'm pretty sure that's not true at all, considering all the things I've read in combat manuals."

Mavis had very little confidence in the "wisdom" of Mile's homeland. Such aphorisms were about as credible as the Japanese folktales she told.

"W-well, anyway, this is fine. The real question is, what do we do from here?"

Reina was also correct.

"We know at least that the orcs are strong," said Mile. "What we don't know is, why? We already felled eight orcs, so we should be able to find any stragglers easily. With the combat strength we have now, they shouldn't be any problem. Even if we come across some goblins or kobolds or jackalopes and they're several times stronger than normal, we can deal with it. The real problem here is..."

"Ogres, right?" asked Mavis. "There's the strength of a normal orc, and then there's the strength of those orcs we faced earlier. If you applied that same difference in power to an ogre, then..."

"Yes, we'd see the birth of a hyper ogre. The Aura Road is opening. It's the 'Ogre Battler Dunbine!'"

This time it was Mile who completed Mavis's sentence. No one had the faintest idea what she was talking about, but they got the gist of what she was trying to say, and ignored the rest.

"Well, what should we do?"

"Ain't much that we can do."

This time it was the dwarves who joined in.

"We may've won now, but if we don't get rid of the rest of these monsters it'll be the end of the village. As long as the old-timers in the village are the ones callin' the shots, we're never gonna be able to go and ask other humans for help. Given the amount of time this village has left, and our budget, we're probably never gonna have another chance to have such a powerful group here to help us—especially not one with two skilled healers that the elders can tolerate. This is our first, last, and *only* chance. I hope you girls don't mind, but we'd like it if you would stay by our side."

The members of the Crimson Vow all looked to one another.

"Um, I'm only thirteen years old, though... It's still a little soon for me to be accepting any formal proposals."

Reina karate-chopped the top of Mile's head.

"That's fine," said Mavis, "but there aren't any dragons living around here, are there? And there aren't any swarms of souped-up dragons roaming around here, right?"

The dwarves went pale and shook their heads rapidly.

SIDE STORY |

# Copy

"THIS SUCKS..."

Something was troubling Mile.

"We're leaving on a job tomorrow, and I still haven't finished this manuscript... I need to finish the book in the next three days and get it sent out in the Guild post going out four days from now or I'll never make my deadline on time... Ugh! What am I gonna do?!"

Apparently, she had hit a block. She had no ideas for her next manuscript.

"Mmnnh, I've never missed a deadline before! Ngaaaaaah!!!"

Mile rolled around in her bed in the middle of the night, cloaked by a sound and vibration barrier.

However, all the flailing in the world was not going to help her.

There was nothing at all that she could do. Or rather, there shouldn't have been...

MIGHT WE OFFER YOU SOME ASSISTANCE?

A spirit of salvation appeared to her, calling out in its silent voice, one that was transmitted directly to Mile's eardrums, not via sound waves running through vibrating air.

PLEASE LEAVE IT TO US!

The next morning...or rather, sometime before dawn, as it was still dark outside, Mile sat in the middle of the Crimson Vow's rented room covered by a dome-shaped barrier that blocked all sound, motion, and light. She could not see out of the dome, and no one could see in. No sound would pass through.

Reina and the others were fast asleep, but even if they woke and saw the dome, at most they would think, *Ah, she's up reading or writing again*, and ignore it. It was not at all rare for Mile to use such a dome when she did not wish to be interrupted. In the event of an emergency, Reina or Pauline could blast the dome with a spell or Mavis could strike it with her sword. While nothing would change inside the dome, Mile would at least be aware that she was being attacked.

The conversation that was currently unfolding inside of the dome went as follows...

THIS IS THE LIVING ROBOT, "MILE-001."

"Whoooooaaaa! It's a real live Copy Robot!"

There before Mile sat a robot crafted in her spitting image.

I WOULD LIKE FOR YOU TO ENTRUST CONTROL TO
ME IN THE EARLY ACTIVATION STAGES, SO THAT I MAY
CORRECT ANY MALFUNCTIONS IN THE INITIAL OPERA-
TION. JUST THE EARLY STAGES IS FINE. MY PRESENCE IS
NECESSARY FOR THE EARLY STAGES!

"Hey, Nano, you... Wait, *you're* going to run this thing?"

YES. I AM THE INDIVIDUAL WHO OVERSAW THE PRO-
DUCTION OF MILE-001.

"Hm? So, you give the directions for this, then?"

YES. I AM MOST FREQUENTLY IN YOUR PRESENCE,
AND THEREFORE THE MOST FAMILIAR WITH THE FORM
OF YOUR BODY, LADY MILE. THUS, I WAS PERMITTED TO
OVERSEE THE DESIGN PROCESS AND CRAFT THE BLUE-
PRINTS FOR THE ROBOT. I CAN PROMISE THAT THE SIZE,
SHAPE, COLORATION, AND POWER ARE ALL A PERFECT
REPLICA OF THE ORIGINAL...

"Gy..."

GY?

"Gyaaaaaahh!!!"


"*Hff hff hff...* A-anyway, Nanomachine... Actually that's actually a little hard to distinguish. Let's give you a name. Hmm, well, you kept saying, 'early stages,' so I guess we can call you that? 'Early Stage...'"

OH, WHAT GREAT HONOR, WHAT GREAT FORTUNE,
TO BE GIVEN MY OWN UNIQUE NAME!

The overseer nanomachine seemed to be overjoyed by this.

"So then, um, Early Stage..."

YES, THE "EARLY STAGE" WILL EXTEND THROUGH-
OUT THE NIGHT.

"Wait, so what are you trying to saaaay?!"

HM?

The nanomachine was dumbfounded, unable to understand just was it was that had pained Mile so...

"All right, so this trip'll be three nights and four days. We're in charge of taking out a goblin settlement that's popped up near a mountain village. Let's go!" said Reina.

"All right!" replied two of her fellow party members.

"All right..." came the last party member's reply, a bit behind the rest.

"I really thought I was supposed to be the party leader," Mavis muttered—a bit bitterly. Her comment was completely ignored.

"I wonder how long it is until we get to the village this request came from," Reina muttered.

"6.274 kilometers remain. At our current velocity, the remaining travel time will be 1 hour, 18 minutes, and 26 seconds."

"Uh..."

Mile's immediate and incredibly precise reply left the other three stunned.

"I... I see. Thank you."

Reina was always surprised when Mile gave a reply that was actually on the mark, but there was something particularly out of character about this response. Her face was deadpan and serious; she did not appear to be joking.

Reina had brushed it off as best she could, but a strange suspicion began to gather in the back of her mind.

"So, that's where most of the goblin sightings have been, right? We'll aim for there tomorrow," said Reina, as they sat in the village elder's house, getting briefed about the goblin situation.

Just then, Mile held out a slip of paper.

"Based on the provided information, I have plotted a diagram of the locations of all of the sightings and made further calculations based on the timing of those sightings. As a result, we can predict that the goblin settlement will be in this general region. We can assume that the goblins' typical hunting grounds are located in this area."

A cry of stunned praise rose from the village elder and the villagers who had come to give their witness statements.

The members of the Crimson Vow, however, were silent.

What was with her?

They all stared at Mile, warily.

This living robot, Mile-001, was not a machine in nature, but a manmade—or rather, nano-made—facsimile of a living body.

However, it did not possess the mental faculties to operate on its own. It was controlled by an army of nanomachines, each in charge of their own part, under the direction of a single nanomachine. Its speech and actions were entirely controlled by the nanomachines, all of which had made a desperate rush for the position of director.

They had been collating speech and movement data regularly, so it was unlikely that any discrepancies should arise. The individual nanomachines' dispositions might have some minuscule amount of influence, but that was still within permissible bounds.

"I think it should be somewhere around here. All right, let's all split up, and..."

"I've spotted it—the goblin settlement! It looks like they're living in those caves."

Before Reina could even finish speaking, Mile announced her discovery.

The other three were quiet, and then Pauline said, a bit surprised, "Mile, you should pace yourself!"

"Yeah, Mile. Let's take this one step at a time," Mavis added.

For some reason, Reina looked a bit peeved.

"Okay then, let's go check out the situation nearer to the village. No matter how thoroughly we trounce the settlement, if we let even just a few females or children get away, their numbers will just start multiplying again right away. If that happens, then we can't really say that we fulfilled our clients' expectations."

"I've confirmed the situation with my surveillance magic. My survey shows no signs of any other goblins in the surrounding area. If we just crush their settlement now, I don't believe we should have any problems."

The other three fell silent again. Reina was now in quite a foul mood.

"Let's do this!" she shouted.

"All right!!" replied two.

"All right..."

Each time, Mile's response came just a little bit late.

"Fireball!"

"Ice Javelin!"

"Wind Edge!!!"

Mavis's Wind Edge, Reina's fireballs, and Pauline's ice javelins were an exercise in applied magic, each fired at high number in miniature form. Against a horde of goblins, such techniques were far more effective than any more powerful, more straightforward magic. But then...

"Super Laser Beam, Fire!"

Suddenly, a spray of countless beams of light went flying from Mile's fingertips.

In an instant, not a single goblin was left standing.

Again, silence fell over the party.

"Let's head into the caves and wipe out the rest! We can't let a single one get away!"

"All right!!"

"All right..."

The Crimson Vow headed into the cave mouth, with Mavis and Mile in the lead.

*Okay, so we're only fighting goblins, and most of them are already gone. I don't think I'll need to use the Micros or my True Godspeed Blade to deal with the rest. I'm not gonna rely on them— I'm gonna fight with my own strength and let my true powers shine!* Mavis thought to herself. Just then...

*Tmp!*

*Smacksmacksmacksmacksmack!*

"It's over."

"M-Miiiiiile!!!"

The walk home was a silent affair.

They had completed their job without a scratch, the villagers were overjoyed, and everyone thanked them. However, three of the members of the Crimson Vow seemed to be in a very bad mood, and the remaining member, Mile, began to fret.

*This is strange! Our actions have been within the bounds of Lady Mile's abilities, and we have been using the same manner of speech that Lady Mile uses, so why are the others now in such a foul mood?! We've worked so hard... If this ruins the relationship between Lady Mile and her companions, she will never forgive us...*

The silence deepened.

*Mile's been especially capable on this mission. She's made sound judgments and acted quickly,* thought Mavis.

*Mile didn't once slip up or make any stupid jokes this time. She just battled fiercely,* thought Pauline.

*Mile was straightforward and serious this whole time. She didn't even mention anything weird,* thought Reina.

*...But that's not like Mile at all!!!*

The three seemed to be sharing each other's thoughts.

And so the Crimson Vow hurried home, saying nary a word to one another.

"All right, done! Volume 1 of my newest work, *Here Comes the High Ogre*, and Volume 3, the concluding volume of *Giant Orc*, are complete!! Now to hurry to the Guild, and..."

The morning of the party's departure, before the others awoke, Mile switched places with Mile-001 and slipped out of the inn.

After the other members of the Crimson Vow had left town, Mile had rented a separate room and holed herself up inside, frantically continuing her writing—not as Mile, the C-rank hunter, but Miami Satodele, the author.

And now, her manuscripts were finally complete.

"If I don't hurry, the Guild's post wagon's gonna leave without me..."

Mile rushed to the guildhall, her manuscripts hastily stuffed in an envelope.

"Phew! Made it just in time!"

As Mile exited the guildhall, dabbing the sweat from her brow, suddenly, in the distance before her, she saw the Crimson Vow approaching.

"C-c-c-c-crap!"

Mile's visual acuity was still leagues beyond that of Mavis, who possessed the next best vision among the members of the Crimson Vow, so while she could see them clearly, the Crimson Vow—save for Mile-001—were still not within range to spot her. But if anyone in the area should happen to spot two Miles standing near each other, the jig would be up.

*Light beam refraction, stealth mode!*

She quickly used her light-warping magic to cloak herself.

It was too soon to swap places with Mile-001. She, the original, knew nothing of how their mission had gone, so if she was with them when they went to the Guild to report on the completion of the job, there was a chance that discrepancies might become obvious. The timing of the exchange had to be just right...

*Auuuugh! But then, when we're having dinner to celebrate, we'll probably start discussing what happened on the job, so I can't swap back before then, either! I'm gonna miss out on our special celebration meeeeeal!!!*

Though she was practically crying tears of blood by now, Mile was utterly resigned. She had brought this all upon herself by procrastinating on her manuscripts.

After the celebratory meal was through, as the Crimson Vow

headed back to the inn, Mile (001) spotted, for but a moment, the silhouette of a human in the corner of her vision.

"Hm? Um, I'll be back in a minute!"

"Huh? Wait, where are you running off to?"

Reina tried but could not stop Mile 001 as she went dashing off to the right, down an alleyway. Not even a few seconds had passed, however, before she came running right back.

"Sorry, I thought I saw this cat that I like over there, but it ran off. It was probably just another cat that looked similar."

*Huh?*

Nothing had changed about her. Not her face, or voice, or smile.

And yet, somehow, a sense of profound ease suddenly swept over the other three members of the Crimson Vow.

There was a silence, and then Reina said quietly, "Mile, you don't have push yourself so hard. You might be absentminded, or act silly, or slip up, or talk about weird things, but that's just part of who you are. There's no reason for you to act weirdly serious or try to smooth out the quirks in your personality... What I'm saying is, that attitude of yours was really pissing me off! You can't just try and do every single little thing all by yourself! That's really annoying!!!"

"Huh? What??"

Mile had no idea what was going on.

"She's right, Mile. We're your party members and your friends, so just be yourself. You have to have faith in us when it comes to our work and split up the responsibilities. And you can't just go and upstage me when it's time to show off my sword skills! Like, seriously!!!" Mavis added, sounding somehow a bit desperate.

"......?"

Pauline, for some reason, just tipped her head silently.

*What?! Did they not already go over all of this at the dinner discussion? Why are they all being so weird?! What's going on here? Nanos, you told me that everything was completely fine!*

OUR DEEPEST APOLOGIES. IT SEEMS THAT THE BONDS OF EVERYONE'S HEARTS ARE BEYOND WHAT WE ANTICIPATED.

By now, the nanomachines had exited Mile-001 and returned to their normal functions. The robot in question, meanwhile, had been packed away in Mile's alternate-dimension inventory.

*Ah... I-I see. Well, I guess that's not your fault.*

Believing that she was being told that this happened because the bonds between their hearts were so strong, Mile was happy not to complain.

THAT'S NOT IT!

*Nanos, did you just say something?*

NO, NOTHING AT ALL!

*Really? Still, it's too bad. You went through all this work to make this thing for me, and it seems like this is the only time we'll get to use it.*

At this, there was an outcry among the nanomachines.

The Mile-001 was their masterpiece. Getting the chance to operate it and act like a human, specifically Lady Mile, had quickly become an aspiration of every nanomachine, something for which they would gladly wait their turn. Now, no matter how diligently they performed their everyday functions, it seemed that guiding star was going to collapse before they ever got their chance to bask in its glow. If the robot was stuck away in storage forever, it would be a dreadful thing.

The nanomachines, of course, would never be allowed to construct something like this or operate it of their own volition. This was a Super Ultra Rare creation, able to be made only because it was in accordance with the desires of Lady Mile, authorization level 5.

H-HERE'S AN IDEA! HOW ABOUT NEXT TIME, YOU CAN GO TO YOUR JOB, LADY MILE, AND I—OR RATHER, THE LIVING ROBOT—CAN WRITE YOUR NOVEL FOR YOU! I BELIEVE THAT WAY, THE NOVEL PRODUCED WILL BE EVEN MORE INTERESTING THAN WHAT YOU, LADY MILE, CAN WRITE YOURSELF... the nanos said confidently.

*Wh-wh-wh-what?!*

I'VE ALREADY GOT AN IDEA FOR IT. IT'S THE STORY OF A ROBOT IN THE SHAPE OF A LITTLE GIRL, OFTEN MISTAKEN FOR A BOY AT FIRST GLANCE BECAUSE SHE'S SO FLAT-CHESTED, WHO TRAVELS THE WORLD ON HER MOTORBIKE. I'LL CALL IT, "NANO'S JOURNEY." IT'LL BE A BIG HIT, I JUST KNOW IT!

*Wh-wh-wh-wh-wh-wh-wh-wha?!*

NATURALLY, OF COURSE, THE LIVING ROBOT WILL BE A GOLEM, LEFT OVER FROM ANCIENT TIMES, AND THE MOTORBIKE WILL BE OPERATED BY MAGIC...

"Go back to the part where you said 'mistaken for a boy because she's so flat-chested'—are you talking about me?! That robot was made to look just like meeeeee!!!"

"Eek! Wh-why are you shouting?! And what exactly are you shouting about?!"

Mile had accidentally shouted her frustrations out loud. At the top of her lungs.

"Oh, no, um, I, uh, just, suddenly remembered something that I really didn't want to remember."

"I see. Well, you shouldn't worry too much about that." Reina offered warm words of comfort.

Judging by what Mile had shouted, she had some guesses as to just what it was that Mile "didn't wish to remember."

Pauline and Mavis could, of course, plainly see why it was that Reina was suddenly being so nice to Mile, but neither of them would ever be foolish enough to voice such a thing out loud, so they kept their mouths shut.

"Looks like we have our usual Mile back," said Pauline. Reina and Mavis nodded.

"Still, I didn't really mind the serious, capable Mile..."

"Mile the hard worker, never saying or doing anything weird..."

"I get the feeling that version of Mile would earn us a lot more money..."

"What?!?!"

Did Mile's allies actually prefer the copy over the original?!

If so, it would be a grave blow to Mile's self-esteem. However...

"Even so, this version is a lot more fun. I prefer this one."

"Me too."

"Yeah, me too. Having fun is what's most important when you're with friends!"

"Wuh? Uhn... Nnnnnnn..."

Mile was not sure if she should be angry or glad. Swept up in this complex emotion, she could only grumble.

HOW SPLENDID! YOU'RE BLESSED WITH SUCH WONDERFUL FRIENDS!

*Y-you keep out of this!!!*

# I Saw a Bird

*C*HIRP CHIRP...

"Did you hear something just now?" asked Reina.

"No, I didn't," Mavis replied.

Just then...

*Chirp chirp!*

"Listen, there it is again! Where is that coming from?"

This time, they all heard it clearly. Reina, Mavis, and Mile began to search for the source.

The incessant chirping sound...

"U-um, well... Eheheh..."

...was originating from Pauline's cleavage.

"...So you're saying that you found it in the grass when we were taking a break earlier and decided to pick it up?"

"Yes... It would have died if I'd just left it there—I know it!"

A cute little bird, roughly the size of a sparrow, was poking its head out from between Pauline's breasts. Or at least, it was the size a sparrow would be when it was full grown. At the moment, it was still partly covered in down, so one could assume that it was a chick or an adolescent, and that it still had a little while until it reached its full size.

The spoiled, friendly little bird nibbled happily on a scrap of bread that Pauline offered it.

"It's so cute!" the other three sighed.

"L-Let me hold it for a bit!" Reina demanded.

"No, I should be first, I'm the party leader," said Mavis.

"N-no, me! You should give it to me, Pauline!" cried Mile.

However, Pauline gave only a heartless reply.

"None of you have enough *padding*. Chirpy might get crushed."

"........"

"I'm sorry! I really didn't mean it. Please cheer up, everyone!"

Pauline was starting to fret. The other three were still down in the dumps, not yet recovered from her inadvertent attack that afternoon. Since then, they had hardly said a word, and now it was dinnertime.

"W-well, I guess I have no choice here. I'll allow one of you the privilege of sleeping next to Chirpy tonight. But I'll leave it to you all to decide who..."

*Twitch. Twitch twitch!!*

*Fwap!*

"Yes, it's mine!"

"Heeeeey!!!"

To everyone's shock, Mavis, who always yielded to everyone else, had made a mad dash to secure Chirpy.

"Heheh. Ehehehehehe! You're gonna be sleeping next to me tonight, Chirpy!"

"Grrrrrrrngh." Reina and Mile grumbled bitterly.

Pauline called out to Mavis worriedly, "Please try your best not to roll over in your sleep and crush Chirpy!"

The next morning, a safe, living, and blessedly uncrushed Chirpy was stored safely back in Pauline's "breast pocket." It was the safest and coziest place for the bird during travel.

The other three seethed jealously.

"Ow!"

"What happened?! Pauline, are you all right?!"

It seemed that Pauline had tripped on a small rock and twisted her ankle. Of course, a little injury such as that was easily patched up with a bit of casual healing magic. While Pauline was on the ground, applying a healing spell to herself, Chirpy suddenly flew out from her shirt.

*Chirp! Chirp! Chirp!*

The bird landed beside her, chirping desperately at Pauline's injured ankle.

"Thank you, Chirpy. I feel like the pain is starting to go away already..."

Chirpy then turned its head and looked toward the rock that had been the source of Pauline's fall, giving a single shriek. The rock appeared to move slightly, as though it had been flicked. Everyone observed this curiously, but figured it was just their imaginations, and put it out of their minds.

Once Pauline's ankle was all healed, the Crimson Vow started down the road again.

That evening...

"Mine!"

"Oh!!"

This time, it was Reina who snatched up Chirpy, leaving Mile to grumble.

The next morning, as Mile prepared breakfast...

*Chirp!*

*Fwoomf!*

"Huh? Did the fire just light itself?"

"It's my turn tonight!"

There was no one who could argue with Mile's assertion. It was in fact her turn. Not even Pauline could object—she had Chirpy to herself all day long, and tomorrow night would be her turn.

As long as she slept face up, Mile's chest would be a perfectly safe place for Chirpy. The little bird nestled into the small crevasse and fell fast asleep.

"S-so cuuute!!!"

The next morning, Mile awoke before dawn, short of breath. She slowly opened her eyes, to see...

"Gyaaaaaaah!!!"

"Wh-what's going on?!?!"

The other three awoke with a start at Mile's scream. Beside them, they saw Mile, stretched out on her bed, and nearly covering her, something huge, fluffy, and roughly the same size as Mile—a giant bird.

"Wha-wh-wh-wh...?"

"A-a bird monster?"

"Is that Chirpy?"

In fact, it was Chirpy, who had ballooned to massive size overnight.

"S-so Chirpy's a magic bird?"

"You knew this, didn't you, Mavis?"

"Well, there are birds who look like normal birds but possess magical power and can use simple spells. They don't have any magic when they're first born, but after their mother breathes some magical power into them, they grow up quickly and can start using weak wind magic and such... Still, I don't think they're supposed to get this huge, and no matter how fast they're supposed to grow, I don't think it's supposed to happen overnight..."

In reality, the mothers did not "breathe their magic" into the babies. It was simply that they were lending them some of the nanomachines who were under the mother bird's influence and allowing the baby to use them for its own growth. Of course, the people of this world knew nothing of these principles. Besides, given that most birds were very small by nature, any magic they possessed would have been miniscule, causing most people to hardly pay them any mind.

As though awoken by all the commotion, Chirpy shuffled off of Mile and alighted on the ground.

After taking a good, hard look at Pauline, Mavis, Reina, and Mile in turn, it made a motion like bowing its head and trotted out of the tent.

Everyone rushed to follow it, only to see Chirpy look back just one time, spread its wings, and then take off into the air, flying away.

"Oh, Chirpy..."

Pauline watched as the bird flew into the distance, looking as though she was going to cry. Mavis, however, looked grim.

"What's the matter, Mavis?" Reina asked suspiciously.

Mavis replied, hesitating, "Oh, ah—I mean, maybe it was just my imagination, but... I thought I saw Chirpy use a little bit of magic the day before last, when Pauline twisted her ankle. And then yesterday, when Mile was making breakfast, the fire seemed like it lit itself..."

"Huh? So then, based on the people involved...could it have been that it was 'breathing in its mother's magical power'? So when it was sleeping next to Mile last night..."

"It was breathing in some of her ridiculous amount of magical power!"

"*We've just created a monster bird!!!*"

"Well, that's not *my* problem!" said Reina.

"I-I had nothing to do with this, either!" said Pauline.

"Nor did I!" said Mavis.

"Well then, anyway..." said Mile.

And the four agreed as one: *"Time to hurry along to the next country!!!"*

The Crimson Vow began to book it down the road.

It would not be until much, much later that they would hear rumors of the giant bird who swooped down to help lost and injured people in the forest...

# Didn't I Say
## to Make My Abilities
### *Average* in the
#### ——— Next Life?!

# Afterword

LONG TIME NO SEE, everyone. FUNA here.

At last, we've reached Volume 8 of *Average*. Volume 10 is just around the corner...

The publication and manga adaptation of *Average* have been going smoothly, as have the publication and adaptations of *Working in a Fantasy World to Save Up 80,000 Gold Pieces for My Retirement* and *Living on Potion Requests!* by Kodansha's K-Ranobe Books imprint. My days have been passing by relatively problem-free, outside of the luxurious worry of being so busy I hardly have time to do anything.

Of course, given that I only leave the house a few times a month—and when I do it's only to go to the supermarket that's a three minutes' walk from here to stock up on the soba and cup noodles that are my main staple—I can't really say that it's not like I don't have any problems these days.

In this volume, Mile's birth home, the land of the Ascham family, is invaded by the imperial army, and though Mile no longer feels a connection to that place, she can't bring herself to abandon it. In order to repay all the favors Mile has done for them over time, the other three members of the Crimson Vow do a number of devilish things...

Then, we see some old faces: Marcela and the Wonder Trio! And *then*, the Crimson Vow heads to the east!

**MILE:** "Next up, the *Touhou Project*!"

Y...yeah.

Production planning for the anime version is progressing smoothly, or rather, it seems to be coming along.

The supervisor and staff seem to be making a lot of decisions, anyway.

Perhaps it'll air next year...

Also, I'd been assuming that the English-language print volumes and e-books were only being sold in the U.S., but apparently, they're also being sold in a number of other counties. They're trending in Amazon's comic and graphic novel categories in Canada, Australia, Brazil, Mexico, the Netherlands, and others...

Don't tell me—am I really becoming an international author? No.

No no no.

*No no no no no no no!*

P-perhaps I can achieve world domination with my light novels...

**FUNA:** "Just one more step closer to my dreams..."
**MILE:** "Dreams, magic, and rock'n'roll!"
**REINA:** "I have no idea what you're talking about!"

The manga serialization of *Average* can be found online at Earth Star Comics (http://comic-earthstar.jp/).

And the manga serializations of *Potions* and *80,000 Gold Pieces* are doing very well at Wednesday Sirius (http://seiga.nico-video.jp/manga/official/w_sirius/).

You can continue to look forward to both the novel and manga versions.

And finally, to the chief editor; to Itsuki Akata, the illustrator; to Yoichi Yamakami, the cover designer; to everyone involved in the proofreading, editing, printing, binding, distribution, and selling of this book; to all the reviewers on *Shousetsuka ni Narou* who gave me their impressions, guidance, suggestions, and advice; and most of all, to everyone who's welcomed my stories into their homes, I thank you all from the bottom of my heart.

I hope to meet you all again soon, either in Volume 9 of *Average* or in one of the other two works in the three-part set

I'm calling "Flat-Chested Girls Who Look About Twelve or Thirteen."

And I hope you'll stick with us just a little while longer to help make my hopes, the Crimson Vow's dreams, and the reality of a completed anime adaptation come true...

—FUNA

# Didn't I Say
## to Make My Abilities
### *Average* in the
### Next Life?! ——

# AFTERWORD?

MARCELA, WHOM I DREW FOR NO PARTICULAR REASON.
MARCELA, WHOSE HAND I WANT TO GIVE AWAY IN
   MARRIAGE FOR SOME REASON.
MARCELA, WITH HER HUGE CURLS THAT
   I DESIGNED HER WITH BECAUSE
   I FELT LIKE IT.
MARCELA, WHOM I HAVE NO IDEA
   WHEN WE'LL SEE NEXT...

ITSUKI
AKATA

# Experience these great light**novel** titles from Seven Seas Entertainment

See the complete Seven Seas novel collection at
**sevenseaslightnovel.com**